TRIPLE TROUBLE

A Cassidy Callahan Novel

by
Kelly Rysten

CCB Publishing
British Columbia, Canada

Triple Trouble: A Cassidy Callahan Novel

Copyright ©2009 by Kelly Rysten
ISBN-13   978-1-926585-41-3
First Edition

Library and Archives Canada Cataloguing in Publication

Rysten, Kelly, 1960-
Triple trouble : a Cassidy Callahan novel / written by Kelly Rysten.
ISBN 978-1-926585-41-3
Also available in electronic format.
I. Title.
PZ7.R98Tr 2009   j813'.6   C2009-905424-8

Cover artwork by Kelly Rysten.

Publisher: CCB Publishing
              British Columbia, Canada
              www.ccbpublishing.com

Dedicated to the memory of my father
Henry Daniel Saastamoinen
who always believed in me and encouraged me
to share Cassidy with others.

PART 1

TROUBLE TIME

I was pulling out of the grocery store parking lot when a large, scruffy man yanked open the door of my Jeep and jumped in. He pointed a grimy, worn gun in my face and yelled "Drive!"

I was so shocked I froze. After using guns my entire life including a stint in the Marines you'd think I could keep a cool head in a simple carjacking. My second reaction was, oh no, trouble has found me again. Wherever I go, trouble follows. Sometimes it follows at a distance, teasing, and sometimes it attacks like this, with driving force and violence.

Chapter 1

When I was a kid my propensity for trouble didn't bother me as much. In fact, I felt honored when my father's workers called me Trouble. I thought I was tough, and the name made me feel tough. It made me feel like I ought to look for more adventures. And that usually got me into trouble so it was kind of a self-fulfilling name. My real name is Cassidy Callahan. Most people think of me as Skipper meets GI Joe. I'm a petite blonde, and I've always looked like a kid, but in my mind I'm a dynamo.

As I grew up, my life changed but my attitude didn't. I was a decent, if distracted, student. I graduated from high school. Then, after a boring summer where I imagined myself stuck on my parents' ranch forever, I decided there was a whole wide world out there just waiting to be explored. After a big to-do where I butted heads with my parents, I joined the Marine Corps and took off to prove just how tough I really was. Having grown up on a ranch, in a place that was physically demanding, I thought I was prepared. I'd wrestled skittish horses and helped round up cattle, backpacked, hiked and tracked, and was physically fit. The Marines, however, had a very different idea of what fit was. I met all their tortures with firm determination and was proud when my determination paid off and I was a soldier. Men laughed when they saw me in full gear. At times, I looked like a walking uniform. Put me in fatigues, boots, helmet, backpack, give me a weapon and sunglasses and I disappeared. Put me through a morning of calisthenics, send me on a long hike in the desert heat and I could drop several pounds in a day.

Four years as a Marine had kept trouble at bay. I'd married an Air Force test pilot named Jack and settled down a bit. I was almost a normal housewife except for sudden longings for the great outdoors. The nearby mountains called to me until I gave in and took off into the woods. Give me a daypack with snacks and a bottle of water and I was good to go. Jack went too, occasionally, but I often found myself alone up in the hills. I was free there, I could feel the ground beneath my feet and would awaken to the sound of birds. We were happy like that, him in the sky, me on the ground. He wasn't going to stifle my free spirit and I wasn't going to hold him down. We had reached a silent and contented agreement when out of the blue my worst nightmare occurred and I found myself a widow at twenty-four. As a test pilot, Jack's life was cut short. Trouble fell from the sky and shook my world. It nearly knocked me flat but I was gaining it back a little each day.

Then one day I was running errands and had to stop by the grocery store. How in the world can someone get into trouble going grocery shopping? I patiently went up and down all the aisles finding the things I needed and went back through all the aisles for the things the first trip reminded me about. I'd smiled when I checked out and hit all the buttons right on the debit machine. I'd packed up my Jeep Wrangler with a few days' worth of groceries, hopped in, headed for home and gotten carjacked! Leave it to me to be the only one at the grocery store to get carjacked.

"I said drive, bitch! Hit the gas!" the man yelled and stomped down on my foot. My Jeep shot across two lanes of traffic, barely missing being broadsided by a white step van and a Brady Bunch station wagon. Tires screeched and the step van rocked and weaved as the two drivers slammed on their brakes. I frantically turned the wheel to avoid the median and that put me going west on Main. I felt his foot come off mine, but I kept the pedal down as much as I could. This guy was obviously in a hurry. I took a deep breath. My mental faculties were catching up with the situation. I had a desperate man in my car. He wanted to go somewhere fast. That left a lot of likely possibilities. I didn't like the sound of most of them. This obviously wasn't a joy ride and he wasn't going to be the perfect date. Nope, this guy meant business.

The speed limits are fast in my city but we exceeded every one of them. I prayed for a cop to catch me.
"Where are we going?" I croaked.
"Just keep driving," he barked back, "I need to figure this out."
"Okay," I said. "I could use some thinking time too."
"Don't you think, just drive. Get me far away from here."
Thinking and driving go hand in hand for me so I just kept on driving straight as fast as I could. I ran red lights when I could and stopped when I couldn't but the gun was always there menacing, pushing me to do stupid things. My first inclination was to drive to the sheriff's station but that was almost directly behind me. I kept it as an option but I couldn't count on it.

Joshua Hills is not a large city, but neither is it a small burg. It's 150,000 plus population was sending tendrils of housing tracts out across the desert floor. It didn't take long for me to hit the outskirts of town. Old houses gave way to new houses and new houses would soon give way to houses under construction.
I didn't want to continue in this direction. I could see the agricultural belt on the west side of town and beyond that was foothills and desert. I was

nervous about getting off in the boondocks with this guy. I didn't know what he intended to do but I might need people handy. I steeled a glance. The gun was still there.

"You married?" he intruded on my thoughts.

"N-n-no," I replied, "widowed."

"You're kind of young to be widowed."

"Not if my husband was a test pilot."

"Got kids?"

"Not the maternal type." And there wasn't time, I thought.

"Where d' you live?"

"Directly behind us. Past where we came from," I said. And past the sheriff's station too.

"I need a hideout for a few days so you're gonna have company. You try anything and you'll be sorry. You cooperate and it'll buy you time."

"You want to go to m-my house?"

"That's what I said."

Traffic was thinning and we had reached the construction that marks the city's slow, outward expansion. I hung a U-turn and headed back the way we came, thinking ahead, analyzing the route for possible ways to escape. As we neared the middle of town he became antsy again, not wanting to get too close to something. He fidgeted and looked around nervously. The barrel of the gun swung towards my face but he was just motioning with his hand. "Turn off this street and go down to the next light," he said, real antsy, real paranoid.

I turned left at the next light, took Hampton down to Thompson and turned right. I was disappointed because that took us off the route to the sheriff's station. I tried turning right on Division to approach the station from behind, but I got a whack on the side of my head with the butt of his gun. "Keep going straight and don't try anything," he growled. I wondered if he knew the city, knew what I'd tried to do. I had to assume he did. I continued down Thompson nervously.

"How are we supposed to get to my house if you won't let me drive?"

"You just keep driving. I'll let you know when to do what."

As we neared the street where he'd earlier jumped into my Jeep, the carjacker took a long look up the street. Red and blue lights flashed at the corner of Santiago and Main.

"Fuck and damn!" he said, "Keep going."

My brain was working overtime trying to come up with some way to get out of this before we reached my house. The next traffic signal was red and there were very few cars around. My training told me a moving target is always harder to hit than a still one. I was thinking of making a run for it. I reached for the door handle, yanked it hard and was halfway out of the Jeep when the butt of the gun came crashing down on my head. Pain exploded behind my right temple and I felt myself being hauled back into the Jeep. The carjacker slid over to the driver's seat and took off with a squeal of tires. Two more blows from the gun butt followed, presumably to teach me a lesson. I felt the Jeep bump along erratically. Sharp turns, quick bursts of gas, jerky shifting. It had been a while since he'd driven a standard.

After my failed escape, I found myself on the floorboards of the Jeep with my head against the passenger seat. Aside from the bruise on my head, I felt I was in a much better position now that I didn't have to drive and plan at the same time.

"Where the hell is your place?" he demanded, "I gotta get you tied up so's you can't try anything else."

I peeked over the edge of the window.

"Stay on Thompson till you get to Desert. Turn left. It's a bunch of cul de sacs. I'm on the third one."

I righted myself in the passenger seat and studied the neighborhood as we drove in. It was midday. Quiet. I lived in a small house in a well-kept older neighborhood. One window faced the street.

I pointed at my small desert sand stucco house with blue trim and he pulled into the driveway signaling that I should open the garage. I pushed the button and the door went up to reveal a wall of boxes. Somehow we had moved in and were comfortably settled with only half our possessions unpacked. I've heard this isn't unusual. Mr. Carjacker wasn't happy about the garage situation. He closed the garage, then backed the Jeep so it was visible from the living room window.

"Now, I want you to go in the house, nice and easy. I don't want to have to shoot you in the yard. That would cause a scene and I need things to stay nice and quiet."

"No," I said, "I am not letting you in that house."

A grim expression crossed his face. His eyes narrowed. "Okay, well, then I guess I'll have to choose another house. How about that house on the end? Looks like there's more hostages down there. 'Course, I only need one. And I'd have to take you with me. Can't leave you alone to go calling the cops."

I looked down the street. Mrs. Gonzales was outside with two of her kids cleaning up the yard. I'd let him kill me before I'd sick him on another person. Okay, so I'd go in the house. I could hear barking coming from the living room. It was my dog, Shadow. He wouldn't be any help in my current predicament. He was too friendly. I hoped he wouldn't end up with a bullet through his brain.

"You didn't tell me you had a dog."

Like I was supposed to give him my life's history.

"You didn't ask and he won't hurt you. If you're looking for valuables he'll probably show you where they are. And he's obedience trained so he won't be a problem. Just give him a minute to get used to you."

"Yeah, right. Dogs hate me."

Smart dogs.

I gathered up the groceries in two heavy armloads and we walked up the sidewalk to the front door, the gun pointed at me discreetly. I noticed the rose bushes were getting ready to bloom and the grass needed cutting. I wasn't much of a gardener. The roses were there when we moved in, and somebody else had given them a good start. I awkwardly unlocked the front door and pushed my way in. Shadow immediately jumped on our unwelcome guest to say 'hi' then he backed off avoiding contact. Smart dog.

"He'll be fine in a minute, just pet him and let him smell you."

After I put the groceries down I went to see how things were progressing in the dog department. Shadow was in sheepdog mode, positioning himself so he could see everybody.

"Sit," I said in a commanding tone. Shadow sat, gazing at me for further direction. "Stay." The gaze intensified waiting for the release word. "Is it okay if I put the groceries away? I'd like to get the stuff in the refrigerator at least."

"Just don't get out of my sight."

I looked down at Shadow. The gaze was still anticipating. "Good Boy!" I said and he bounded after me.

I put the milk in the fridge and then put the deli meats and cheese in the drawer. The vegetables and fruit went in the vegetable bins, the meat in the freezer. I saved out a package of chicken, putting it in the fridge, just in case I was still alive to cook dinner. I took it for granted he wouldn't call out for pizza.

I continued until all the groceries were put away. I couldn't keep still. I was too nervous and I felt like I had to keep busy, demonstrate that I wasn't going to turn on him, let him think he could trust me, buy some time. Predictable motion promotes trust, was my theory. He walked down the hall, taking inventory of the rooms and any problems they might cause. He unplugged the phones, locked the three bedroom doors and closed them, checked the back door to make sure it was locked and the curtains were drawn, took my cell phone and pocketed it. I was glad he didn't check my bedroom closet. There were two rifles, two handguns and plenty of ammo in there. Now they were safely locked up. I was half glad and half disappointed. That might have come in handy to make my escape, but intuition told me to play along with him for now.

"So," I said, "what's the plan?"

"I need a place to stay for a few days that's nice and quiet. Soon as I get ahold of a friend of mine, he's going to pick me up and we'll be outa here."

"So, what's the plan for me?"

"You do what I say, nobody gets hurt. You foul things up, you're gonna get hurt. You foul things up bad, I'll kill you. I don't want to kill you. I need you for insurance. Plus shooting makes a lot of noise and usually draws the cops. I don't want that."

"And when you leave?"

"Depends on the circumstances, no promises."

Okay, I could deal with that. In fact, it was better than I expected.

Things quieted down after that. Shadow seemed to accept his new visitor. After a while Shadow's afternoon routine brought him pacing in front of me. Shadow is a Shetland sheepdog, commonly known as a sheltie. They are smart but they tend to recognize patterns and once things become routine they lock into that pattern. It was mid afternoon and to Shadow that meant lunchtime. I could ignore him for a while but Shadow knew what time it was and he was going to keep reminding me.

"Shadow says it's lunch time," I said. "Is it okay if I feed him? All I gotta do is put a cup of food in his bowl and he'll leave us alone."

"Okay," he replied warily, "but I'm gonna follow you."

I went to get Shadow's bowl, took it to the dog food bin and measured out the right amount, poured it in the bowl and took it back to his spot. Sure enough, carjacker dude followed every step of the way. Shadow knew the routine. He sat waiting for me to put down the bowl. When he was a pup he bowled me over trying to get to his food, so we established this routine. I get the food, he sits and waits for the okay. I set the bowl down.

"Okay", I said brightly, "You can get it!" The magic word was spoken so he was free to eat. He dove in enthusiastically.

Five seconds later he was back, but the routine had been followed so I was off the hook. Normally, Shadow was a working dog out of a job. A sheep dog with no sheep, he took his position in the house seriously. I was his lone sheep and it was his job to keep track of me. Now with another person here, there were two sheep. Two boring sheep. He looked at me like the job was getting too cushy. Normally I helped fill his day with doggie chores. We played fetch and did obedience exercises in the backyard. Since sitting and staying and heeling weren't much in the way of work, we started adding agility equipment to the backyard. The agility course was calling to him, all those fun obstacles for a sheep dog to play on. It wasn't complete. I had several more obstacles I needed to build, but to him it was like doggy Disneyland. I could see it was calling to him. Sorry, boy.

We sat in my living room, the gun always pointing at me. He seemed calmer. I was getting bored and antsier by the minute. It felt like I was sitting on a time bomb.

"Look," I said, "I don't know about you, but just sitting around is driving me nuts. Can't we cook dinner or let the dog out or do anything besides sit here? How long has it been since you ate?"

"Eating is overrated compared to staying alive. Let me worry about the staying alive part and then we'll think about the eating part."

He took out my cell phone and programmed a number into my speed dial. He hit the number and quickly hung up. I got up and paced, anything besides sitting. The more I sat, the tighter I felt. Action. I needed action. Even risky action. Okay, not too risky. Think, I told myself, as long as you are stuck, you can think. How can we get out of this fix?

Just then the doorbell rang. We both looked up. What to do?

"Don't answer it."

"I better. If it's my neighbor she has a key. If she is here to borrow something she knows she can come in and get it. We borrow stuff from each other all the time." Okay, so it wasn't true, but I needed to be able to answer my door in case help showed up.

"Get rid of her. Don't let her in. If you want her to live you'll get rid of her."

The bell rang again. I opened the door just wide enough to see out. It was a kid.

"Hi, Mrs. Callahan, I'm selling candy for my school and I was wondering if you'd like to order some chocolate or cookies. We have other stuff if you're on a diet." He thrust the catalog at me and the gun jabbed me in the side.

"I can't right now," I said, "I'm right in the middle of something. When is it due?"

"Next Thursday," he said.

"Can you come back next week? I'll buy something from you then."

"Okay, I'll try."

I closed the door with a relieved whoosh and almost sank to the floor.

"What makes you think you'll be here next week? Maybe I'll take you with me when I go. Maybe you'll mess up and make me use this gun. Maybe we'll still be sitting here next week picking off candy salesmen with my .45. You can't count on next week."

I hadn't even turned around to reply when there was a knock on the door. Scared to answer, I turned around. The knocking turned to banging and I knew it was the kid next door. He wanted to go get his basketball from my backyard.

"This'll only take a second," I said with a glare.

I opened the door. It was Aaron, like always.

"Lose your ball again?" I asked, masking the fear in my stomach with a cheery voice. "I'll throw it over the fence in a minute."

Aaron ran home and I turned to my unwanted guest.

"I know you want things kept quiet, but in this neighborhood the best way to do that is to keep things normal. All I need to do is retrieve the ball and toss it next door."

We went out into my backyard, found the ball and tossed it over the fence. Aaron yelled, "Thanks!" and resumed dribbling.

"What's all this junk back here?" the carjacker asked.

"It's not exactly junk. This is an agility course. When Shadow gets bored he wants to come out here and run the course. See, this piece is a hurdle. This piece is called the Weave Poles because the dog weaves in and out of the poles in a straight line until he reaches the end. Here's a tunnel. This is an A-frame." The A-frame gave me an idea, but it wasn't time to test it. The A-frame was only a few feet from my back fence and would give me easy access out of here if I had to make a run for it. "Do you want to see how it works?"

"Sure, why not, just remember I got the gun."

"Shadow isn't used to having people here but we'll see how it goes. Shadow! Heel." I commanded. Shadow trotted up and stood at my left side. I walked over to the hurdle. I wasn't sure he would listen to me with distractions, so I put him in a sit-stay several feet from the hurdle and walked to the other side of the hurdle.

"Jump!" I called. Shadow looked around, unsure. "Jump!" I tried again. He stood, ran a few steps and jumped over the hurdle. "Heel." I said and walked to the next obstacle. Since this one was easier to do from a walk, I headed right into it "Weave," I said, "weave, weave." Shadow weaved in and out of the poles. "Good boy! Good weave!" We went on to the next one, the tunnel, "go through!" Shadow shot through the tunnel. He really liked the tunnel. He liked to go through the course at a run but I thought if I did anything sudden I'd get in trouble. Shadow was holding back and he wasn't too happy, just obeying.

"What about the ramp one?"

"We just started that one. I'll see if he'll do it right. If he doesn't I'll have to correct him and work with him or he'll develop bad habits."

We walked over to the A-frame. It was set at a gentle slope and peaked at about 4 feet. "Up!" I commanded, "Shadow, go UP!" I walked beside the ramp showing him the direction he was to go. He had gone over the A-frame but he wasn't yet ready to take it flying like some of the other obstacles. If I was doing this on my own, I would have food and a leash and I'd take it at a jog so he had some momentum going, but I didn't have those things. Shadow walked up the "up" side and peered down the "down" side. Going down was harder than going up. He started the down side and slid a little because of his hesitant attitude. As soon as his paws hit the ground on the far side I praised him.

"Good boy! Good dog!" Shadow jumped around and around barking.

"We usually do the whole thing at a jog. And we have other obstacles that we need to build."

He gestured to the course and I took that to mean we could go through it once more so I jogged off with Shadow trotting next to me. "Weave, weave." I said, "Go through. Jump!" Now the A-frame, "Go up, come down, good boy!" Shadow was really stoked now. He was in his groove and it was time to stop. I got an idea. Since all this activity seemed to be okay, I walked over to the A-frame, unhooked the chain and raised it another foot. I might be able to use that additional height later, and I could fit the change into the training without suspicion.

"One more time, Shadow! Weave, weave, go through. Jump! Go up! Come down! Good boy, what a good boy! You did the high one! Good job!" There, the A-frame was ready in case I had a chance to use it. Mission accomplished.

It was getting on towards dinnertime and I hadn't had lunch yet. Staying alive was more important than lunch but I was debating whether it was more important than dinner. I rose to go to the kitchen and the gun immediately swiveled my way.

"Where do you think you're going?" A warning voice but his demeanor was calmer. This was a good thing.

"It's dinnertime. I'm going to cook dinner. You want to eat eventually, don't you? And do you have a name? I'm Cassidy."

"Manny," he said and let me cook. So much for the tying up threat. Maybe his hunger was outweighing his fear.

I'm not much of a cook, but I won't ever starve to death either. I learned all my cooking from watching Martha, the ranch housekeeper, and Martha cooked for a crowd. I grew up on a ranch with four ranch hands, so dinner involved cooking for at least nine. Big men with big appetites. So there I was, single and cooking for a crowd. I've cut back some, but my Texas skillet is still the most used pot in the house. I thought of my options for chicken trying to think of a dish with lots of cutting and preparation time so Manny would get used to me walking around with sharp knives.

I chose my biggest, sharpest knife and cut the chicken into strips and put the pieces in a gallon size Ziploc bag. I added a bottle of Jamaica Mistake and squished the bag up to get all the chicken pieces coated. Then I let the bag sit while I cut up the vegetables.

Manny sat at the dining room table watching every move I made, punching numbers on the cell phone and grunting when the call didn't go through again. Shadow stared at him since he was sitting in a place where food magically appeared on the floor. If I were alone, he'd be sitting under the cutting board because sometimes food magically appears under that, too.

I went to the refrigerator and got out onions, bell peppers and mushrooms and cut the onions and peppers into strips.

The best way to cook the meat would be to grill it, but that involved another trip to the backyard. Since the barbecue grill was just outside the door I hoped he'd let me use it. The more things he observed me doing in a calm manner, the more he'd be taken off guard when I made my break. I shook the meat bag a few more times and headed for the back door. I was met with a gun to the side of my head and my heart did a little flip flop at how fast it appeared there.

"I'm just lighting the barbecue. You don't want this cooked on the stove. It just isn't the same."

He lowered the gun and watched me closely as I opened the back door. Shadow shot outside to sniff around. I lit the grill and called Shadow back in the house. A few minutes later, I scraped the grill and added a grate so the chicken strips wouldn't fall through. I did a final squish of the bag and placed the chicken on the grill. I went inside and sautéed the onions, bell peppers and mushrooms. I flipped over the chicken and then set the table. Nothing fancy. When you live alone, fancy doesn't seem worth the bother. I microwaved some tortillas so we could eat the chicken soft taco style. I brought in the meat and mixed it up with the veggies. I set the whole mess, still in the Texas skillet on the table. Manny dug in and I got us each a glass of Coke.

This is the way I usually ate. I fixed a big batch of something and then ate the leftovers for a week straight. It looked like I wouldn't have to do that this time. Manny was definitely going to help out in that department.

"I never want to see another hot dog or bologna sandwich for as long as I live," he said.

"I'm not much of a cook but I don't think you'll starve to death here. Only thing is, I only keep a couple days worth of food at any one time here."

Manny looked like he hadn't eaten in days. He was really getting into this meal. In fact he hardly noticed me as he ate. I made a mental note of that. I was hoping to get some information out of him, but I thought I was getting more information just watching him than if I talked to him, so I stayed quiet. He never set down the gun, but his focus was on nothing but the plate in front of him. I got up and went to the kitchen and pretended to look around for something. His eyes flicked up but his hands and mouth kept working on the food. I thought of making a run for it right then but something told me to hold off. Still, I was forming a plan for later. I fingered the keys in my pocket.

By the time dinner was over it was dark out. Shadow got his share of dinner, a teaspoon of people food in his bowl. There were two more failed attempts at the phone call, each followed by mutterings and cursing. There had been a plan and that plan wasn't going smoothly right at the moment. I cleaned up the dishes and Shadow was ready for his evening run. I always went out with him in the evening to cool off and he went out every evening for a last patrol. He started the pacing and staring thing again. I ignored him until he tried it on Manny. After a while Manny got the idea and opened the back door. Shadow stood at the door and stared at me. "Come on sheep!" he seemed to be saying, "You know what you are supposed to be doing." Well, I did. I knew I was supposed to be getting out of this house alive. I took Shadow out quickly and was waved back in again with the gun. Didn't he ever put it down?

I sure wished I had a real name to go with the face. I'd like to know who I was dealing with, even if the name didn't mean much to me. Manny, short for Manuel? Dark skin. Scraggly gray hair. Looked like his hair used to be black. Mexican? He didn't look particularly Mexican. He just looked tanned. And unkempt. He wore an old undershirt with a torn and worn flannel shirt over it. Baggy faded jeans that were too long for him bunched up over scuffed black shoes. He looked like he'd stolen his clothes from the Goodwill drop off box and then worn them for a week straight.

As night settled in the stress level built up again. I could feel the tension rising. Manny was getting nervous. He poked me with the gun.

"Let's go," he said, "I need to find some stuff."

We went out to the garage and he dug through the workbench until he came up with duct tape and a pocketknife.

"Lace your fingers together."

He taped my fingers so they couldn't move, then taped my wrists. We went back in the house and he shoved me to the floor. He brought my hands down to my knees and taped my hands and knees together and then my ankles. I wasn't going anywhere. He made some more calls on the cell phone, finally getting through to somebody. I heard a one sided conversation.

"Oscar, where the fuck are you? I've been trying to get through all day.... So, you did it?... shit... yeah, I got a car and I got a hostage. Cute one, too.... It's quiet here." Long pause. "You better get outa there.... We can use my hostage and your car. It'll be faster if we have to run. You did manage to get the keys... What do you mean you're pinned down?... Shit! I could make a run for it without you. And you know I will if I have to... Two days. You have two days. I'm not waiting any longer than that and I'm only saying that because I got it good here. I'm all set."

He hung up and almost threw the phone across the room. Instead he slugged the wall, sending sheetrock crumbling and knocking a picture off the wall. He threw the picture, missing my head by inches. He strode over, kicking me in the side and rolling me over so he could look me in the eyes. "Looks like you're gonna be stuck with me for a long time. Things aren't looking too good right now but things could change. Two days. Looks like you've got two days." He cut off a strip of duct tape and put it over my mouth.

As the hours wore on I was glad for my training. I'd slept in worse places than this. Carpet was nice and comfy compared to foxholes and tents in the desert. I'd slept standing, sitting, hanging in trees. Only my thoughts kept me from sleeping now. Two days. I had to escape tomorrow. That's it. That's the plan, only half formed in my mind, but I did have options left to me. I didn't know if I was willing to go down fighting. I wanted this to end peacefully with this guy behind bars, but the likelihood of the police strolling by was slim to nil. My mind was racing through all the possible outcomes until I felt like a rat in a maze, and then the maze became a haze and I dozed.

Chapter 2

Morning dawned, but it was overcast. I couldn't see out a window but I could tell there was a blanket of clouds out there because the jets from the Air Force base were flying under the cloud cover. The room was dim. If I were free, I would rejoice in a cloudy day. I would use the break from the sunshine to do my outside work. Shadow and I would run the agility course and go to the park or hike in the mountains nearby. Today I knew I had a day of tense waiting. And watching. Maybe the watching would keep it from being boring. Maybe it wouldn't be boring because I'd be fighting for my life. Watching came first; watching for a break, no matter how small. I'd built up some trust. Now I needed to make that trust work for me.

Shadow was out of sorts. He was used to sleeping in his crate and he had been loose last night. Now he wanted to go out but I was still all taped up. Sorry boy!

Manny didn't wake up until close to eight o'clock. About 8:30 he cut the tape on my hands and legs and allowed me to do the morning routine minus a shower. I rushed through washing up, brushing teeth, brushing my hair. The bathroom had no windows, no way to escape.

I started breakfast and I only had two eggs left, then I was short on bread so I got out a sticky pad and started a list, more out of habit than anything else. Eggs, bread, toothpaste… He never yelled at me for writing so I filled the front page with bogus grocery items and turned to the second page and wrote, "Help me get out of here. Call the police. Have them seal the neighborhood. Send someone at 6:00 p.m. ARMED. No uniforms, pretend to be a neighbor with a question." Extra insurance. Boy Scout motto "Always be prepared." I tore off the list and the note and silently slid them into my pocket. Occasionally I would take the list out and add to it. One time with the list out I turned and quickly separated the two sheets of paper stuffing them in different pockets. I made sure the list was in my left pocket and the note was in my right pocket, the pocket that would be handy if I had to answer the door. I kept cooking, giving up my two eggs but silently celebrating the fact that I had the note. I wasn't hungry anyway. I was too tense to be hungry.

Later in the morning the doorbell rang. I almost jumped out of my skin. I looked up. Manny gave a slight nod that I took as permission to answer. I knew the rule, just get rid of them. He stood behind me at the door out of sight. I opened it slightly, felt the gun against my side and looked out. I almost sank to my knees right then and there because at my door was a man with a badge. Not only that, he was the most handsome detective I ever saw, even on TV. I didn't even think they grew them like that! He was dressed in jeans and a tweed sport coat but he would have made anything look good. His sandy hair was windblown and set off his blue eyes, serious at the moment, they held the promise of a quick smile. More importantly, I had to keep my head on straight here. Think Cass, think! I wasn't thinking. I was only hoping. My heart was doing a hundred miles an hour and my hands were shaking and he hadn't said a word yet. His eyes took me in and I think just my expression might have tipped him off that something was going on here.

I tried to speak, but a lump formed in my throat.

"I'm detective Rusty Michaels," he said displaying his badge. His deep voice rumbled like soft thunder. He snapped his badge closed and dropped it in his shirt pocket. "I was wondering if you've seen this man." He held up a piece of paper with Manny's picture on it. Manuel Silva it said. Finally, I had a name.

I leaned in closer to the door pretending to look at the paper closely, but I was really blocking Silva's view of my pocket.

"N-no", I said shakily handing back the piece of paper, "I don't know him and I haven't seen him."

"I have a witness that says your Jeep was leaving the High Desert Bank when a man fitting Silva's description jumped into your vehicle and took off in a big hurry. The plate number and description match your Jeep."

"Oh, um," I stammered. Think, think! "That was my brother. I was there loading groceries at the store and John got hungry and said he was running over to McDonald's. He went to McDonald's, got a snack and I picked him up on my way out of the parking lot." My hand slipped into my pocket and I silently stuck the note on the front of the door. Michaels glanced at the note and gently pulled it off the door. His expression grew serious. He knew Silva was here but didn't want to leave me in this predicament. He didn't know if others were involved or not. He didn't know anything except that I had something in mind and it happened at 6:00 p.m. He ran his hand through his hair, thinking, trying not to act, trying to keep his cool. Hoo, boy.

"So, what was the big hurry leaving the parking lot?" he asked. We had to play this out now, even though he knew he had Silva cornered.

"I was really late for something and thought I wouldn't get there in time. I didn't realize I was going that fast. I was just rushed."

"And you've never seen this man before?" I couldn't help it, my eyes glanced left.

"No."

"Here's my card. Can you give me a call if you happen to think of anything that might help? This guy's wanted for bank robbery and murder so we're kind of in a rush to get him off the streets." This last part didn't seem to be information he'd pass on to a potential accessory. Of course, if I'd helped Manny with the getaway I'd probably know these things anyway.

He turned to go and I turned to close the door. It was very tempting to run for it right then but I felt the gun and I knew I could improve my chances at 6:00 p.m. I just prayed 6:00 got here before Oscar. When I turned around I saw anger, only anger. Silva knew the police were out there. This was a grim reminder.

"You were smart not to pull anything. Here's what you can look forward to if you try anything. And I mean ANYTHING." He hit me with a punch to my eye and another left punch to the stomach. I slumped forward and he brought his knee up cracking me in the jaw again. He then picked me up by the front of my shirt and tossed me across the room. I lay stunned and more determined than ever to beat this guy.

The day passed in a constant state of tension. I was fighting anxiety and at the same time trying to play up the little trust that Silva had in me. I'd stood up to the police once. He knew that. Actually the tension in the air made Silva think he had me scared and I guess in a way he was right. I wasn't afraid of the pain. I'd felt pain in many ways before. It always goes away eventually. I was a little afraid of dying but I was too proud to think I'd let that happen. I was more afraid of failure. I didn't want this guy to get away. In fact, I was determined to get Silva and Oscar both behind bars. It just seemed like a heavy responsibility.

When Shadow's afternoon feeding came, I only pretended to feed him, dropping just enough kibble in his bowl to make noise. I got some thick, juicy steaks out of the freezer, defrosted them and put them in marinade. Seems like I marinade everything.

I baked potatoes. Four o'clock rolled around. Walking by the mirror I took a glance. I had a shiner of a black eye and a couple of lumps on my head from my airmail flight across the living room. Michaels would be sure to notice that if he came back at six. Nothing said it would be him that came, but I thought I could count on somebody. The clock seemed to stand still. I tried not to look at it too often.

At five o'clock I scooped the insides out of the baked potatoes, then mashed them up with some butter, sour cream, grated cheese, salt and pepper. I put the mess back in the potato skins and topped it all with cheese, then stuck the casserole dish with the two potatoes into the oven. I started the barbecue grill and heated it up. After scraping the chicken gunk off the rack I added the steaks. I prepared a salad and placed the bowl on the table. I was trying to stay busy so I wouldn't panic. Panic was very close to the surface but I pushed it down. Shadow was following my every movement. He was hungry and I was counting on him to stay that way.

At ten till six I took up the steaks and set the food on the table. Five minutes later we sat down to eat. I could have sworn the clock died. Time stood still. Seconds felt like minutes and minutes felt like hours. Silva dug into his steak. I didn't want him to finish eating before things started happening so I got up a few times to get things out of the fridge; steak sauce, then salad dressing. If he was tired of hot dogs and bologna, a good steak should keep his attention.

Shadow had his eye on the table. Good boy.

A few minutes after 6:00 p.m. the doorbell rang. I jumped. I looked at Silva for direction and he nodded, giving the okay. I walked to the door like a zombie. My legs wouldn't work right. I had the shakes. Glancing behind me Silva was still at the table watching, his gun pointed in my direction. The doorbell rang again. I guess time was working faster on the other side. I opened the door and there was Michaels, this time wearing faded blue jeans and a t-shirt advertising outdoor gear. Just a neighbor here to ask a question.

"Hi, Cassidy," he said brightly, "I was wondering if you could help me out with something. Wow, what happened to your eye?"

"Umm," I stammered, "Don't worry about it. What's up?"

"My girlfriend bet me a six-pack that I couldn't cook dinner, so now I need to come up with something she'll like and I was wondering how to make meat loaf."

Is he serious? I thought. Meatloaf?

"Meatloaf? Why meatloaf?" A glance at Silva. "Sure, I can tell you how to make meatloaf but that's not exactly a meal that is going to impress a girl. Meatloaf is what housewives make if they can't think of anything else." I glanced at Silva. He rolled his eyes and started eating his steak.

Michaels looked at me quizzically, like okay, what would impress a girl? Was he enjoying this? I felt like a jellyfish. My legs were all wobbly. I was barely thinking. I was watching for my break.

"Okay, I'll bite. What would impress a girl?"

"You have to make something like she'd order at a restaurant. There's easy ways to make dishes like that, too. When is she coming over?"

"Tomorrow."

"That gives you some time. Go to the store and buy a bottle of Jamaica Mistake. It's a marinade." Gee, I guess I do marinade everything. "Get a package of boneless chicken breasts. Put the two in a big Ziploc bag and marinade it for a few hours. Cook the chicken on the grill and steam some vegetables to go on the side. You can cook rice to go with it."

I stole another glance at Silva. He was getting impatient. Good, that was just what I wanted. He rose and stood at the door of the dining room. He caught the tablecloth on his way out and his plate scooted towards the edge of the table as he got up. Even better. Shadow stared at the plate. He *really* wanted that steak but he knew he had to get the code word first. His ears pricked, begging for the code word. He drooled a little.

"*Chicken?*" he said. "You think she'll like chicken?"

"Better than hamburger. You can do the same thing with steak but I like it with chicken better." Check out the dining room. I looked Michaels in the eye and slid the car keys out of my pocket pointing at the electric blue BMW Roadster parked on the street. A barely noticeable nod affirmed he got it.

Chatting with a neighbor was not the same thing as getting rid of them. Silva was debating between heading off something at the door and sitting down to his steak. This is what I was waiting for. I glanced at Shadow. He was so close to that plate all he needed was…

"Okay," I said, and then louder, "Get it!"

Shadow lunged for the steak. There was a clatter for silverware and china and Silva turned. He lunged for the dog. I hopped out the door, closing it behind me. I slid the key in the lock and heard the bolt slide in. I dashed for the car. There were a lot more cars on my street than usual. Men in uniform hunched behind them. My hands were shaking so bad I couldn't find the keyhole. Stupid key! Come on! The curtains were thrust aside and a shot went wild over our heads shattering my front window. The key slid in. I heard the snap of the door locks disengaging and we jumped in. I turned the key, threw the car into gear and took off. Zero to sixty in 5 seconds. Thank you, Jack! I love this car. I screeched around the corner and took the left turn that led out of the neighborhood, then immediately had to brake to a stop at the police barricade.

"Whoa, little lady. You can stop here. This is the where the good guys hang out." I pulled to a stop beside the group of police cars. A uniform walked up to Michaels, checking us out.

"Everybody okay? We heard a shot."

"Yeah, I think so." Michaels answered. "You okay?"

I got out of the car and sank to the ground, sitting cross-legged in the dirt. Too much. I was wound up too tight. I had to sit. But not in the car. The car oozed stress, too. Okay, just sit. It'll be fine.

Michaels walked around the car and knelt down in front of me. All I could do was stare at the ground. He put his hands on my shoulders looked me in the eye. "Did Silva do this to you?" He touched my black eye gingerly.

A single nod, "Yeah, but that's not what hurts."

"I know," he almost whispered and sat down on the ground with his shoulder against mine. I listened in stunned silence to the crackle of the police radios and the quiet talk in the background. Even with all the action and tension around me, it was relatively quiet compared to the noise of my mind for the past ten hours. The warmth felt good. Just the touch pulled some of the tension away. We sat that way while the cops closed in and did their thing.

"Do you want to tell me about it?"

"That's cop talk for 'we need the rest of the story so we can put this guy away for a long, long time.'"

"You're right. But it's also from someone who knows what it's like to be kidnapped, and beaten, and shot at. It'll help you to get the story out."

A big sigh escaped, almost a sob, but I was determined not to cry. "He's got my dog and my dinner. And I can't go back. And you guys are going to have to watch my house for a few days."

He grew grim again. Long pause.

"Why's that?"

"Silva is expecting company in a day or so. That's why I was determined to get out of there today. You'll probably want to pick him up, too. Name's Oscar. I think he might have met with more trouble than Silva did, so there will probably be some charges filed there, too. He'll probably be driving a stolen car. Sounded like something sporty but big enough for two guys, a bag of loot and a hostage. Something fast."

Michaels stood and spoke with one of the uniforms.

"Look, I need to get back and wrap things up. Will you wait here for me?"

I nodded numbly, "One more thing you should know."

He knelt down in front of me. "Yeah, what's that?"

"The master bedroom closet has two rifles and two pistols in it. Silva doesn't know they are there, but if he hides back there he could discover it. He'd have ammo for a long stand off."

"That might be good to know, thanks. You sure you're okay?"

I nodded again, "I'll be okay as soon as this is all over."

Michaels spoke to another officer. She came over and sat with me, but it wasn't the same. He jogged back to my house, disappearing behind the Wilson home.

A fire department rescue squad drove up and two paramedics jumped out and spoke to the officers standing around. One of them approached me.

"Let's get you checked out."

"I'm fine," I said. "A little banged up but I'm not injured in any way."

"A black eye and three lumps on your head and you're not injured?"

I let him go through his routine exam and declined a ride to the hospital for further testing. All I really needed was a little peace and quiet and all the lumps and bruises would take care of themselves.

After a while it became apparent that things were not going well for the police. I couldn't figure out what was wrong. Silva was trapped in my house. How could he not be caught? I thought this would be a simple matter of breaking the door down and storming the place, but time went on and I got the distinct impression that something was wrong. A helicopter came flying overhead circling the neighborhood. I was relieved no shots had been fired, but the silence was grating on me. I was getting impatient and antsy. I was just getting up to start pacing when Michaels jogged up.

"Silva's not in there," he stated. "The house is empty. There's no sign of him in the house or the yard. That's a good-sized fence in back and the lock is still on the gate. Any ideas where he might be?"

"Empty house and empty yard?"

"Yup."

Then I remembered! Plan B! Silva had used my Plan B and jumped my back fence using the A-frame just like I was going to!

"I know where he is!" The two looked at me like I was nuts. "Well, I don't know right now but I can find him." I took off at a fast walk toward my house. I don't know why I didn't think to drive, maybe because you can't track in a car and I was suddenly in tracking mode. I was only two short blocks from my street. Michaels dashed after me pulling me up.

"Oh, no, you don't. You're not going back there."

I spun around to face him. "I am and I know what I'm doing. You can come along if you stay behind me. I need to see where I'm going and what I'm doing. I won't go too close. I promise."

"Why? Why do you think you have to do this?"

"Because I can. I know I can. I know what he did to get away and I have tracked all my life. I've been watching him for two days. I know his walk and his mannerisms. It's where my talent lies, in observation and tracking." I let the determination show on my face. It's a little hard to get my five foot four inch frame to stand up to a six-foot hunk of a guy, but I'd been doing it since I was old enough to walk and he backed off.

I walked into my neighborhood. It was spooky quiet. Did they evacuate it? My house was taped off and men walked back and forth through the front door. I passed up my street and went to the next one. I knocked on the door of the house directly behind mine. Michaels followed.

"What are we doing?" Michaels asked me.

"Plan B. We're doing what I was planning on doing if you hadn't showed up."

Lorraine wasn't answering her door. "Lorraine," I shouted, "It's Cass! I need to talk to you. The police are with me. It's okay." The door opened a crack, then opened wider.

"What the hell are you doing out. With all this ruckus, you should be locked in your house!"

"Been there, done that. I need to see your backyard. I think the guy the police are looking for came through here." She blanched. She looked at Michaels, who showed her his badge.

"Okay."

I walked around to her side gate. It was swinging open. Her backyard was still dirt for which I was very grateful. Michaels tried to go first but I held out my arm.

"I need to be able to read the signs. His footprints are right here so we know he left this place but we need to see what he did back here. It'll tell us a lot about his frame of mind."

I followed the clear footprints to a pile of junk by the back fence. I almost laughed. I was right, Silva had used the A-frame in my yard just as I'd planned to and jumped the fence. He crash landed on this pile of junk and rolled off. There were clear prints of his hands and knees in the dirt beside the pile. He had crouched beside the junk pile, probably listening for the police and checking out Lorraine's house as a possible new hostage situation. He'd decided to run for it and his dash for the gate was plain. He was in a hurry, and he was pushing himself. His footprints were not the pattern of a seasoned runner. These footprints showed desperation. Then he had staggered off through the gate and into the neighborhood. I took mental notes on his footprints; big feet, the pattern of the tread, how he favored his right foot. The tread was more worn down on the left side of his left shoe. It all matched up to what I'd already observed while I'd been captive.

When I returned to the gate, I was back to guessing. I looked up and down the street. There had been a police cruiser stationed at the end of the cul de sac preventing him from jumping that wall. He had to go straight but how did the police miss seeing him? I put myself in Silva's shoes and the large bushes directly across the street beckoned. I crossed the street and poked around behind the bushes. The footprints in the soft soil behind the bushes were plain. He'd crawled through the bushes and made his way from yard to yard taking advantage of the landscaping. When he'd gotten to the end of the street there was more cover, but I thought he would aim for the vacant lot at the end of Joshua Street. I jogged down to the end of the street and stopped at the curb of the pavement. The streets in my neighborhood all drain this way so there is always a big puddle at the end of Joshua Street. Silva didn't know that.

The construction companies in these high desert communities tend to buy up several acres of land and plant a neighborhood smack dab in the middle of a large vacant lot so around the edges of Joshua Hills little four and five block neighborhoods dot the desert floor, all surrounded by desert sand, perfect for tracking. My neighborhood was no exception.

"Stay here," I instructed, "I'm not going far." I inched around the puddle. There was a scuff on the near side. He'd seen the puddle in time to avoid it. I needed to make certain it was Silva that came through here. Anyone could have made the scuff recently. Kids hunted tadpoles here all the time. On the far side, Silva's clear print showed. He was running. I signaled Michaels that he could follow me again.

I was glad Silva didn't expect to be followed on foot. He wasn't being careful at all. His trail was clear, leading in a straight line through the vacant lot. He'd stumbled once on a loose rock and kept going. I didn't see sign of a chase. He must have cleared out before the police saw him get away.

My thoughts ran on ahead as my feet and eyes followed the trail. He was going to get tired quick. This guy wasn't used to running. He was going to look for cover real soon, and the cover up ahead wasn't what I wanted him to go for.

There was a mobile home park to our right with a short wall. Inside it was all cement and pavement again. If he went in there, I'd probably lose him. I was hoping he would go for the other mobile home park across Elm Boulevard. It had dirt streets and the trailers were less populated. If I were Silva, I'd go for the older one. More chances of finding a hiding place there. Michaels was keeping up easily. I was walking fast, only verifying the sign. When I was looking for lost kids, I studied the trail, learning all I could about the person I was tracking. In this case, I knew as much as I wanted to know about Silva. I just wanted the trail to end. The signs continued past the fancy mobile homes. Like I thought, the skirted homes didn't offer the cover he wanted. I headed for the next park.

Silva had stopped at Elm, probably waiting for traffic to clear. We had to wait, too. The light was failing. A police cruiser headed our way and Michaels flagged it down and asked for a flashlight.

"What are you doing out here?" The cop asked.

"We're tracking Silva. We've followed his trail this far."

"Are you shitting me? We've been looking all over. He just vanished."

"You've been driving the streets," I said, "Silva's not out walking the streets. He's looking for cover. His trail is very clear. He went that way."

Traffic cleared and Michaels and I trotted across Elm.

"I don't like the feeling I'm getting off this trailer park," he said, his voice just above a whisper.

"I know. That's what makes me think he's in here."

The black and white pulled into the park.

Silva's trail got messier after he crossed the street. He'd stop and turn, presumably to check for occupants in the trailers. He'd stop outside a trailer, pause, then run on to the next one. All the trailers he stopped at had lights on. They were better off, too. Some had skirting around the bottoms. Silva's trail turned when he got to an old silver trailer. It couldn't be called a mobile home. The back of it was surrounded by sheds offering dark hidey-holes underneath. The windows were dark; the flimsy screen door hung ajar, not quite fitting right. It banged in the wind. Trees blocked the little light there was left, casting the tiny yard in shadow. I signaled Michaels to stay. I had to make sure this was the right one.

I examined the tracks. Silva had vaulted the three-foot wall surrounding the park and landed heavily on the other side. He'd paused, walked forward two steps, then paused again. He'd turned this way and that, listening. He'd crept to the side of the trailer and put his ear against it, his footprints shifting the soft sand. A little Bermuda grass grew here, but it was mostly just dirt. I noticed sandy handprints on the side of the trailer. The footprints went all the way around to the other side, where he'd peered in a window. He'd circled the trailer and entered. He was here and he was trapped.

I looked in the window and saw a trashed out interior. Food wrappers and dirty clothes covered the floor. Silva was rooting around in the junk, presumably looking for something useful. He didn't know he'd been spotted yet. He thought he was in the clear. Another quiet hideout to hole up in till Oscar could pick him up.

I was turning to go back to the wall and find Michaels when two beady eyes appeared in the window.

"You!" he yelled. He pointed the gun at me and fired. I leapt to the side. Curses filled the air and the trailer started shaking as Silva fought his way through the trash and junk on the floor.

I rolled under the trailer and came out on the other side. I stood up and Silva filled the doorway of the trailer, gun in hand. Simultaneous explosions rocked the small yard. The smell of gunpowder stung my nose as I made a mad dash for the wall. Pain seared through my shoulder as I vaulted over. I sat on the other side, sheltered for a bit from the violence behind me.

Sirens filled the night and seconds later the flash of lights told me the police had closed in.

Michaels! Where was Michaels? I thought I had heard two shots. I assumed Silva's shot was meant for me. But what if he'd seen Michaels? Silva wouldn't hesitate to shoot him. He was in escape mode.

"Cassidy!" I heard, "Cassidy, where are you?"

I poked my head up over the wall and there he was, searching underneath the trailer, glancing around, afraid of what he might find.

"Over here," I said standing.

He rushed over, the relief clear on his face.

"You've been hit!" he exclaimed as a bloodstain spread down the arm of my shirt.

"It's just a scratch. Stupid trailer, I caught my shoulder on an old lawnmower blade down there."

Following the police, paramedics came in and cleaned me up a bit. It was just a cut. It bled like crazy but didn't need any treatment. Silva wasn't as lucky. They took him away on a stretcher.

My part in this mess was over. I turned to leave, sadness and tension bubbling up inside of me. I heard footsteps approaching from behind and Michaels joined me. We walked quietly back to the Roadster still parked outside my neighborhood. I looked up into his eyes. I saw kindness coupled with worry and uncertainty, but there was something else, too.

"I heard the shot." He swallowed hard.

"I know. Me too."

"Look, you haven't had any dinner. I haven't had any dinner. You need some space from all this and I need a statement. Let's go to the interrogation room and get a bite to eat."

"The interrogation room?"

"Or Zeke's, come on. You need some space."

I looked at the Roadster. This was Jack's car and I hadn't driven it much. Driving it brought back too many memories, but I knew it could get me out of a jam and Jack would have been glad I used it. The keys dangled from my finger and I glanced around at all the police. My driver's license was at the house. Michaels' car was at the house. I held out the keys to Michaels.

"What's this?"

"I left my driver's license at home and I didn't think I should drive off with a cop and not have it."

"That's the reason?"

"Yes."

"You sure?"

No, I wasn't sure. The car was just too much to deal with right now. The memories, the tension I felt driving it. But I just said, "Yeah."

"Okay, but I wouldn't give you a ticket."
"Thanks."

We got in the Roadster and it slid out of the parking spot and cruised down the road. This car was a perfect match for Jack. It flew. It even had vanity plates that said FLY LOW. That was Jack. Jack flew. My Jeep Wrangler suited me, too. I thought about all the fingerprints on the Jeep. It would be dusted when I got back. Everything would be dusted. I hoped it wouldn't be busted. My mind was spinning in little bitty circles as we rode along. In a way, I was glad. It kept me from staring at Michaels. It also had me worried about Shadow. What had Silva done to him? Maybe the police crashed my door before Silva caught him. Shadow was fast and my house was set up in a way that made it impossible to catch him. We often played tag in the house and Shadow always won. Maybe Silva had given up on dinner and made a run for it.

"I hear the wheels turning in that brain of yours," he said as he drove along.

"Just thinking," I replied.

"About what's behind us or what's ahead of us?" He pulled into a parking lot and found a parking place. It was crowded.

"Pizza?"

"Sure. Nothing is better for taking your mind off stressful things than a nice busy, noisy pizza place and a big pizza with all your favorite toppings. Zeke makes the best pizza."

"I left my pack at home, too. No money."

He guided me in. Guess money wasn't an issue.

"Look, I've been cooking, getting beat on, sat around without a shower with a gun pointed at me. I've been tied up, thrown across a room, sat in the dirt for an hour and rolled around under a dirty trailer. It's possible I might need to go wash up."

I found my way to the ladies room and had to wait in line. At least the crowd led me to believe the place might have good pizza. I was surprised I hadn't been to this place before. I thought I had visited every restaurant in town. Cooking wasn't my favorite thing to do.

I finally got in and looked in the mirror. Yikes, my hair was a tousled mess. I had red tape lines around my mouth. I looked at my wrists. Yep, tape marks there, too, and strips of tape residue. My eye was purple and green. At least it wasn't very swollen. I dusted off my clothes, washed up, and did what I could with my hair. It wasn't much. I didn't have a hairbrush. If Michaels was worried about my appearance, he didn't let on. I joined him in the foyer.

"Feel better?"

"Not after what I just saw in the mirror."

"Don't worry about it. If I ask you out for dinner and you have time to prepare, then you can worry about it. If I yank you out from in front of a firing squad, I don't expect you to put on make up on the way."

Some women would have taken offense to that, but having been in the firing squad position a number of times, it didn't faze me.

"I was going to play the video games but I didn't think you'd like to be in the arcade with that shooting game going on."

"Actually, I don't mind being on the shooting end of a gun. Believe it or not, I can shoot. Silva didn't know it when he locked all the bedroom doors, but he locked up four guns and plenty of ammo. He'd have been set for a stand off, but he locked it all up."

I'd told him about the guns before, but it still drew a curious look.

The pizza place bustled with activity. Booths lined the outer walls and tables filled the open spaces. No tablecloths. Plenty of beer. I noticed they served pasta, too. A waitress seated us at a booth with a worn but polished wooden table. Menus stood at one end. Michaels ordered pizza. I added ice tea; he added Coke.

"You look like you're feeling a little better."

"I am. Thanks."

"How bad was it?"

"It could have been worse."

"It can always be worse."

"The psychological stuff was the worst. The physical stuff I can take." He looked at my small frame and childlike face and seemed amused. I continued, "I was pathetic. I knew what was supposed to happen. But somehow, in real life, other factors crowd in and all the self-defense classes in the world can't help you when instinct tells you not to use it."

I was talking myself into a corner. Michaels was probably wondering just what kind of a girl he had here, and he wasn't getting anywhere on the interrogation. He looked at me and his eyes softened. There was a gentle pause.

"Just tell me what happened."

I started at the beginning, when Silva jumped into my Jeep, and went through the whole story. He winced when I told him about getting hit with the gun butt and the time when Silva had hit me after Michaels left.

"You don't know how hard it was to turn my back and walk away. You can't imagine it."

"I know. But when you came this morning, I had a gun to my head. I knew I could improve my chances if I waited."

"So, now we're expecting this guy Oscar to show up. Do you have a place to stay? Your house is going to be watched and the investigation will go on for a few days. You can't stay at home until we nab Oscar. Where will you go?"

I knew where I was heading, but I didn't want to tell Michaels.

"I've got a place," I said. A place far away that nobody else knew about. "I'll check back in a few days. Oscar won't show if the place is surrounded by crime scene tape and police cars."

"We'll try to get everything out of the way tonight. Where are you going? Is it safe? Does Silva know about it?"

"It's in the mountains, just far enough away. No, Silva knows nothing about it. Yes, it's safe enough for me." This was my place. Not even Jack knew about it.

"If Silva thinks you're too much of a risk he could call someone to eliminate you."

I remembered my cell phone. Silva had it. "Will we be able to pick up a few things from the house first?"

"I think so. We'll go see. Okay, on the lighter side, Jamaica Mistake?"

I laughed, "No, I thought I pulled it off pretty much as planned."

"I didn't mean…"

"I know what you meant. And, no, I wasn't kidding. It's great stuff. The story is on the bottle."

"It took me a while to figure out what I could ask you about. I was going to tell you I had a computer problem, but I didn't know if you even had one. Do you like to cook?"

"No, but it's kind of a necessity of life. I grew up with lots of good food around and I hate eating alone in a restaurant. So that means I cook."

Michaels was right, Zeke did make good pizza. I was sorry when the meal ended and it was time to go. Michaels paid the tab and we got in the car and drove to my house.

From the Jeep I pulled a daypack. I pushed the front door open with my foot in case they didn't want more fingerprints. It would need to be replaced after being kicked in. Shadow came bounding around the corner, barreling into me. Relief flooded me. What a good dog. He even misbehaves when he's supposed to. I filled a Ziploc bag with kibble and stuffed it in the daypack. I got a change of clothes and my other daypack and combined the contents of my hiking pack and my purse pack. I dug my camping box out from the garage and pulled out a few packets of backpacking food. I filled a plastic bottle with water.

"You're going camping? After being through all this you can't go into the hills alone."

"Why not? It's what I do when I need to get away. This seems like an excellent time to me."

"You don't have enough gear. Where's your tent, your sleeping bag?"

"I've got that stuff in the Jeep."

"Are you sure you'll be okay for three days?"

"I'm sure I won't be in any danger."

"I really wish you'd tell me where you're going."

"It doesn't have an address."

"I could follow you."

"Not if I don't want to be found. I'd lose you in five minutes. Like Crocodile Dundee. I'm there, and the next thing you know, I'm gone."

"Does that mean you don't want to be found? I've been at this for a while."

I thought for a second before answering, "When I want to be found I'll take you there, but right now you have work to do and I have to stay out of the way. I'll be back. It's the only place I have left, so there's no point in worrying about where it is."

I took a shower and changed into camouflage pants, a khaki t-shirt and moccasins. No fingerprint search in my bedroom. It had been locked. All the bedroom doors had been knocked in during the search for Silva.

Walking outside, I looked longingly at the Jeep. I'd rather take the Jeep than the Roadster. I wasn't comfortable leaving Jack's car in the woods. Nobody touched the Jeep. It blended in. Just like me, my Jeep was at home in the woods. I didn't have that assurance with the sports car. It begged to be stolen.

"Can I take the Jeep? I really would feel better if I had the Jeep."

Michaels conferred with the team investigating my house. They checked a note pad. They knew it was the getaway car.

"Yeah, you can take the Jeep."

"Silva gave Oscar two days to show. I'll check back in three."

Shadow jumped into the Jeep. I held up Michaels' card, then stuck it in my pocket.

"You be careful," he called as I drove away.

Chapter 3

This wasn't a good time to be heading for my camp. Night had already fallen and it took a little over an hour to reach Creekside Campground. It then took three hours to hike in. I headed east until I reached Millerton Road, took Route 138 east, then took the first turn off onto Route 2. This brought me up into the mountains and forty-five minutes later I was parked at Creekside Campground. I put the fourteen dollar camping fee into the drop box, hung my Adventure Pass on the Jeep's rearview mirror then pulled my sleeping bag out from the back. I tended to disappear like this at a moments notice so I kept the pack and the sleeping bag in the Jeep, ready to go. I only took a tent if I was going somewhere else. I walked Shadow around a bit, popped the passenger seat back flat so he would have a bed and locked him in the Jeep. He used to sleep on the ground under the table, but after being attacked by raccoons he now slept in the car at night. I unrolled the sleeping bag on top of the picnic table and climbed in. I didn't know what time it was and I didn't care. I'd had a full day.

In the morning I woke up with the sun. I loved mornings in the mountains. The campground was always filled with the chatter of birds. That's one thing I missed by hiking to my camp. The Stellars Jays, Gray Jays, sparrows and finches all seemed to prefer the campground where they could count on finding people food. Only the truly wild birds were found at my camp. I rolled up my sleeping bag, stuffed it in the Jeep again and drove down to the trailhead.

The trail out of Creekside Campground follows a pleasant little stream for several miles. After two miles, another stream flows into it, and this was where I left the trail. I climbed a rugged canyon, sometimes rock climbing, other times hiking. I crossed a few meadows and inched my way up short rocky cliffs. Eventually I reached a tall pine tree and a flat rock overlooking the creek and I was home; my home in the wilds. Shadow tagged along beside me. He always finds his own way up. Maybe I'd have had an easier time of it if I'd followed him, but I'd developed my own route and he'd developed his. He seems to know where we are going and occasionally he will beat me there and be sitting on the flat rock when I arrive. I ate trail mix and beef jerky as I hiked and when I got to camp, there was a stash of food in an ammo box.

Even from the flat rock the camp can't be seen. The small area looks like a flash flood hit months ago. Two trees fell between two standing trees resulting in a perfect place to make a tent. I brought a huge tarp up one summer and anchored it over the two fallen trees. I cleared the floor area making it flat and smooth, then I covered the whole thing with branches. The forest grew up over it and now it just looks like a very wild patch of forest. There is no door. I lift a flap of tarp, usually having to search around a bit for it, and slide in. The inside is watertight and cozy. I keep a sleeping bag, my ammo box of food, several books, a fluorescent lantern, a large jug for water, and a tiny one-burner camp stove inside. My food cache is for three days, but I have stayed here for 10 days before living off the land part of that time. I like it up here. It is a rugged, lonely outpost. I have never seen another person up the canyon this far. Once I get about a quarter mile off the trail, the tourists seem to fade away.

Shadow and I have great fun up here. In the meadow, we play a stalking game. When the deer are in the meadow, we see how close we can get to them. Shadow creeps forward like a cat and when the deer look up he freezes. I do the same thing. One time I came close enough to touch a deer, but then Shadow appeared and the deer bolted, almost taking my head off in a jump of fright. The trouble is, Shadow tends to think of the deer as sheep and I tend to think of then as family. Skittish family, but always welcome in my neck of the woods.

Sometimes Shadow and I play hide and seek. I put him in a down stay and take off. I release him and he searches. He always finds me eventually, but not until I ease up and make myself visible. He is definitely a sight oriented dog.

Up here, life swells around me and the cares of the valley begin to melt away. The memory of Silva and Oscar was fading. The memory of Michaels, on the other hand, refused to fade. Every time I turned around, I wanted to show him something, a funny animal, how to set up a snare to catch dinner, a birdcall I had never been able to identify. That was strange, because even Jack had never been here. This was a place I went to be alone.

I hiked up the canyon, trying to enjoy the outdoors. The canyon got more rugged as I went upstream. More rock climbing and less hiking. There were little tumble down waterfalls and shady nooks in the rocks to stop and rest in. The water was frigid. It was snowmelt from the very tops of the mountain peaks.

When I got back to camp I fixed one of the backpacker dinners. I boiled some water on the tiny stove, then added it to a pouch of dehydrated food and waited. Beef stroganoff. Yummy. Backpacker food wasn't my favorite but I was used to it. My favorite meal to eat up here was teriyaki steak. I'd mix up brown sugar, soy sauce and ginger in a mayonnaise jar, stuff a semi-frozen steak in and hike while it marinated. I always pictured all the doctors and dieticians out there cringing. I pictured my mother telling me I was going to die of food poisoning out in the mountains somewhere. When I got to camp I'd cook the steak over a campfire. It's the best steak in the world. Today, backpacker food would do. It fit my lousy mood.

I found myself moping. This was the pits. Usually my camp was a place of refuge for me, but today it felt like a prison. Tomorrow I'd hike out and drive around in the mountains, maybe spend a night in one of the other campgrounds. Maybe Oscar had already made his appearance. Maybe he and Silva were safely locked up, waiting for trial. Perhaps I should consider heading back to town. It's not like I would be in danger there. I just couldn't go home. I had to admit though, another night on a picnic table held more appeal than a hotel.

After dinner, I laid down on the flat rock beside the stream, listening to the water rushing past. This was no burbling brook. This water was in a hurry and it was a steep downhill tumble all the way to the valley floor. I watched the stars come out. It was pitch black and I counted the constellations within view. Some of them were lost because there were too many stars. Shadow kept bringing me pinecones and dropping them on the rock. Every once in a while, I threw one away and he'd run after it. I never knew if he brought back the pinecone I threw or a different one. I wondered how he could even see them as they disappeared into the darkness.

I woke up in the middle of the night, still on the rock. It was chilly, so I crawled over to the hideout, lifted the flap for Shadow, and followed him in.

In the morning I didn't know what time it was. The bird chatter was still going on but it sounded muffled to me. I peeked out from under the flap and was met with a blanket of white. The clouds had blown in from the coast, then hit the mountains and stopped. The wind pushed the clouds until they filled every nook and cranny of the woods. I was sure the few that made it over the mountains had dispersed, leaving the valley below sunny and warm. From town it would look like huge white breakers flowing over jagged rocks. From here, I was socked in. No hiking up the canyon, no stalking the deer. They would be hunkered down just like me. I could try and hike out if I wanted to fall and break my leg but no thanks. I wasn't in that much of a hurry to get out of here.

Once, I did try to hike blindfolded. It had heightened the awareness in my feet. I always walked in the woods with my feet, not my eyes. Eyes are for seeing with, not for walking. My feet lead the way feeling the ground while my eyes watch things. I broaden my vision when I hike, taking in the big picture. When I settled into this way of looking at things, I saw deer deep in the forest. I saw movements and irregularities that signaled animals, people, and potential dangers. Most people walk down a trail and all they see is the trail. I see everything else while I follow my feet.

I let Shadow out and pulled back inside. I lit the lantern and started arranging things for a long wait. After a while, Shadow whined outside so I lifted the flap and let him in. His fur sparkled with moisture and the hideout filled with wet-dog smell. I dug out the books, three novels, a sketchbook and writing paper. I found my pocketknife and a hunk of wood I had stashed in a nook last time I was up here. I wasn't much good at whittling, but it passed the time. I looked at the wood, trying to figure out if I was going for a duck or a dolphin. I couldn't find any place on it that looked like a tail so I decided it was a duck.

I read one of the novels and packed it into the daypack. I'd take it home and bring one back that I hadn't read yet. Days like this were precisely why I brought books up here. I ate backpacker food, trail mix, beef jerky. Had I been able to stand I would have paced. Instead I took a nap and ventured out of the hideout when nature called but scuttled back in as soon as possible. Cold was settling in. I wished I'd brought a jacket, but I hadn't been careful with my packing as my thoughts had been centered on the events of the day. I'd be plenty warm in the sleeping bag but it might be a chilly hike out tomorrow. Day blended into night and night blended into day. I slept off and on, read off and on, and tried to sketch, but couldn't think of what to draw. Michaels came to mind, but I was never good at drawing people, and wasn't sure I'd remember his features right. I thought about drawing Jack and was saddened to think I definitely couldn't remember his features well enough. When I thought of Jack it was his whole body and his face wasn't clear. In my memory he was always doing something; flying, or driving, or walking through Disneyland, or chopping wood. We had gone camping together, but we hadn't ventured out in the woods like this. The woods were my world and the sky was his.

I stuck my head out of the flap and it was daylight again. I wondered what time it was, glanced at the fog, and decided it was still morning. The fog was lighter. I could see trees and rocks several yards away. I could hike out today. My mood brightened and I pulled back inside to start packing up. I pulled all the food out of the ammo box and the daypack. I saved one meal leaving the rest in the ammo box for next time. I made sure the book I read was in the pack, rolled up the sleeping bag and stuffed in it a big plastic bag I kept for that purpose. I turned off the lantern, made sure the camp stove was off and cold and put it all back together with its little nest of pots and pans. Pretty soon the hideout was just as I'd found it. I put the daypack on and crawled out the flap and stood, easing out the aches from being cramped up for a whole day. One of these days I would have to dig out the floor and leave more head room in the hideout. The chill air settled around me. The fog teased me. I figured there would be less fog as I lost altitude so I headed down the canyon and trekked off into the woods. I decided maybe I'd follow Shadow down this time. He wasn't good at rock climbing and I didn't think rock climbing in the fog was a wise thing to do so I followed along behind as Shadow trotted through the undergrowth.

Shadow got his name because of his black and white coloring, but it was also a name that I could speak without drawing a lot of attention. When we were belly down in a meadow with a herd of deer close by a whispered "Shadow" blended in with the forest. Shadow also tended to follow me everywhere so he was like my own shadow in many ways. He picked his way down the mountain and when he was too far ahead and I couldn't follow his lead, I'd call out to him. He'd quickly return for me acting as if I sure was a dumb sheep.

Halfway down the canyon the fog thickened again and I couldn't see the ground in front of me. I started casting around for a place to hole up. I headed for the side of the canyon. I thought I remembered an overhang and an overhang could mean a cave. Wisdom said to stop and wait out the fog. Wisdom also said that if I found the overhang and it *was* a cave, there would probably be a critter in it. Shadow's route down the canyon really was easier than mine, so I continued to pick my way along, feeling with my feet, gazing into the white blanket surrounding me. Shadow was the easiest thing to see in the fog because his black fur stood out, but as we walked along his fur became covered with water droplets until he looked like a sparkly ghost. When Shadow came back to check on me I'd swipe the droplets from his coat so I could follow him more easily.

We came to a crevasse where water had worn a trough in the rock. Shadow picked his way down and I followed keeping my hand against the rock wall of the canyon. Suddenly something moved underfoot, a rock turned and I rolled down the trough landing in a thicket at the bottom. Thorns poked when I moved, fog rolled around me, and everything else was still. No bird calls, no rustling noises. I tried to stand and the thorns closed in. I flexed my arms and the thorns bit into my skin. I curled into a crawl and inched out of the torture chamber on hands and knees. The thorns tore at the pack but I fought my way free. I stood up again, scratched and bleeding but whole. I really felt like I should stop and wait out the fog but now I had itchy scratches all over me and all I wanted was a shower. The knee of my pants was torn. The shoulder seam of my t-shirt was ripped. Wisdom is the better part of valor, but misery is better dealt with over a cup of hot chocolate and a toasty fire at home. I'd had my share of miserable hikes but this didn't need to be one of them. I was going to get out of there and back to my own bed and my old routine. No more carjackers, kidnappers, shooting or fog. I was going home.

I had better luck with the rest of the canyon and when we hit the trail the fog began to thin. The hike back to Creekside was always faster than the hike in because it was almost all down hill. The two miles went by quickly and without mishap. I stumbled down the trailhead and heaved a sigh of relief at the sight of my Jeep.

I turned the rearview mirror so I could see myself and assessed the damage. Oh, man, there was no way I was going back to town looking like this. My black eye had faded a little but now I was covered with scratches from the top of my head to the tops of my shoes. I drove into the little town of Wrightwood, stopped at a convenience store, and bought a hairbrush and a bar of soap. I went to the public restrooms at a park and washed as well as I could in the icy water. My scratches stung like crazy when the soap and water hit them. I washed my hair in the sink until it was blonde again and then dried it with the hand dryers. After much brushing it settled down to a manageable mess. I stepped into a stall to change clothes only to realize I'd left my extra clothes at camp.

As soon as I left the mountains the weather turned sunny and warm. It was windy just like it always is when the clouds are coming in but the chill was mostly gone as I reached the outskirts of town.

I meandered around town until I pulled up to my house. The window was fixed but I saw the yellow tape and my heart suddenly felt heavy again.

I drove to the police station. I'd driven by it thousands of times, but I'd never been in there before. It was a modern gray stucco building located in the center of town. I walked through the double glass doors and approached the counter that filled one wall of a lobby area. I asked to see Michaels and took a seat on a chrome and plastic bench.

After a few minutes I saw Michaels look through the small window of a utilitarian, fake wood door. The door swung open and he strode across the room sitting on the bench facing me. He was grim-faced.

"What happened?" he said his voice sounding like thunder.

"It's nothing, just a stupid accident on my part. I was just hoping I'd have my house back. Surely it hasn't taken them this long to take a few finger prints."

"Come in to my office and I'll tell you about it."

I followed him down a hall, around a corner and then down another hall. My skin prickled. I could feel eyes on the back of my head. People peered around corners and stuck their heads out of doorways as we walked by. What's with these people? I was sure they were used to seeing all sorts of people walk down these halls. What was so interesting this time? Sure, my clothes were torn and I looked like I'd been in a fight with a giant pincushion, but all the looks seemed odd to me. Michaels didn't seem to notice. He stopped at his office, entering through another fake wood door with a little window in it. Everything was utilitarian. His desk had stacks of files on one corner. All the walls were beige just like the rest of the station. He had a plant on his filing cabinet but it needed some real sunlight. Two chairs faced his desk. There weren't any photos on his desk or pictures on the walls. He closed the door behind us and looked at me. Reaching out he touched the tear in the shoulder of my t-shirt taking in the rips, the scratches and the black eye.

"Now tell me what happened."

"Nothing happened. Nature just hasn't been very kind to me this week. First I got carjacked and kidnapped and shot at. Then I hiked up into the hills. I was so lonely and the mountains felt so empty. I usually like it up there, but this time I couldn't stand it. Then the fog closed in and I spent a whole day stuck in a little rat hole on the mountain. I tried to hike out on the third day and I slipped on a rock in the fog and fell into a thorn bush and here I am." I shrugged, all part of being Cassidy "Trouble" Callahan. "But my house is still taped up and I can't do anything and I don't want to go back up there. I can find a place to stay but I was hoping my house would be there and..." I was babbling and was ashamed of it.

He reached out and I saw a big hug coming and then he checked himself. Instead he studied me. I felt his gaze go right through me and I toughened up inside. I adjusted my stance.

"Have a seat."

I sat in the chair facing his desk while he folded himself into the other one. He turned it to face me. I was glad because I didn't want that big desk stretching out between us.

He began, "Oscar didn't show up till this morning." Thank goodness for fog and thorn bushes, I thought. "Jefferson and Rubio were watching your house and everything went according to plan. He had a stolen car and a bank bag like Silva. He's being questioned." Michaels remembered something and walked around the desk, opened a drawer and removed a small object. He handed me my cell phone. "We took this off Silva at the trailer park. I don't think he had a chance to call Oscar about the change in plans because picking up Oscar was easy."

"Then why are they still investigating?"

"They should be done soon. When Oscar came to your house a neighbor walked up. They tried your door, walked around the side of the house. They waited for the neighbor to clear out before they nabbed Oscar. Let's go see if they're finished. Maybe I can get them to speed things up a bit."

"I need to get back to my car anyway. Shadow is out there."

I felt the eyes on us again as we exited the building.

Shadow started barking as soon as I stepped into view. He danced around on my car seat, wagging his tail and barking. I took him out on his leash and made him sit in the back. Michaels climbed in and we took off.

It didn't take long to get to my house and there was little conversation as we rode along. Michaels seemed to be thoughtful. Like most guys, he probably preferred to drive. As we pulled onto my street they started taking the crime scene tape down. I pulled into the driveway and we all got out. Shadow ran for the front door.

"The window is fixed," I pointed out.

"I thought the house should look normal when Oscar arrived. I didn't think he'd stop if the place looked violated so I called a glass place and it was fixed the next morning."

We entered the house and a sense of familiarity settled over me. I picked up a lamp that had fallen over and fingered the dent in the wall where my foot had almost penetrated when Silva threw me across the room. I found the plate that held Silva's steak in the far back corner of my bedroom. It looked like Shadow finally got his dinner. I put the dishes that had been left out into the dishwasher. Things weren't too bad, considering. I went out to the backyard and dragged the A-frame away from the back fence. If Silva could jump the fence from up there, Shadow could easily. Michaels glanced around the backyard.

"I need to mow."

"Nah, I wouldn't worry about that yet. You have a lot of other things you need to do first."

"Like what?" I asked, curiously.

"Doesn't all this bother you? You know we have teams of guys at the station. When someone has some violent crime committed against them they go in, find out how to help the victims and they put a work crew together.

Sometimes it's something easy. There's a burglary and the victims would feel better with just a motion detector light. We install one for them. Maybe they were attacked from some creep hiding in their bushes. We can take out their bushes so they feel safe coming home again. That's one reason it was easy to get your window fixed."

"I think I'll be fine," I said, curling up in a corner of my couch.

"Do you have someone who can come stay with you?"

"I'll be fine, really. Silva is caught. Oscar is caught. My window is fixed. My lamp didn't even break and I'm surprised at that, the way I hit it." Oops. Too much info. His expression softened and his eyes saddened. Next question, could *he* put all this behind *him*? I thought he'd be used to this, that it was routine police policy: get the job done, put it behind you. Now I wasn't so sure.

"No, I don't have someone who will come stay with me. We were stationed out at the base. I was Marines, Jack was Air Force. We were only married a short time. Does the name Jack Callahan mean anything to you?"

"Yeah," he said, "He was a test pilot out there. A lot of the guys at work have friends out there. They spoke highly of Jack. Lots of them attended his funeral when his plane went down."

"That was my Jack. My stint with the Marines ended shortly after we were married. We were worried, with him in one service and me in another that we'd get shipped in different directions so I didn't sign up again. He was career so here's where we stayed. We bought this house. Jack crashed. Now I'm in limbo. I'm doing okay for now. I've just been spinning my wheels, building junk for my backyard, training Shadow, camping a lot. Eventually I'll have to get a job, but I don't know what kind that would be. There's not much use for a cowgirl, Marine, tracker."

"The pictures on the mantel?"

"That's Jack and me. Some of the pictures are of my mom and dad, sister and brother-in-law and their two kids. That's my family. They live in the central part of the state. They have a big ranch. They've all got each other and I've always been a loner."

"You shouldn't be that much of a loner."

"How'd it go with your girlfriend?"

"My girlfriend?"

"The one you were going to cook dinner for."

"You know I don't really have a girlfriend."

"I do?"

"Cassidy, I don't have a girlfriend."

"Jamaica Mistake?"

"Not yet, but I'm a little worried that I might."

And that is how I met Rusty Michaels.

PART 2

TROUBLE TRACKER

My house felt more comfortable, yet I was getting more and more restless. Occasionally I spoke at elementary schools, telling kids how to stay safe in the woods, what to do if they ever became lost and how to prevent becoming lost in the first place. I would tell them the story about finding a missing boy in the mountains and would then take their questions. It was a way to contribute and I hoped the information sunk in.

Michaels called every few days to check up on me. Our visits were always warm and casual. I got the feeling he was sitting on the sidelines waiting to be called into the game. What kind of game he was watching intrigued me. I certainly couldn't find anything remarkable about the Cassidy Callahan game, but I enjoyed his calls.

I remembered the day I had escaped from Silva. Michaels had already known my name and in a way that felt nice. He had probably found my name from the DMV records while checking my license plate number from the bank robbery. It still felt good that he had used it. That had helped him look like a true neighbor with a real question that day. I never asked him about it, but I certainly speculated.

Chapter 4

Trouble seemed to be taking a break from my life for a little while. Maybe that is what made me feel so restless. Maybe my life had become so hum-drum that trouble got bored and left. That would be a good thing, except I was bored, and when I was bored trouble was usually close on its heels. I just had to ignore the boredom. Don't go looking for adventures, I'd tell myself. You know what happens when you do that.

Michaels could feel it, too. He knew change was in the wind and I was afraid he would do something about it. I thought it might involve a date and I wasn't ready for a date. A date would cause guilt and guilt was bad.

A week went by and for some reason Michaels hadn't called. I thought he had just gotten busy at work and dismissed it wondering how I felt if this stretched on for two weeks. I was in my box-filled garage sawing on a two by four, trying to build another obstacle for my backyard, when the phone rang. I dug the phone out of my pocket.

"Hello?"

No "Hello" or "How are you doing?" this time.

"I'm probably going to hate myself for doing this," Michaels said, his voice strained, "but can you come down to my office?"

"Sure," I replied, "just give me a chance to wash up. I'm building something and I'm full of sawdust."

He paused. It seemed like no matter what I did it surprised him for some reason. "Thanks," he said. "I'll be here."

I took a shower, blow-dried my hair, and used a curling iron a little bit to flip the ends out. I brushed on mascara and eye shadow, changed into jeans, a little eyelet tailored blouse and moccasins. I switched my daypack contents to a real purse and slung it over my shoulder. I made sure Shadow had water, said good-bye, and jumped in the Jeep. I was curious what was going on with Michaels that made him call me to his office. If it was a social call, he would have stopped by the house.

I pulled up in the police station parking lot, locked the door on the Jeep, and went in. There was a black woman at the reception counter and she eyed me suspiciously. I went to the desk and asked to see Michaels. A white woman's head appeared from around a doorway. There was a silent conversation between the two that involved lots of finger pointing, head nodding and glares at each other.

"Okay," she said uneasily, "I just got one question. We have this thing going on in the office and it was agreed on that the person at the front desk next time we saw you would ask you something."

Uh oh. I smiled waiting for her to go on, "Yes?"

"We want to know what you done to Rusty."

"What I did? I didn't do anything to him."

"You sure enough DID! It's a well known fact that one minute he was his own self, same ol', same ol, Rusty. Then he gets involved in that Silva case and he changed. Oh, he changed something awful! The day after the hold-up, he charged in here, went straight to his office and called in Schroeder, his best friend on the force. And he told Schroeder not to let him out of this building for the rest of the day. Then he starts planning like he's invading a foreign country. Schroeder don't know what's up neither. He knew it had something to do with the Silva case, but Rusty's keepin' quiet. An' Rusty won't budge. Nobody could talk to 'im. He's gotten better since Silva got captured but he still acts really weird. All the women in this office have been after Rusty since they started working here and none of 'em have had any luck. Then you come along. And you say you didn't do nothin'. Humph."

Now this was very interesting. But it made me a bit uneasy. Was that why people were watching when I came to the station before?

"I swear I didn't do anything. But he did ask me to meet him at his office, so can you tell him I'm here?"

"Harumph" she picked up the phone and buzzed Michaels' office.

"I've never even called him Rusty!" I said in self-defense.

"Do you remember where his office is?"

"Yeah." She opened the door and I walked down the beige hallways to the fake wood door with the little window. I peeked through the glass to make sure it was the right one. Michaels brightened a little, but his expression was worn. He was sunburned and tired. His sports coat was hanging on a chair nearby and he had his shirt sleeves rolled up like he'd been working hard.

He opened the door and stood filling the doorway, just looking.

"It's good to see you again. You're looking great."

"I feel almost human again." I glanced around him. There was a topo map spread out on his desk. The pile of files had grown. "What's up?"

"I told you I'm not going to like myself for doing this, but you're the only person I know who might be able to crack this. We've had rangers out, search and rescue." He resigned himself to his cause and bent over the map.

My curiosity perked. This was a tracking case!

"We've got a forest ranger missing." He glanced at me, still unsure if he wanted to share the information. He knew I'd take it. He knew I'd jump at it. What was holding him back?

"Here, you can see the area. He started out at Piney Point camp and he hiked this trail." He ran his finger along a 20-mile section of trail. "To Elk Meadows campground. He was supposed to take notes on where the trail needed repairs. He was fixing minor things as he went along but he only had a week to complete the trail. It's now been a week since he was supposed to be back, and no sign. There are rough spots in the trail up on the ridges and places where the trail needed marking."

I sighed. It was a rough trail. And it would take longer to track it than hike it.

"You say there have been others over the trail? There may be no tracks left to read. How much of a search have you conducted so far? And why do you have the case? Do they think this is crime related?"

"I don't have the case. Guy's name is Kelly Green. We go rock climbing together. I went out with the search and rescue unit. I thought you might be able to see things we missed."

"Why didn't you call me in the first place? This would be a lot easier when the trail was fresh. Now we've got tracks on top of tracks and wind and weather have deteriorated the trail."

"Do you think it's worth a shot?"

"Sure, it's worth a shot. I'd hike the trail just for the fun of it at the drop of a hat. This will be interesting. I'll need a day to prepare. Every minute we sit around here valuable information is being lost. And you can't expect me to get through this trail in a week. I will have to walk slow and read sign. This won't be like tracking Silva. Silva was a piece of cake. Soft desert sand is ideal for tracking. And that was minutes after he ran. This is a week we're talking about, and it'll be another week before I complete the trail. Green might not even be along the trail. He may have left it. There's a lot to consider."

"I know. I've considered the hell out of it."

I knew I could hike the trail in a week. That was no problem. I knew I could have found him before any searchers went through and covered his tracks. Now the outlook wasn't promising. On the other hand, this was a man used to being in the woods. He was in good physical shape and he would have gone out prepared. If anyone could make it after this time, it would be him. Still, I had plenty of questions. I hadn't worked with the officials here. I'd found a lost boy scout and spent plenty of time in the woods, but I hadn't tried anything of this magnitude.

"How will I keep in touch? If I find him, I'm going to have to be able to call in my coordinates so help can get in."

"I can get one more team together. We can set you up with a radio. I'll check on a GPS system for you. Cell phones work from certain points along the trail. Here, here and here. One of the perks of living close to L.A."

"You really think I can do this?"

"I'm betting on it."

"Betting what?"

"Just be careful. I could go with you."

"You've got bad guys to catch."

"There's better things to do than catch bad guys."

"I'd work better alone."

"I knew you'd say that. I don't think I can let you do this. Let me get some guys together. Nobody is ready to give up on Kelly. I can have a team ready by morning."

"I can't work with people looking over my shoulder. At times when the reading gets tough I have to take my time. It's like a puzzle. I can't ask a whole team of people to just sit around while I figure something out. I would feel pushed, and this is one time when I can't be pushed. It has to be right before I go to the next step."

"Then what can I do?"

"Nothing. It needs to be done, and I'll do it. You knew I'd do this when you picked up the phone. You knew I'd jump at it. You can fill me in a little on site. I have to have something to start with. It would be helpful to see a picture, to know Green's height and weight. If he was wearing work boots, does he have another pair I can take a look at? Or even a pair of his every day shoes. There are wear patterns on the soles that give me lots of clues. Does he walk weird? Does he favor one foot over another? Has he had any injuries that would affect how he travels? How far do you think he got? I need to examine the exact spot where he left his vehicle. Anything like that will really help."

"I'll go talk to his wife, pick up a pair or two of shoes, some pictures, and get any information I can from her."

"A photocopy of a picture would be helpful, too, so I can question other hikers that I meet. I'll go pack up and buy some gear I'll need."

"And I'll pick you up at eight?"

"The earlier the better. I can be ready at five. It'll give me more time on the trail before the sun sets. I'm pretty much restricted to daylight hours on a search like this. Too much important information gets skipped over in the dark."

"Okay, I'll shoot for five."

He walked me to the Jeep. Driving home I made a mental list of the things I needed to accomplish before the end of the day. First on the list was to get Shadow to a kennel. I didn't want to pack a week's worth of dog food on top of all the things I would need, and I didn't want him in the way if I had to call in search and rescue.

Dropping Shadow off at the kennel was always heart wrenching. I knew how bored he would be. At least he was used to this and I trusted the kennel to take good care of him. I was always amused at his reaction to their mushy doggie woggie talk. He was used to a firm command and they gushed all over him. I dropped him off along with two weeks worth of food and a couple of toys.

I drove to a sporting goods store and bought ten different packages of backpacker food, some pepper spray, two hundred feet of light climbing rope, and a new topo map of the area. I stopped at Sam's gun shop and picked up a new box of ammo. Then I stopped at the grocery store and bought a tiny notebook, a box of hot chocolate mix and a box of instant oatmeal. I didn't really like oatmeal, but it was one of the best breakfast foods to eat on the trail. A hot breakfast on a cool morning always made a good start.

At home I pulled out my backpack. I'd need more gear than the dayback would hold. Hell, I might even need more gear than the backpack would hold. I'd have to pack light, taking only essentials. I started by pulling out the daypack, a box of camping gear, my tent, and a down sleeping bag. I took the bulky fiberfill bag out of the Jeep and then stuffed my down bag into the tiniest stuff sack I owned. I checked the gas in my stove, and made sure I had an extra bottle. The stove came with its own pan and handle. I put a small fork in the pan too. I packed one change of clothes. It was going to be a major decision whether to change halfway through the trip or save the good clothes for when Michaels picked me up. Luckily, I was used to grunge and could live with it. I packed the heavy stuff in my pack against the small of my back and the lighter stuff against the zipper. This would make the load much easier to bear.

I checked everything: tent, sleeping bag, stove, fuel, clothes, first aid kit, rope, food, water, water purifier system, matches, pepper spray, notebook, pencil, tiny hair brush, and a flute. The bamboo flute I had bought at a craft fair years ago. Although it only played in one key, it was light and made lonely nights deep in the woods friendlier. I could play a few tunes in that key and had made up a few others that seemed to fit the mood of the woods.

I made sure my 9mm was loaded, jammed it into the holster and set the webbed gun belt beside my packed gear. I brought along eight bottles of water and would decide at the trailhead how much of it I should pack in. A pint a pound the world around, the saying goes, and I wanted as few pounds as possible.

Holding the pack, I stepped on the scale which showed 151 pounds with no water. Setting the pack down I weighed only 116, which left a thirty-five pound difference. That was the best I could hope for. I could ditch the tent but if it rained I'd appreciate the shelter. I could ditch the water purifier but I didn't want to risk getting sick on a trip of this magnitude.

I battled over my choice in shoes. I preferred hiking in moccasins, but this trail called for hiking boots. Patches of the trail were littered with shale and other sharp rocks. I'd have to cross a few streams and climb a steep butte. Plus, if I ran into trouble my own trail had to be easy to follow, so the hiking boots won.

I couldn't put my finger on what I was feeling about this trip. I was excited to be on a mission again, but something didn't feel right about it. Green was experienced in the woods. He'd hiked these trails. He knew the wildlife and understood the necessary precautions. He was physically fit. I knew a single misstep could land him off a cliff, but I couldn't believe that's what happened. Possibly it was something else, and I clung to the hope that he had made it past the tourist point and left the trail occasionally. If he left the trail, it would be very recognizable and I'd have clear signs to follow.

I slept fitfully, and 4:30 came way too early. Scenarios kept flitting through my mind. They all seemed to happen a few days down the trail, but I couldn't figure out why. Something niggled at the back of my mind, which bothered me and yet, in a way, gave me hope. Eventually it would surface, and I hoped it would surface in time.

I showered and blow-dried my hair. No sense in putting on any make-up. It attracted bugs, looked smudged and awful after half a day on the trail, and went down hill from there.

Until I found Green it was necessary to stand out, so I slipped on blue cargo pants that converted to shorts, and a red long-sleeved t-shirt. If he was out there, I wanted him to see me. I pulled on thick socks and hiking boots. The boots felt stiff on my feet after the moccasins but I'd eventually get used to them. They were well-worn older boots that conformed to my feet.

I was arranging things on my dining room table when Michaels rang my doorbell. Letting him in, I noticed a slight tinge of light on the horizon.

"Looks like you're ready," he said.

"Yup. I've checked and double checked."

He hefted the pack estimating its weight, looking at me dubiously.

I'd shopped and tried on a dozen packs before I found one that was just right. It suited me and had been my hiking companion for many years. I took the pack from him.

"Are you sure about this? Twenty miles lugging this thing around for a week? I've seen part of this trail on the first search, and that was the easy part."

"Look, you can start worrying about me after a week. If I were just hiking straight through, I could do it in four days. But I told you I need to take it slow. I need to read the sign and sometimes that means spending a long time figuring out what those signs mean. It's all very subtle, and subtle clues take some detective work. And, if luck is with us, I won't find him until the end of the trail because that will mean less time spent in whatever situation kept him from finishing the hike. He'll have gear, food and water up until very close to the end, and hopefully he will still have it when I find him. The more time he spends with his gear, the more likely he'll still be alive. I have ten days worth of dinners and twelve days worth of breakfasts. I have jerky, trail mix, a couple of energy bars, and water. I can live off the land for a few days if I need to. Been there, done that. I'd pack more food, but more food means more weight. The less weight, the faster I can go."

He eyed the gun on the table. "You licensed for this?"

"Of course."

"Do you expect to use it?"

"No, it's only for self defense. I am going to be hiking through bear and cougar country. I won't use the gun unless I have to, but I like to be prepared. Would you rather I left it behind?"

"No, you wouldn't take it if you weren't comfortable using it. It's just that a 9mm won't do much to a bear."

"By the time I get scared enough to shoot a bear, it will be pretty close."

"You sure aren't making me feel any better about this."

"What *would* make you feel better?"

I could hear the gears grinding in his head and see the struggle on his face. It was scarier than facing Silva. He was going to cancel the search.

"Let's go," I said, first strapping on the gun then shouldering the pack. We loaded it into the back of his dark blue Explorer. I pulled a small cardboard box from the Jeep and brought it along, too. We climbed in and hit the road. I asked him to stop at a coffee shop near my house. The manager and checker greeted me by name. I ordered a white chocolate caramel macchiato and a big piece of New York cheesecake. Michaels ordered black coffee and a zucchini/walnut muffin. We ate on the road. I poked the cheesecake out if its little envelope and ate it like a candy bar.

"Gotta get my cheesecake fix in. I'm going to be deprived for a week." Michaels pulled off pieces of his muffin and ate them as he drove. "You're eating your muffin upside down," I said. This brought a smile to his face.

"How do you eat a muffin upside down?" he asked.

"The flavor all rises to the top, so you take off the wrapper and eat the bottom first. That saves the best part for last."

"I'll have to remember that for next time."

The drive to Piney Point was quiet and I could sense the tension building as we got closer. Michaels' driving became tighter, and his grip on the wheel was almost white knuckled. He stared ahead, arguing with himself. This couldn't go on.

Desert scrub and Joshua trees gave way to pine trees and junipers. We stopped at the ranger station on the way and I was glad for the break. Maybe some conversation with the rangers would calm him down.

I hopped out of the Explorer and climbed the steps up to the ranger station two at a time. I waited at the door for Michaels to catch up, then stepped inside.

"Hey, Cassidy! Are you stopping in for a wilderness pass again? Which direction are you off to this time?"

I smiled. This was good news. It was Paul, and he was always issuing me wilderness passes. If anybody could make Michaels feel better about this hike, he could. Paul was short and potbellied. His hair was thinning on top and sprung out at the sides of his head. Hat hair. He stretched the buttons on his ranger uniform, and he was warm and friendly, always cheerful.

"She's going after Kelly Green," Michaels said matter of factly. "We're stopping in to get fitted with radios and GPS."

Paul looked at me just like Michaels did. Oh, no.

"Aw, no, Paul, not you too! You know I've been all over these mountains. I found Thomas Parker when he wandered away from his Boy Scout troop. I brought you a pinecone from the top of Waterman Mountain just to prove that I'd been there. Look, that's it on your windowsill. I recognize it. It's split on top and lopsided but it is from the top of Waterman. You'll dare me to climb a mountain but you don't want me to hike from Piney Point to Elk Meadows?"

"It's not the hike Cass. I don't want you to be the one to find Green. Something just doesn't smell right about this whole disappearance."

I stared down Paul. "Why didn't you call me in while the trail was still fresh?"

Michaels and Paul looked at each other. Michaels took a deep breath and blew it out with a huff. "I think she's dead set. We'll just have to fix her up the best we can."

Paul nodded. He called another ranger in from the back room to hold the fort and we followed him into the room housing the radio station. Paul took out an orange two-way radio, popped the back off and dumped the batteries in the trash. He then went to the refrigerator, pulled out new batteries and inserted them into the radio.

"I'm not taking any chances. You're going to stay in touch, right?"

"Right."

"Cell phone charged?"

"Yup."

"You know how these things work. I'll be here days, Larry will be here nights. I'll inform him that you're out there and he'll keep an ear out for you. Test it just to make sure it works and test it just before you hit the trail. Check in every day, rain or shine, preferably on my watch. If you haven't called in and Larry doesn't hear from you by midnight, he's gonna be calling me and you don't want that to happen. We'll keep a log of your calls, what time they come in and where you are."

I pushed the button on the radio. "Test, test," I said quietly. I hated the sound of my own voice across a radio. It never seemed right to me.

"Here's the GPS system. This shows your location. The coordinates appear here and here. Keep it on you at all times. We don't care where your pack is. We want to know where *you* are."

"Is this supposed to tell *me* where I am or *you* where I am?"

"Both. If something happens we'll know where to look."

"Then why the radio?"

"A dot on the screen is not an update. We want to know you're okay out there. Some of us wimpy guys just gotta hear your voice. And if you find Green, we'll need instructions."

I clipped the radio and GPS system to my belt.

When we pulled into Piney Point the campground was nearly empty. A motor home had taken one of the nicer camping spots with a big rock off to one side. It's funny how a single rock or a stand of trees can make or break a site. A young couple on motorcycles and camping in a pup tent had the spot next to the camp host. We rolled on quietly through the campground. It was still early. The couple was up making coffee. No one stirred at the motor home. At the trailhead we stopped at the first parking spot.

"Do you know where Green's truck was parked?" I asked.

"Vaguely." He opened the side door to the Explorer and pulled out a cardboard box. From the box he pulled out a worn pair of work boots and a framed photo of Green and his wife. "This is Kelly and his wife, Rhonda. He's about six one, a hundred and ninety pounds. Here his hair is short, but by the time you find him it'll be down over his collar. I asked his wife about any injuries he had, and she only mentioned a climbing accident from five years ago when he bashed up his ankle. He's got a long, ground eating stride."

The picture showed a nice looking couple. Green had dark, curly hair and a quirky lopsided smile that made him look like a bit of a smart aleck. In the picture, he was wearing tan shorts and a Hawaiian shirt.

"Let me see the boots," I said pulling out my own cardboard box. I removed two pieces of sketch paper and a drawing pencil that had been sharpened for rubbings. Unfolding the paper, I centered it on the shoe and made a careful rubbing against the sole. I did the same to the other one. I examined the soles of the boots and made notes with little arrows. "Heel and ball very worn. Heel hits first. No drag marks. 6-1, 190 lbs, injured ankle 5 yrs ago." I sprayed fixative on the rubbings, waved them in the wind to dry then placed them in my pack. Michaels watched with interest.

"You take this pretty seriously."

"Green would want to be taken seriously."

"Anything else?"

"Yeah, there's a couple of things we need to do." I took out the map and spread it on the hood of the Explorer, but it was too high for me to see properly. Taking it to the back, I opened the hatch, climbed in and spread the map out so that it faced Michaels.

"Show me again where the cell will work." He pointed to three areas and with a pencil I marked them with a nice clear C. "And where can I expect to find water?"

"I don't know that one. I've only been this far," he said pointing. "Call Paul and ask him. You were supposed to test the radio anyway."

I unclipped the radio and put it to my mouth, pressing the button. "Test, test," I said.

"I hear ya, Cass."

"I have a question."

"Shoot."

"I'm marking waterholes on the map but I forgot to ask you where they were."

"Hold on. Let me get to my map. I gotta get oriented here." As Paul made his way to the front counter I could hear the sounds of shuffling and then the map unfolding. I assumed he was marking a reference map from the display model used for tourists. "Okay, Cass, can you hear me?"

"I hear you."

"You got three for sures and two maybes. You got one at the 5-mile mark where a stream crosses the trail. Easy to spot. You won't have trouble finding that one. The next one is about six miles further. If I remember right there's a sharp bend in the trail and then it starts a steep climb. If you cut off the trail to the east, you should see cottonwood trees. That should be your mark. There's a spring there. Unfortunately, the next water hole that you can count on won't happen for a while. On your map, find Elk Meadows, then go back two miles. You should see an area on your map similar to Elk Meadows. There are several meadows leading up to the campground and the spring is on the far side of one of them. The south side of the meadow is all swampy, so you'll want to get to the source. It's up in the rocks on the south side. You won't see the meadow from the trail, so you'll have to keep track of your progress with the GPS and the map." I marked the locations on my map with big Ws.

"Okay," I said, "Where are my maybes"

"See the point where the trail crosses the PCT? There's sometimes a creek running near there. It's kind of iffy. Then there's another mostly dry creek after the shale mountain." Shit. So I might need to carry 3 days worth of water and one bottle for Green. "I got it." I said, "I'll take the map along. Thanks."

"Over and out. And Cass, please be careful."

"Will do."

I broke out the water bottles and guestimated my water needs; one cup a day for the backpacker food, plus one bottle a day for drinking, plus one bottle for Green. That meant I'd have to bring 7 bottles. Double shit. I had to pack it in, though, because even trustworthy watering stops could prove problematic. One time I had reached a spring only to find a dead deer laying in the water with flies and maggots crawling on it.

I unzipped the pack, removed the contents, and then repacked it with most of the water, the stove, radio, and rope in the back. Then I layered everything else on top, leaving the map and notebook easily accessible. I slid one bottle of water into the outside pocket.

"Let's go see where Green parked." I brought the rubbings along, hoping to match them to a print in the parking lot. If I was lucky, Green did a lot of walking around his car before heading out.

"What's all the rope for?"

"After day two I'll have to hang my pack in a tree at night. I also brought it in case I need to do some rock climbing."

"Nope," he said. "No rock climbing off by yourself in the woods."

Yeah, right.

"Only if I have to. I'm not planning to."

"I think this is the spot."

I unfolded the rubbings, trying to match it to any of the prints found around the parking area. I found the tracks of at least ten people crisscrossing the spot where the truck had been; men, women, kids. I wondered how far the little girl with the Lilo and Stitch sneakers would get before her parents had to carry her. The tracks of a boy about ten led straight to the trailhead and raced around. He'd jabbed a walking stick into the dirt impatiently while waiting for his parents to get out of the car, work the kinks out, and drag themselves down the trail. And I saw the faint size ten work boots of two rangers, identical tread on both. Big, smooth wear points on the soles of boots used to putting miles beneath ranger feet. One of the men walked toes straight ahead. The other man tended to twist and turn, backtracking a lot, probably forgetting things in their truck. His toes pointed out slightly as he walked. Michaels watched my circling and reading of the ground with interest. He squinted at the ground, attempting to identify what I was able to see so clearly.

After I'd read the parking area as well as I could, I traced around two semi clear footprints for each man.

"Which one is Kelly?" I asked. "This man is heavier. Could be because he's wearing a pack, could be because he's heavier. This man walked around the truck several times, like he still had unfinished business. Would Kelly Green have been the one to quietly put on his pack and be ready to go, or would he be the one to have to put things together?"

"He'd have his pack ready to go. There wouldn't be loose ends with Green. This was a routine trip, normal ranger duties. He'd be ready to take off so he could finish up quicker."

"Have you watched him walk? Which set matches the man I'm after?"

"It's still consistent. He's the straight toed guy with the backpack on."

"Check." Now comes the awkward part where Michaels kicks himself in the ass.

"Cassidy," he said squaring me in front of him, "what's your mission?"

"Find Kelly Green."

"And?"

"Be careful?"

"And?"

"Call the ranger station every day?"

"And?"

"Call you when my cell works."

"And?"

"Meet you at Elk Meadows?"

"Or come out with the search and rescue team."

"So, Rusty Michaels, what's your mission?"

"Follow you on your long and perilous journey, defend you from lions and tigers and bears, build romantic campfires, and make love to you every night under the stars."

We both knew this wasn't going to happen, but it was out there. The thought hung between us, fluttering around and around and I didn't know whether to reach out and capture and hold it close or swat it down like an annoying bee.

I wrapped my arms around him, snuggling into his tweed jacket, the same one he wore to my door so long ago. It felt like ages. Four weeks. A big lump formed in my throat.

My voice cracked, "Try not to worry. I promise to check in. You can call the ranger station every night if you want to." He squeezed tighter and rested his chin on the top of my head. I felt the reluctant nod.

Chapter 5

I shouldered my pack and Michaels followed me to the end of the trail. I picked up the logbook and entered my trip information, "4-10 Hey guys, it's Cassidy Callahan off to Elk Meadows. ETA 5-10 days." Then I read some of the other entries.

"How long is the one mile loop? It feels like ten!"

"You guys need to put the waterfall closer to the campground."

"Great hike, nice views, will do it again."

"Do something about the fucking motorcycles. They're going to kill somebody!"

And, in little kid's handwriting, "Ritchie, age 8, I saw my first deer and I almost caught a fish in the creek with my bare hands and I want to be a ranger too."

It was time to go. "I'll call in. I'll track till dusk. Then I'll find a tent site and make dinner. I need to eat and clean up before dark to discourage critters. I don't go by a clock, so keep your eye on the sky. If it's truly dark, it's a good time to try the station."

I turned at the first bend and looked back. The blue Explorer was still there, Michaels leaning against its dusty side. I waved, but couldn't see if he waved back. I shifted my pack, straightened my back and set off at a good clip.

I didn't really expect to find much on my first day. The book had shown twenty entries since Green had signed it. That meant twenty sets of footprints obscuring Green's tracks.

The first half-mile is always the hardest for me. My pack felt heavy, and bulky, and I hadn't quite gotten into stride. I knew that the pack would settle soon and become part of me. Then the trail would ease up and I'd be comfortable, ready for the long haul.

In the first mile I saw footprints of every shape and size. Tourists out for the day, unused to the elevation or hiking. The tracks going in were always spry and energetic. The tracks coming out were worn and tired. Feet dragged. Most city folk hiked in to the waterfall, splashed around a few minutes to cool off, then hiked back. I tried to guess which footprints were Ritchie's. I decided his were the tennis shoes that were mostly worn out and untied most of the time. He sounded like a kid who would keep going until his shoes wore out or fell off. Green's path was lost in the jumble.

I didn't see many hikers out, but it was still early. Most hikers made the mistake of sleeping in and taking off after a leisurely breakfast, then they hiked in the heat of the day. By the time the tourists hit the trail, I'd be miles ahead of them. Still, I kept a photocopy of Green's picture handy in case I ran into anybody who might have seen him.

At this stage in the game, I was watching for any place that a person had left the trail. The first mile, it was kids running up the sides of hills chasing lizards or peeking downhill, and then being jerked back by parents who didn't remember what it was like to be a kid. Or maybe they did, and that's why they worried. The day was warm and the forest was open, providing little shade.

The second mile held my first breakthrough. Green had stopped to pull a large branch off the trail. The small branches along one side were cut off and the branch was strategically placed to discourage hikers from going down what could have been mistaken for another trail. The false trail ended in a thicket. Green's boot prints were deep but faint where he had straddled the branch. Two indentations at the foot of a tree showed where his frame pack had dug into the soil. Not many people used an exterior frame pack anymore, so it was something to remember.

As I hiked along these first few miles, my thoughts drifted and I allowed them to flow. I was watching for obvious signs, and the breaking pattern of footsteps off the main trail alerted me to stop and pay attention. My thoughts ran along the lines of how to get into tracking as a profession, how to make it my job so when kids wandered off, I was the first person the authorities or the parents called. Then I wondered how Michaels would feel about me taking off at a moments notice to parts unknown. I knew there were very few trackers around. I'd heard about real trackers being flown in to remote areas, but I didn't think I'd find much support for that. The trick was to prove to Michaels that I was capable, and that meant I would have to spend time in the woods with him. I had to prove I could not only follow a trail but could also handle myself in tough times. Spending time out here with Michaels held some appeal, but I still hesitated. Time in the woods meant time alone and nights together. And what would that mean? A hot flash of desire exploded in me and bounced around. I recognized it, stuffed it down, and turned to a safer subject. And how could I make tracking pay anything? I certainly did not want to charge people to be found. I had never found people for money. I found them because they needed it. It was the thing I did best.

Even as a kid I had practiced tracking. If my dad sent me after one of the ranch hands, I knew the tracks to follow. I would cast around the barns and corrals until I picked up their trail, then I followed it to them. I knew Randy had a hole in the right heel of his boot and Zack walked with an uneven gait. He tended to walk several steps and jog a few steps and walk again. He was always in a hurry, keeping himself to a walk when he could and breaking into a jog when he couldn't. He must have been hyper or something. I knew the sorrel that Randy rode had smaller shoes than Steve's buckskin, and that the buckskin tended to stumble easily until it got into work mode, then it took off like a shot.

I knew when mice had been active around the barns, or when a coyote had neared the house. I could find my dogs and sneak up on them anytime of the day or night by following their paw prints in the sand. I used to play hide and seek with them in the woods. I'd lead them in there then disappear, keeping out of sight until they gave up searching for me. I brought home rabbits I had snared in the woods. My mom would get mad at me for catching them because she didn't want to cook them, but they were good when fried, almost like chicken.

The ranch hands hated to be snuck up on, so I started a game with them, too. I'd stay out of sight until I tracked them down, then pop out of nowhere. They were fond of me. The younger ones thought of me like a sister while to the older ones I was more like a niece. Old Frank had encouraged me in my tracking. He wasn't a good tracker himself, but he knew how to get a kid thinking. If I was tracking something, he'd ask me why a rock was moist side up instead of dry side up, or why one spot of grass grew opposite to all the others. I learned volumes from him, because he was the one who took my penchant for trouble seriously. I suppose he also felt responsible when the boss heard of my shenanigans. He yanked me off of more green-broke horses than I care to admit, and splinted my arm the one time I was bucked off and thrown into a fence. He was also the one who spotted me atop the old yellow tractor as it pulled out of the barn and sent Steve running off to pull the brake before I broke the corral fence, my neck, or both. I didn't break my neck but I did knock over the fence. Old Frank couldn't run, but he could sure holler.

I began to see Green's boot prints on the left side of the trail. They were still mostly covered with other prints, but I took out the rubbing and held it up to the prints I found. I should have asked Michaels if Green was left handed. I made a point to ask Paul when I called in. Surely Paul or Michaels would know that if they had worked and climbed together. It would make a difference in the choices Green made on the trail. I wished I had paid closer attention when I came to the branch he'd cleared. The boot prints would have leaned differently as he cut branches if he were left handed. I debated calling Paul and asking him, but then decided I could do without the safety lecture that would follow. I'd call after I made camp.

The pack was fitting more comfortably and I was in better spirits now that I was seeing sign. A wash crossed the trail and I saw that several deer had followed the wash down the hillside. I could see them in the trees. Little tawny flecks moved in and out of the brush, antlers blending in with tree branches. The wash was dry. Luckily it wasn't one of my water holes.

The sun rose in the sky and I was glad to have a few miles behind me. I stopped and dug out some trail mix and jerky. I had made a mix of nuts, dried fruit and M&Ms before I'd left. I ate some before the M&Ms melted. The trail mix was always better the second day out, once the M&Ms had melted and then hardened again to make the whole mix into chocolaty chunks. I took a drink from the first water bottle, wishing it was my only water bottle and reminding myself again why it was necessary to lug five pounds of water up and down the trail.

The day passed uneventfully. I arrived at the waterfall by midmorning, and knew the chance of running into other hikers was growing slim. I left the main trail to see if there were hikers down there. A young couple sat cooling their feet in the water, with their backpacks leaning against a tree.

"Good morning," I said in greeting. They smiled. The girl wore a halter top and was fried to a crisp. The guy wore a loose t-shirt and baggy shorts. "I'm looking for a lost hiker. Which way did you come from?"

"We left the Pacific Crest Trail and now we're looping back towards Piney Point," the guy said.

"Did you notice anything unusual? Have you seen this guy?" I asked, digging out Green's photo and handing it over.

"Nope, we haven't seen very many people. It's still kind of the off season," the guy answered.

"At least it is cooler. I wouldn't want to do this in summer," added the girl.

"Thanks," I replied, pocketing the picture. "It was worth a try. Enjoy the rest of your hike." I headed back up to the trail.

"Good luck," the guy called out as I found the trail again.

Few people would venture further than a few miles from camp. The people I met now would be seasoned hikers and backpackers out for the long haul. Hopefully, some of them would have come from Elk Meadows, but I couldn't count on it. Twenty miles on foot was not something the average Californian was up to.

I ran into all the signs of Green that I had expected. He'd cleared off that branch, taken a leak, stopped to take note of a washed out spot and a sign covered with graffiti. I was making good time, but it was because everything Green had done was normal. This was packed dirt with softer soil to the sides. For some reason, Green managed to hit that soft dirt often enough to keep me going at a good pace. There had been some windy days up here, and the tracks were eroded but recognizable. Fortunately, winds around here usually came from the west, and I was on the east side of the mountain.

The trail rose from the campground, following the creek. Past the waterfall it continued along a hillside up a canyon and hugged the mountainside. It zigged and zagged through little pockets of shade, then came around a big, bald face of the mountain. The face was steep with tree trunks curving upward, dotting the barren mountainside. A few trees had lost their footing and slid down, keeping their hold to the earth with a few deep roots, then the tree had turned and once again started its reach for the sun. Rocks and boulders littered the trail. Green had spent some time clearing rocks along this portion of the trail. The larger rocks were placed on the downward side of the trail to keep people from venturing too close to the edge. The smaller rocks were swept aside in a futile effort. The rock encroached on the trail relentlessly.

Around the bend, I met laborious switchbacks. Switchbacks usually required maintenance because people tended to cut across them. Where they were handy, branches or rocks had been moved to discourage hikers from crossing over. The switchbacks provide security because they keep hikers to a safer speed, but when hikers cut across them, it creates places for erosion to start, which in turn causes the trail to deteriorate. It was hot, dry, open ground and each switchback meant another uphill trudge. There was no place to go but up, and I followed the trail, taking note of how long it had been since I'd seen a Green boot print.

The switchbacks began snaking further into the mountains, and then suddenly I found myself splashing through a small stream; my first water hole, and the five-mile marker. I reached for my nearly empty water bottle and debated whether to refill it or not. I still had another half dozen more, with only a distance of six miles to the next spring. I dumped out the tepid contents and filtered in some cold water. At least this would be an improvement. I packed up the filter system and pulled out the map. The switchbacks had taken more time than I cared to admit, but I still had several hours of light to go. If I hiked five miles a day, it would only take four days to get to Elk Meadows, but that meant possibly four days that Kelly Green had to survive. I opened the map looking for a likely tent spot. Much of this trail was on the sides of mountains with no flat spots to pitch a tent. Where had Green camped? After these switchbacks, the trail headed west over a pass between two mountains. There was bound to be a tent spot there but it was two miles further. It seemed like a plan to me. I looked around the creek area for signs of Green, and found boot prints similar to mine, doing the same things I was doing; cooling off and enjoying the green forest in this small oasis. The ground was always moist here and footprints tended to degenerate quickly so the tracks were rounded with age, but still legible.

Just in case, I took a quick excursion up and down the creek, but found it to be a simple water stop. Green had continued up the relentless switchbacks. I was huffing and puffing and thought these were the switchbacks from hell when I topped out, and the trail gently followed the top of the pass and entered a barren expanse.

The wind whipped around, blowing my hair in my face. One thing I didn't like about mountaintops is that they receive the full force of the wind. There was plenty of space here for a tent, but I didn't want to camp in the wind with my tent flapping about me all night. I scoured the area looking for a spot where Green might have camped. There were a few lonely fire rings, but not one of them held the now-familiar boot prints. Taking note of the wind direction, I continued down the trail hoping the wind would be less severe on the other side of the hill, with some flat spots to make camp.

I found a little niche next to a rock. Dusk would come late way up here but there was little assurance of a camping spot if I started the tedious switchbacks going down the other side. I figured I'd made good time. I'd have time to eat, call Paul, and set up my tent before dark. I assembled my little camp stove, struck a match, lit the burner, and set a pot of water to boil. I sorted through my pack looking for an interesting packet to rehydrate and came up with chicken Alfredo with broccoli. I was going to crave fruit and vegetables by the time I got out of here. I poured about a cup of boiling water in the pouch and closed the bag, trapping the heat. I let it sit while I unpacked my tent.

My tent was old, but once I have a good piece of equipment, I hate to part with it. I unrolled the tent fabric and staked down the corners, not bothering with the side stakes. I put the tent poles together and threaded them through the casings, making sure the ends were seated well within the pockets. Unzipping the tent, I checked to see if I had swept it out well after my last outing. Sometimes, sweeping out meant shaking the tent upside down, and other times it meant a thorough cleaning with a whiskbroom and a damp cloth. Satisfied there were no sharp rocks or sticks under the tent, I pulled out my sleeping bag. I was now set for the night. I checked the contents of the foil pouch; dinner wasn't ready yet, so I resealed it.

Unclipping the GPS system, I checked the readings and wrote them in the notebook for no particular reason. I wrote everything I could remember of Green's route so far. Since I was on top of a mountain, I checked the reception on the cell phone. This wasn't one of the call spots marked on the map, but I had a couple of bars on my phone.

I ate the chicken Alfredo and washed it down with water, while wishing I had one of those mayo-jar steaks. After dinner I rolled up the pouch, I stuck it in a small, plastic trash bag, and then stuffed it back into my pack. I never forgot the backpacker's rule: pack it in, pack it out. I unclipped the radio and buzzed the ranger station, hoping Paul was still on duty. I pushed the button. "Test, test, can you hear me Paul?"

A short pause. He was probably coming in from the next room.

"I hear ya, Cass, and I've got you on the screen at the 6.8 mile mark. How's it going?"

"As well as can be expected. As far as I can see, Green made it up here no problem. I was going to go further but I don't see any place to camp for miles. What do you think?"

"Negative. Stay where you are. There's word of a nasty mother bear on the down side and you'll want to make a nice big racket when you hike that area during daylight hours. You know the drill: hang the canteen on the outside of your pack so it makes an annoying racket."

I'd only brought plastic bottles, but I knew what to do.

"Your boyfriend stopped back by here on his way to town and threatened me within an inch of my life if I didn't keep track of you."

"He's not my boyfriend. He just seems to care an awful lot."

"Well, you could do worse."

"I've got two bars on my cell phone. I'll try to call, but if I don't get through, expect a phone call from him real quick and tell him I'm fine, that I checked in with you as planned, and I just had an iffy connection."

"Ten-four."

"Thanks, Paul. I'll talk to you tomorrow."

"Take care."

"You, too. Bye." Well, that wasn't so bad.

Now for the cell phone. I flipped through the phone book until I found Michaels' phone number. I didn't really know what I was going to say, but I'd told Paul I would try, so I would. This was going to be awkward. Then I figured if I called him myself, he wouldn't hear about the bear from Paul.

"Hello?" he answered on the first ring.

"Hey, it's me. I don't have much of a signal but I promised I would call when I could."

"It's early."

"I know, but I'm almost seven miles in and there's not a good place to stop for several miles."

"You made good time."

"It was easy reading. Very straightforward. Green stuck to the trail except for a few rangerly exceptions. There was just enough of a trail to keep me going at an almost normal pace. I forgot to ask Paul. Is Green left handed?"

"Yeah, I think he is. I'm picturing his climbing technique and I do believe he is left-handed. You got that from following a week old trail of footprints?"

"Mostly partial foot prints, but yeah. I just wanted to verify that because it will affect things that he does later. I should have asked you that right from the start."

"How are you?"

"I'm okay. Tired, a little sore. I'll feel better in the morning. How are you?"

"A nervous wreck," he said wearily.

"I'm sorry. Try not to let it affect your work. I heard you've been a real bear at the station."

"I have?"

"Yup, ask anybody."

"Okay, I get the point. Who did you hear this from?"

"It doesn't matter. They all care about you. Be nice to them. Well, I need my charge to last a week, so I better go for now. Take care."

"You, too."

I wandered around the mountaintop until it started getting dark. I hadn't brought a light, so when the sun went down I turned in. Best to get an early start in the morning.

Morning dawned early, as it always does on top of a mountain. It would take an extra hour to reach the valley below. I got up and stretched all the kinks loose, then stuffed my sleeping bag back in its little stuff sack. Dismantling the tent and shaking it out, I removed the poles and rolled it up, putting it in its little pouch. I bungeed the tent and sleeping bag to my pack and then got out the camp stove. I then heated two cups of water in the pot that came with my stove; one for hot chocolate and one for oatmeal. Breakfast was always a two step process due to my lack of supplies. Backpacker dinners were eaten straight out of the foil pouch. Breakfast was eaten out of the one little plastic cup I packed. I made hot chocolate in the cup and drank it, then put the oatmeal in the same cup and added water, stirring it until the oatmeal was mushy. It was a joyless, but important, start to my day. I washed out the cup and added it to my pack, then bagged up the trash.

Taking another look around the mountaintop, I spotted another tent on the east side of the mountain. I made my way towards it and as I approached the tent quietly said, "Knock, knock." A guy poked his sleepy head out from the tent. He was rather rough looking with a shaved head and skull tattoo on his shoulder.

"I'm sorry, I didn't mean to wake you. I'm looking for someone and I was hoping you might have seen him." I handed him Green's picture.

When he replied, "No," I asked him to report any sightings to the ranger station.

"You can hike with me, though. I'll take off in an hour or two."

"No, I really need to press on," I answered, hoping he was heading in a different direction. The wind was still blowing up top, so I was glad to be heading downhill.

On this leg of the hike I needed to be a little more careful. It was necessary to make plenty of noise and keep an eye out for bears. I also needed to keep track of how far I was walking. I didn't want to miss the spring. I had to remember it was a little over four miles from my current location, there'd be a sharp bend in the trail (like a switchback?), and then I was to cut east until I spotted cottonwoods. I hoped I wouldn't pass the sharp bend in the trail. I set about figuring out the noise issue. If the bear was down there and heard me coming, she would stay out of my way. Metal canteens were great as noisemakers while plastic water bottles didn't work as well. I hadn't brought tie-ons either, which meant that attaching the bottles to my pack was going to be an issue. I took out my climbing rope but didn't want to cut it because I might need the length later. I uncoiled it, put the two ends together, found the middle of the rope and then recoiled it. I wrapped the ends around the rope securing it for carrying, and then tied a half-full water bottle on each end of the rope. I slung the rope over my shoulder and walked around. The bottles went *tuckity tuck* as I walked. Not great, but better than nothing. I dug around in my pack until I found my bamboo flute. I picked up a small rock and gave it a tap. The musical rap was louder than any water bottle. Only problem was that it brought to mind the old joke about tapping sticks together to scare away lions. I put on the pack, placed the rope over my shoulder, and with flute in hand, entered the dreaded switchbacks going down the other side of the pass.

The forest became thicker as I descended and trees blocked the sunlight. I found Green's trail almost immediately because he had made a lot of repairs to the switchbacks. People are notorious for cutting across switchbacks, and there was a flurry of activity in areas where Green had taken branches, rocks, and anything he had at hand to steer hikers around the proper way. This time, when I examined the tracks and the manner in which he did things, his left-handedness was clear. The switchbacks had probably taken him the better part of the day to complete. Nearly every bend in the trail bore evidence of his labors. I felt like I was gaining on him. A mile of tracking ten switchbacks and I was on my way, pleased to have the trail so clear before me.

The switchbacks ended and I came around a bend when all hell broke loose. Across the forest floor I heard a noise like a million angry bees. I glanced up from my study of the ground. It was dry and hard here, and I wanted to know for sure that Green had stayed on the trail, so the sound brought me up short. A blue and white dirt bike buzzed past enveloping me in a huge dust cloud. It was followed by another sound, a sound that didn't usually accompany dirt bikes. I jumped out of the motorcycle's way then waited for the dust to settle. What was that other noise? It sounded like *MRAWWW*, and was coming from behind me. The dust hung in the air then gradually floated downward. As the dust thinned I made out the hunched form of the mama bear, all cinnamon brown and shaggy. Oh, no. Behind me was her cub. I could hear the motorcycle chugging its way up the switchbacks with a long bursting buzz followed by short bursts of engine gunning as they eased around the sharp turns. My brain pulled my ears back to the present. Mama was in front of me. Baby bear was behind me. I backed silently away, hoping to let the mother bear know I wasn't after her cub, but she didn't appear to believe me. The ruckus caused by the motorcycle had her riled, and she blamed me for it. She lowered her head as she walked towards me. I backed away further. Her pace quickened. I stood tall banging the flute and the water bottles yelling "Haaaaa, get away!" She didn't slow down. "Oh, shoot," I thought. I took a quick glance around. There was no need to panic yet. I searched the trees, which were all way too tall for me to climb. I noted the distance separating the mama bear and myself, realizing she could run a lot faster than I could. Quick, Cass, form a plan, form a plan! My mind raced. I chose a path and ran for my life. The Fastex buckle released as I shed my pack. The bear attacked it, giving me precious seconds. Tearing at the fabric, she tossed it aside. Grabbing the rope, I screeched to a halt under a good-sized pine tree. The brush was shaking all around me as I flung the water bottle up and over the highest limb I thought I could reach. Thank you, Paul, for warning me about these bears. If he hadn't warned me, I wouldn't have these water bottles on the ends of my rope. I would never complain about carrying water bottles again. The rope wouldn't have made it over the limb without the extra weight on the end. The water bottle sailed over the limb and came back down the other side. I grabbed both ends and climbed. There'd be no further complaints about boot camp either. I'd never climbed a rope until boot camp, but here I was climbing as fast as my arms could haul me up. The bear charged the end of the rope sending me swinging back and forth. She swatted it and all I could do was hang on tight. As the swinging eased, I climbed higher. I was still climbing, my arms burning, when my head hit the underside of the branch. Hauling myself up, I took a second to just breathe. Just breathe, Cass. My heart was pounding. I checked to make sure the bear wasn't climbing the tree and to make sure I could climb further if needed.

Looking down through the undergrowth, it seemed like a giant blender was down there. The furious bear had thrown a royal temper tantrum, shredding all the surrounding bushes. She was still plenty angry with me. I sighed, getting comfortable on the branch, getting ready for a long stand off. I thought about the gun on my hip, but I really didn't want to shoot the bear. She was only a mama bear and she was only doing what mama bears do best. Still, I was going to be stuck here for a while. So much for my earlier enthusiasm.

An hour passed, and the bear was still pacing under the tree. She examined my pack, dug at it with her claws, and helped herself to all my oatmeal packets and hot chocolate packets eating them paper pouch and all. I pulled my rope up out of her reach. Two half full bottles of water was all I could count on for a while, so I had better make do.

Two hours later my radio crackled. I'd forgotten all about it. I reached around and found I still had the radio and GPS system clipped to my belt. I unclipped the radio. It still crackled. I fiddled with the knobs thinking maybe it had different stations, searching for a ranger voice. Finally, I found it.

"Cass, can you hear me? You haven't moved for three hours. Are you okay?"

I sure didn't want to get anybody worried about me. I was worried enough on my own. Still, Paul needed to know so he could warn off other hikers.

"Hey, Paul. Yeah, I'm okay."

"What are you doing? Did you find something? You haven't moved in three hours," he repeated, "and I was getting worried."

"I'm sitting in a tree. You need to warn other hikers about this bear you told me about."

Pause. "Are you sure you're okay?"

"Yeah, there's not much that can be done now but wait. That's one stubborn bear."

"What's the plan?"

"Wait for the bear to leave and climb down."

"You wouldn't shoot it, would you," he accused me.

"No, I won't unless I have to. She's got a cub."

"You want me to stay on line?"

"There's no use. Don't tell Michaels about this."

"Leave your radio on till you know you're in the clear."

"Okay."

My nerves had settled and the day was hot. I tied myself to the tree in case I dozed off. The bears didn't seem as interested in me now, but they also weren't leaving. There must have been a berry patch down there or something.

My stomach was growling and the day was well on when I finally felt safe enough to slide down the rope. I wasn't counting on lunch, though. There was probably very little food left in my shredded pack.

"Okay, here goes," I said to myself. Then, realizing my radio was on, I wished I hadn't said anything out loud. I pictured all the rangers sitting around the radio, holding their breath, waiting for growling and screaming noises. My feet hit the ground with a soft *whuff* and I stood still as a statue behind the tree listening for any bear-like sounds. There was the distinct barnyard smell of bears in the air, but I couldn't hear or see them. I left the rope hanging, just in case, and staying low, looked around for my gear. My pack lay ripped apart, its contents spread around. I gathered up what I could and took stock. I was relieved that the food packaged in foil had survived, but all the food in plastic bags and paper pouches had been devoured. I rolled up my spare clothes and shoved them in, and located my stove under a bush. The first aid kit was scattered so I picked up what was left and stuffed it in a bottom corner where it would stay somewhat together. A few of the water bottles were punctured, with bullet-sized teeth marks marring the plastic. I poured the water into the remaining undamaged ones and found I was left with four bottles of water and nine backpacker dinners. Well, I'd survived on less, but it hadn't been pleasant and at the time it was my only responsibility. I needed to start moving. I had a waterhole to find, a trail to follow, and I wasn't going to make my five miles today. I put everything in the pack, plastered my shirt against the rips to hold everything in, and wound the rope around the pack to secure it all. It wouldn't be comfortable while hiking, but it was necessary to secure the gear I had saved. After a quick search, I located my bamboo flute several yards behind the tree. With several claw marks across it, I now had quite a conversation piece for future hikes. Deep in the woods hikers seem to be drawn to any kind of music, as long as it isn't a boom box. A gentle flute melody or an acoustic guitar is a comfort in the woods.

I gave the bears five minutes to renew the attack but they seemed to be gone.

"Okay guys, I'm off again. I'm turning off the radio."

"Ten-four, Cassidy. Take care," Paul said, signing off.

Chapter 6

As I hiked, the ropes wound around the pack dug into my back. My knee ached and I thought back to when I could have injured it. Nothing came to mind. I thought ahead. The water hole should be three miles down the trail. That was my first goal, aside from keeping tabs on Green. I was dismayed to find that the dirt bike had covered the trail. Well, it wasn't as bad as what the tourists did to his trail the first few miles. I wondered where the dirt bike had come from and why it was here. It was eight miles from any place when I saw it. Of course, a dirt bike could cover eight miles in less than an hour. Still, it seemed strange to see one in here. That note in the book had been right. They were dangerous. Was Green hiking this trail hoping to deal with the motorcycle problem? That could very well be. It also threw a new light on his disappearance. Could it be that Paul and Michaels were reluctant to let me go because of some ranger/motorcycle conflict going on? That could very well be, too, but I was just speculating. I had a trail to follow and three more miles to go before I could think about stopping or eating. It could be closer to four if the cottonwood trees were very far off the trail.

A new development formed in my tracking. Green was now leaving the trail more often but I couldn't tell why. He'd bear off-trail to the left, head into the woods for about a half mile, then turn around and walk back. He must have been looking for something, but what? His off-trail sign was harder to follow but was also more interesting to me because I had to deal with differing surfaces. When he crossed blankets of pine needles I had to look for shifting patterns. New needles had dropped over the past week covering his trail. I got down to ground level, gazing on the seemingly flat surface to see the faint indentations in the bed of needles. On rocky places I had to look for scratch marks where small pebbles had shifted under foot. Occasionally, he would hop from rock to rock like he was trying not to leave a trail. This was becoming more of a puzzle, but this, really, was what Michaels had called me in to do. The rangers and searchers could follow the hiking trail and keep an eye out. It was this invisible stuff they didn't understand.

After following Green down three false leads, I sat down with the map. I got out my pencil and made marks where he had gone off trail and approximately how far he had gone. What was it about these places that made him take off? I studied the map. I knew what all the squiggly lines meant, but they sure could look alike after a while. Here the squiggly lines were close together and there they spread apart. The close together lines were steep places where the altitude changed quickly. The wider spaces were where the slope was more gradual. Then it hit me. Each place he left the trail the terrain had an alluvial fan pattern on the map. A very, very old fan, but distinct nonetheless. I couldn't see it in the forest because the trees had grown and covered it but the pattern showed up distinctly on the map. The fan had formed when the mountainside had eroded, then the forest had grown atop the fan in the rich sediment. But what was he looking for? What did he expect to find? All I could do was push on, but my three miles was stretching, my day was waning, and I couldn't rush the off-trail tracking. Any of these leads could end in Green himself so I couldn't pass them up.

The next place Green pulled off the trail, I followed his sign to the water hole. I filled all the water bottles and decided I had better camp at the spring. I needed all my bottles full when I set out from here because I might not get another water stop for a few days. Four water bottles weren't enough to last but I would have to make do. Here I could use water from the spring for my cooking and save the water in the bottles for drinking. I looked at the sky and it was getting on towards dusk, anyway.

I was setting up camp in a little clearing beside the spring when something leaped to my attention. Toddler sized footprints. Lilo and Stitch tennis shoes. Now, that was odd. The prints were much more recent than Green's. They padded down to the water and then there were toddler-sized barefoot prints. These were very recent, not even a day old. So where was the little girl? I looked around for other signs. I had been concentrating so hard on Green that I forgot to look at the other signs. Yes, they were there. A man's footprint, not Green's. The man didn't move around as much as the little girl. It was like he had stopped to let her run around and play, and then they returned to the trail.

I wondered why I hadn't seen their tracks back on the trail. I needed to broaden my search. It was unusual for a toddler to be this far into the woods, with or without a parent. This had a link somewhere, I just knew it.

I heated water for my dinner and went through the same old routine. Then I called Paul.

"Hey Paul," I radioed.

Short pause. "Hi, Cassidy. It's quite a day you've been having."

"Tell me about it. I'm just checking in. Everything's A-OK."

"Same here. Any more trouble with the bear?"

"No, she just hung around forever. I didn't make good time today, but I have some interesting observations on Green. He keeps leaving the trail for no apparent reason. He hikes off the trail, then just turns around and hikes back to the trail. That's another reason I didn't get very far today. I was off trail a lot. Any idea what he was looking for?"

"Not a clue."

"Another odd thing. A toddler has been up here recently. Probably today, maybe yesterday. The footprints are here at the spring but I didn't notice them on the trail."

"No clue on that one either. We get lots of kids in these mountains."

"Ten miles from camp? Without hiking?"

"Maybe he flew in."

"Very funny. The bear ate half my food and punctured some of the water bottles. I'm down to four. Any word on those iffy water stops?"

"No, most people who walk that trail don't report back in when they finish, so I haven't heard anything."

"Okay."

"Anything else?"

"Nope."

"Okay, check in tomorrow."

"Will do."

My curiosity was running wild. Where did this kid come from? I walked around the spring. There were Lilo and Stitch prints all over the place. I followed the little girl's trail about fifty feet back towards the hiking trail and then it disappeared. The man's trail continued. He must have picked up the kid and carried her. I followed the dad's trail back to the main trail, and then I saw it: they had come in on the dirt bike. The dirt bike had clearly been parked next to the trail, but I had been so intent on following Green that I had missed it. What was a little girl like that doing dirt bike riding with her dad? It still seemed strange, although not as much as before.

Back at camp, I checked my cell phone but there was no reception down in these low lands. I unfolded the map. If Green followed the same pattern, I would be off trail a lot, and my water supply would dwindle remarkably. I found the same fan pattern twice on the map in the next day's travels, and three more times the following day. I needed to make better time and use as little water as possible. Usually those two things didn't coincide, but I'd have to do that if I didn't want to run out. The trail was going to start rising, too, and that meant hotter hiking and more water consumption. This was looking like a very long, hot, dry trail. On the bright side, I was going to clean up. There was plenty of water here. Not a soul in sight. I took off my clothes and slipped into the water. Too bad I had to put those grimy clothes back on when I was through. The little pond wasn't deep. I couldn't really get a good swim in, but the cold water woke me up and I felt the dirt float away. When I climbed out, I felt human again. I washed my clothes the best I could without soap, laid them out on bushes to dry, then crawled in the tent and was out like a light. Some time during the night I woke up cold and climbed into my sleeping bag. I thought I heard a dirt bike in the night, but who would ride this trail at night?

In the morning, my clothes were still damp. Darn. I put them on and shivered as I walked around camp trying to dry them out. I took stock of my food options. I was down to eight packets of food. This was the start of day three, and I was halfway to Elk Meadows. That meant, with any luck, I only had two more days of travel. In that case, I could afford to eat a packet for breakfast. I heated up water from the spring and pulled out a packet. Spaghetti; not my favorite, marginally better than oatmeal. They needed to put some spices in their spaghetti sauce.

After I ate I cleaned up camp, packed everything, and bound it up with the shirt and the rope again, then tracked Green back down to the trail. If it weren't for the rope, my pack would be comfortable now. It weighed less and I was more trail seasoned, ready to face the day, as long as it didn't include face to face confrontations with bears.

I was dismayed to note the dirt bike tracks that covered Green's trail. If Green hadn't strayed so far to the left in his hiking, I would have had nothing to follow.

The trail here began a long uphill climb. The trees closed in and the forest was dark, with little sudden stabs of light highlighting the trail. As I trudged up the long hill, it was easy for me to catch glimpses of Green's boot prints. Slow and steady wins the race. I was beginning to appreciate switchbacks as the trail rose steadily. At least switchbacks broke things up a bit.

After this uphill section, the trail topped out and I'd hike the border of two vast meadows, and then take off from the meadows to a trail that crossed a big rocky mountain. After the mountain, there were more meadows the last of which was Elk Meadows.

I was glad to get an early start, and once I got moving, was also glad to be wearing damp clothes because the heat set in early and lingered. It didn't take long for my clothes to dry, but they felt stiff after having all the dirt rearranged. At least they smelled a little bit better.

I felt hopeful despite the long climb without any water. Green was up to something and this something had gotten him into trouble.

Hiking was toilsome for the first two miles. Conserving water was no fun. This was hot, dry work. I was feeling like this hill would go on forever when suddenly Green made a detour. This time, though, he had to climb a bank. The bank was soft and his footprints dug deep, I followed up the steep incline. It topped out at a meadow. An alluvial fan again, but one which sprouted grasses instead of trees. It was a vast expanse, and I lost the trail as he crossed the meadow through waist-high plants. When he had crossed it, he had left a clear trail of bent and broken plants, but deer had come through several times since then, bending the plants every which way and obscuring the trail. I decided to circle the meadow and find his exit point. I expected it to be down by the trail, so I paralleled the trail walking atop the ridge. If he followed his previous patterns I'd find footprints returning to the hiking trail. If I didn't, I'd have to fight the jungle of tall grass in the meadow to track his movements. I wasn't disappointed. He left the meadow near the trail, but he hadn't wanted to climb down the bank and back up the next one, so he followed the ridge. It was rough backcountry, and he had to weave in and out of foliage and rocks, climb down a shallow gorge and up the other side. He probably wished he had taken the trail. I looked for signs of water in the gorge, but it was dry and the trees upstream looked dry, too.

At the top of the gorge, the woods became denser and Green went into a stalker gait, hiding his tracks and stopping behind trees, pausing and crouching. As Green grew cautious I grew doubly cautious. I was watching the tracks, the ground, the woods. I was watching for movement, listening carefully. I didn't know what Green was hiding from but it could come from anywhere. The woods forced him to zigzag. He was moving carefully, and on the edge of the woods, he had stopped. I froze. Something was not quite right here. Something felt fishy. I examined the trail. I looked around. A faint shimmer of light came from overhead. I was crouched low to see the tracks. I was alarmed to see that if I had been standing up I would have walked right into a trap. Dozens of tiny fishhooks hung from the branches of trees at head height from nearly invisible fishing lines. The light I had seen was the sun glinting off razor sharp points. The place was booby-trapped. I imagined Green standing here observing, not hiding but ready to hide. Had he run into the fishhooks? I stood taller and looked at the trap. I couldn't see blood or skin on the hooks. I don't know how Green had avoided them but I didn't see any evidence that he had tangled with them. Did he know the place could be booby-trapped? According to his tracks he had stood here for a while. What had he seen? I followed his tracks keeping low. I stepped over a cord stretched across the tracks. Another trap? I should not be here, I thought. I should back out of here and return to the trail. But I couldn't abandon Kelly Green. It just wasn't in me. All I could do was press forward, very carefully; thankful I'd been trained to watch for these things in the service.

Green stopped behind a big pine tree. I looked to see why. At first I didn't know what I was seeing. It just looked like a field of very foreign plants. Then reality sunk in. It was an acre-sized field of cannabis, carefully cultivated and hidden away up in the mountains.

"Oh, please," I thought, "don't even go there." Mentally I told him, "Just write it down and go back to the trail." But he didn't listen to me. He didn't venture into the field, but he circled it, hiding at every convenient place. He carefully avoided several trip wires and I followed one of them to see what it was attached to. Fortunately, it was a simple noisemaker to warn the workers of possible detection. When he got to the backside of the field, he stepped into the field just long enough to pick a sample and put it in his pack. Evidence. I followed his trail, now careful that I, too, remained hidden.

When I reached the far side of the acre the dirt bike runs made more sense. They used dirt bikes to get to the fields. There was a doublewide dirt bike trail that I assumed they drove ATVs on when they needed to haul things or cultivate.

I crouched behind a tree and listened carefully for any sounds of people or bikes, but it was silent; only normal forest noises. This was getting spooky. I no longer wanted this bright red shirt on. I didn't feel comfortable changing, not due to modesty but because it involved removing my pack, unwinding the rope, changing, and winding everything back up. I'd be too vulnerable. I'd just have to be careful. I looked around after the distraction, picked up Green's trail again, and followed it through the woods.

It took careful observation on my part to follow him when he didn't want to be found. From this little off-trail jaunt, I learned Green had spent some time in the woods, and not just doing ranger duties. He enjoyed the woods and being part of them. He knew how to hide his tracks and stay out of sight if needed. He also seemed to know he could get his head blown off any minute. Fortunately, he had only himself to watch out for. I had to keep on his trail while watching out for myself.

The more cautious he became, the harder it was to follow his trail, and the more danger he was probably in at the time. So, the closer I came to the source of danger, the less I could pay attention to it. Sometimes tracking involved more than just standing there looking at footprints. Sometimes it meant getting down on hands and knees or flat to the ground to see the prints from ground level. I was almost to that point. I couldn't see the next step or see where he might have hidden it. Choosing between the ground level approach and trusting instinct, I continued in the direction the trail was going, hoping something would turn up soon. The terrain began sloping downhill and soon I could make out light footsteps with pressure points on the downward side, indicating the ground had been soft when he came down the hill. Green paused again, and in front of me was a larger field of cannabis.

I started to follow Green's path to circle the field, then froze. Someone was working in the field. Stealth time. I only moved while the worker had his head down. I found my next move before I left a hiding spot, crouching to keep low. I found shelter behind a dense bush and slid my cell phone out of my pocket. I flipped it open and it came on with a bright, cheerful screen, which I held to my shoulder. I waited until the welcome screen cleared and flipped through the options until I activated the camera. I waited for the worker to look up and quickly snapped a picture of him in case the police could use it later. I also took one of the field. I flipped the phone closed and slipped it back in my pocket. I made sure anything that could make noise was silenced and continued following Green's trail around the back of the field. So far, he was basically doing what I would have done, but when he came to the back of the field, he'd cut into the woods again, leaving the field and trail behind. For a short distance he didn't seem to be worried about being spotted, but I didn't have that assurance. I felt eyes on the back of my head. Then his movements became careful again as he neared a small building. It stood by itself under a canopy of trees. Sandstone stucco and pine green roof camouflaged it from the casual observer and from the sky. Green had approached the building, but I wasn't going to take that chance yet. I'd wait until dark to investigate.

I backed off a quarter mile into the woods and found a hiding spot under a bush. It was going to be a long wait. It occurred to me that Paul was going to worry again, and if I didn't answer the radio call he'd get antsy. I turned on the radio and spoke as quietly and distinctly as I could.

"It's Cassidy checking in. Don't respond. Just letting you know everything's okay. I'm on Green's trail, but I need to stay out of sight for a bit and I didn't want to worry you. I'm turning the radio off. Over."

One thing about hiding in the woods is that you see things that you wouldn't otherwise have the chance to see. Wild animals like quiet surroundings. So, when I sat still and grew patient, the woods around me relaxed, too. I saw a large cottontail rabbit hop by and wondered if it lived on marijuana. It hopped straight so I assumed it lived on traditional rabbit fare. There were many different kinds of birds here. They were birds found around campgrounds and houses, so I thought they might have a food source nearby. I was sitting there speculating about the birds when the little girl with the Lilo and Stitch sneakers walked by. She wore a pink t-shirt and faded jeans. Her hair was a cascade of black curls. I sucked in a breath and held it. Unlike their parents, kids could see down low. My bright red shirt was a dead giveaway. She didn't notice me. She was looking for something specific, and I wasn't it. She looked puzzled, glancing around her like she was lost. "Stay put Cassidy," I admonished myself silently. "Her dad is always near." She began to cry and I shrank deeper into the bush. I gave her half an hour. If someone didn't show up or if she didn't leave within half an hour, I'd take her home. I was concerned about her setting off the booby-traps. I worried that some of them were not simple noise makers. I knew some booby-traps could be deadly.

Maybe I could use this situation. It might be a chance to ask about Green. What parent wouldn't be relieved to have their kid returned to them? They wouldn't have to know that I knew about the fields. Right? I could have found the kid anywhere.

A half hour passed and the little girl had looked around in vain for somebody familiar but had continued in the wrong direction. I snuck out of hiding, strapped on my pack so I'd look like a lost backpacker and took off after the kid.

She whipped around as I came up behind her and looked startled but I knelt down to her level so I wouldn't be as intimidating.

"Hey," I said softly. "Are you lost? Where's your daddy?"

She just looked at me like she'd never seen a backpacker before. Taking her hand we walked back towards the outbuilding, avoiding the fields. I would probably be in trouble if I knew about them so we headed for the outbuilding until we found the ATV track and continued following that. It led to the outbuilding, but then it continued another quarter mile until it stopped at a house. The house had also been built to blend in with the forest around it. Trees leaned over the green roof and the walls were either stucco or rock. A wall surrounded the property. I walked around the wall staying in plain sight and eventually came to a wrought iron gate. I tried the gate, but it was locked. A door opened and a gentleman stepped out on the porch. He was dressed casually in black twill slacks and a dark green flannel shirt, but still managed to look dressed up. He moved with an easy grace that fit in more with a swank townhouse than a mountaintop hideaway. He was middle-aged, with short black hair. He removed his glasses as he strolled down the flagstone walk.

"May I help you?" he asked as he arrived at the locked gate.

"Yes," I said, "I was hiking the trail below looking for a friend of mine. He's been missing some time but I just couldn't shake the idea that he is up in these mountains somewhere. I was following what I thought were his tracks and before I knew it I was off the trail, so I'm kind of turned around. I found this little girl in the woods and she looked kind of lost, too. I knew she couldn't live very far away so I started looking for a house. I was hoping you could help us."

"The girl belongs to one of my employees," he stated calmly. He pulled a cell phone from his pocket and quickly fired off a string of Spanish that I couldn't understand. I only picked up on the fact that the guy's name was Raphael. I'd have to remember that name. I wrestled the crinkled picture of Green out of a side pocket of my pack. His expression changed when he saw the condition of my pack. "Looks like you've met with some challenges in this quest of yours."

"I ran into a bear yesterday. It made off with most of my food and thrashed the pack. I spent half a day up in a tree."

"Quite the outdoorsman."

I held out the picture. "I was wondering if you've seen this man. He probably would have had a 2 day old beard and his hair was usually longer than this photo shows."

He took the photo from me, looked it over, and handed it back. A young man walked up dressed in faded, black, baggy jeans that rode on his hips. Red and white striped boxers puffed out the top. He wore a tight black muscle shirt. He was short, lanky, and tanned from many days in the field. His long black hair was bound in a ponytail.

He spoke to Raphael in Spanish again. I picked out the little girl's name, Amelia. Raphael's face fell. Was it fear I saw? Then in English he said, "She is also searching for the ranger. I suggest you show her where she can find him." My heart leapt. They knew where Green was? The two conversed in Spanish again and then I followed Raphael away.

Something should have kicked in right about then telling me this was too good to be true. Something *should* have told me that if this *was* a good thing, then Green would not be missing in the first place. I felt a little inkling of worry, but I filed it away and followed Raphael and his little girl away from the house. We followed the ATV trail most of the way back to the main trail and then deviated down a motorcycle track. It turned and angled down the high bank to the main hiking trail. It was obvious that this was the way the dirt bikes accessed the trail as I walked down it, yet the trail blended in well and there was no outward sign of the pot farm just over the hill. Raphael led me a short way down the trail and gestured down the side of the hill. There was a short steep hill that fell away to a sandy area below with sharp rocks poking up through the sand.

Raphael hadn't spoken since we left the house and I didn't know how to question him in Spanish. A year of Spanish in high school and the best I could come up with was, "Esta aquí?"

He nodded. I unbound my pack and opened it up, stuffing everything I could into my t-shirt so it would stay in one place. I tied the rope to a tree with a bowline knot, strapped on my pack and backed down the hill holding onto the rope with both hands. When I got close to the drop off I stopped, swung the rope through my legs, around my right leg, and over my left shoulder. Grasping the end of the rope behind me, I was ready for a body rappel down the drop off. Wrapping the rope in this way would give the rope some friction, which would slow my decent and make it easier to control my downward motion. It wasn't a great way to travel because friction causes heat, and heat can be uncomfortable, but it was all that I had. I couldn't take the time to fashion a harness and I didn't have the hardware that makes rappelling easier. I grasped the rope forward and behind and angled over the precipice. I took a last look at the two standing on the trail and the little girl waved. I tipped back, glancing down the cliff. I slowly let out some rope and slowly backed over the lip of the hill. The two disappeared from view and then I felt a wave of shock and nausea as the rope went slack in my hand. Realization dawned as in slow motion I flipped over backwards tumbling, tumbling downwards. I rolled trying desperately to spread eagle to slow the rolling, and then I was airborne. It felt like parachuting, but when I pulled the cord, nothing happened. I landed, *whump,* on my back, and all the air whooshed out of my lungs. I couldn't breathe. Nothing worked. I couldn't breathe, couldn't move, couldn't think. I just lay there, dazed. Slowly, ever so slowly things started coming back to me. A figure appeared overhead. Two shots stung the air and I heard them hit something. Me? The sand? I was still too dazed to find out. Raphael turned, scrambled up the bank, and left.

The first thing I noticed when feeling returned was that my knee didn't hurt anymore. Unfortunately, that was because every other part of me ached more. I couldn't find any broken bones. I was grateful that my sleeping bag made my pack taller then me, protecting my head on impact. I rolled off my pack, thinking all food was now dust in the little pouches. Great, backpacker dust and water. When I got out of these woods, I was going to get a real dinner.

In the tumble down the hill, each of the things attached to my belt had left its own little gadget shaped bruise. There was a radio shaped bruise and a GPS shaped bruise. I wondered if there was even a gun shaped bruise across my thigh. I was scratched and bloody and bruised, but I was whole. I was also standing about ten feet away from Green. Or Green's body. Holy smokes! They weren't kidding. They really did know where Green was.

I ran over to him and checked his pulse. He seemed to be alive, but was unconscious. How long he had, I couldn't tell. He was obviously very much in need of medical attention, but I couldn't be of much help. My meager first aid kit had been scattered by the bear. I only had a few basics. Band-Aids and Neosporin were not going to do Green much good. Water. The first thing Green needed was water. How do you give water to an unconscious man? His injuries made me fearful to move him. He obviously had two very broken legs and he'd been shot twice. He'd stuck a sock in one wound and an undershirt in the other. Next to him was an empty canteen. It was good to see he'd been in survival mode for a little while. I patted his face quietly calling his name, no response.

My mind started running in little circles and I did my best to stop it and look at things logically. Problem one: Green needed help. Problem two: we are both supposed to be dead. If someone came to check, we'd both better be dead. The second problem was a little preventable. I opened my pack and took out my extra set of clothes. I glanced at Green, still out. I took off my shirt and pants. I put on the camouflaged pants and I was just pulling the t-shirt down over the top of my pants when Green said in a raspy voice, "I always miss the good parts of the show."

"Hey," I said, "you look like you could use some help." I brought over a water bottle and held it up so he could drink. "Small sips," I said, "take it slow."

I positioned my old clothes where I had fallen, making the arms and legs bent in odd directions. I found a large stone and put it where my head would be. People tend to see what they want to see. I listened intently for any noise that indicated Raphael or Amelia was still up top. I brought Green another sip of water. I unholstered my gun, stealing another glance up the cliff. I unclipped the GPS device. The screen was blank. I pushed buttons but it was dead, probably crushed in the tumble. I unclipped the radio and turned it on.

"Testing, testing," I said into the mike, "Paul, can you hear me?"

"Gotcha, Cassidy. What's up?"

"I've got Green here, but we can use a lift out. The GPS died. I don't know what my last position was but I suspect it was about 20 feet straight up, so it should be very close to our present position."

"Up as in north?"

"No, up as in up."

Long pause. "What's the status?"

"Green's got compound fractures and two bullet holes in him. He'll need an airlift to L.A. We've got a problem up here. Your guys need to be prepared for some action."

"What kind of action?"

"Possible gunfire. They seem to think Green and I are dead for now but the helicopter just might tip them off."

"Who's *they*?"

"The guys who shot Green."

I heard a bustle of activity at the ranger station, Paul giving orders and people rushing around.

"And what's *your* status?"

"I think I'm fine, bruised from head to toe, but fine. You didn't tell Michaels about the bear did you?"

More chatter in the background. "I had to Cass. He called in to check on you and asked where you were. He put two and two together, and asked why you made only three miles in one day. I wasn't going to lie to him. Plus, you need someone keeping tabs on you. You're nuts. You're going to kill yourself one of these days. We've got a helicopter headed your way with a team of four."

"We're at the bottom of a short cliff right where my last reading was."

"Gotcha."

I turned my attention to Green. He was still conscious, but fading. Keep him talking, Cass. Keep him with us.

I brought the water bottle up to his lips again. He coughed and sputtered. We tried again.

"You heard Paul?"

"Yeah. I was thinking I'd never get out of here."

"You almost didn't. Search and rescue came through a few days ago. They missed you."

"How'd you find me?"

"I tracked you to the pot fields, through the woods. If I'd been smart I would have tracked you here, but I wasn't that smart. There was a little girl that lived at the pot farm and she wandered away from the house. I took her home and asked about you. They showed me where you were, but when I tried to rappel down here, the guy cut my rope so I came by airmail just like you. They took a few shots at me, but I think they missed."

"They shot me on the trail and dumped me over the side."

"That's what you get for poking around where you're not welcome."

"Guess so."

His eyes glazed over.

"Hey, you've gotta stay with me here. There's a helicopter on its way. You gotta hang in there. No dying on my watch."

"I've been in and out all week. Where's that water? Got any food on you? There's some in my pack, but I couldn't move enough to reach it." I looked at his pack. I'd have to move him to get at the food and that didn't look like a good idea. I suspected broken ribs. I dug around in my pack and fished out some backpacker food. I fired up the stove and heated water.

"A bear ate most of my food, but I have enough to share. I don't know what shape it's in after saving me from that fall. It's likely to be powder now, but it'll still taste like something." I held up some foil packets. "Beef stroganoff? Mac and cheese? Chicken Alfredo?"

"Meat. Anything with meat. Mac and cheese is for kids. Speaking of which, how'd a kid like you get to be out here looking for an old guy like me? You said you were tracking me?"

"Right. It's a long story."

"Looks like we got time."

So I told him about Silva and Michaels, and tracking Silva down to the trailer and that Michaels had kept in touch.

"And Rusty sent you in here after me? Because he knew you could track?"

"That's about it."

"I'll kill him."

"No, you won't. He tried to come along, but... it's complicated."

The stroganoff was finished cooking, so I settled in next to Green's head and scooped some up for him.

"Sorry. I only brought one fork; cuts down on the weight. Every little bit helps. Anyway, I wouldn't let Rusty come along. I work better alone, but I have been thinking I need to teach him a thing or two so he's more comfortable with me being out here like this."

He busted out laughing and then grimaced with the pain. Definitely some broken ribs in there.

"You? Need to teach Rusty a thing or two? That's a good one."

"By the way, what's with the color coded names? Rusty Michaels, Kelly Green? If Michaels introduces me to another person with a color name, I'm going to start wondering about him."

"Then you don't want to meet my family. My brother's name is Hunter and my sister's Ivy Lee. She lucked out. She got a double pun name. Get it? Ivy Green, Ivy league?"

"What color is your parent's house?"

"Guess."

I helped him eat his stroganoff mush slowly. I wasn't sure I was supposed to allow him food. I hadn't gotten any instructions on what to do and what not to do if I found him alive. I just knew that if it were the other way around, I'd want to eat whether it was the smart thing to do or not.

"So, what's going on with you and Rusty?"

"Nothing, really. I'm not ready for a relationship, and he seems to know that. But if I *was* ready..." Then what?

"Yeah, what?"

"If I *was* ready, I'd definitely choose him."

"Well, I for one think he really needs you. Not just a girl. He needs *you*."
We heard faint helicopter noises. "Shit. This is going to hurt like hell."

Chapter 7

I'd been thinking, and I wasn't leaving with the helicopter. I still had some information gathering to do. Where was this house? How big of an operation was the farm? And who shot Kelly Green? I would just take a quick fact-finding detour and then high tail it for Elk Meadows. I had been able to find one of the bullets that Raphael had sent down the cliff after me. I dug it out of the soft sand and pocketed it. I hoped the police could link it to the bullets they dug out of Green.

I packed up my stove and what was left of my rope as the helicopter flew in and circled overhead. I stood in the open in my sand-colored outfit waving my arms. I then grabbed my red shirt off the ground and started waving that as well. Two guys were lowered on a cable, and there was lots of radio talk. They loaded Green in the basket and pulled him up into the helicopter. The basket was lowered for me, too, but I shook my head no and told the guy left on the ground that I was headed for Elk Meadows. He took in the bruises, scratches and the blood spots dotting my clothes. He looked at me incredulously.

"We oughta get you checked out."

"No, I'm fine. I have unfinished business."

"How are you getting there from here?" he asked pointing to the cliff.

"I'll have to find my way. There's people up top that think I'm dead. I'd like to keep them thinking that. Take care of Green."

He started to argue, but I lurched into my ragged pack, unsnapped the strap on my pistol, and started walking along the bottom of the cliff, parallel to the trail. He came after me but I picked up my pace, and set my hand on my pistol readying for a stand off. It was more a defensive reflex but it got the point across. He shook his head and climbed back into the basket. The helicopter pulled up and the basket slowly ascended to the bay and was pulled in. I waved to them as they headed west, off to L.A.

I needed to put some distance between the pot farm and me, so I followed the bottom of the cliff. I consulted the map to make sure the trail followed the way I was going. When I figured I'd gone far enough and the terrain allowed me, I climbed up a steep hill to the trail. It was rugged country, all up and down. I fiddled with the GPS system but it was deader than dead. Sorry, Paul.

Once I reached topside again, I found a place to make camp, carefully placing my footprints to be invisible. The spot was off trail by a quarter mile, sheltered on most sides by brush. Nobody would come looking for me here.

Turning on the radio, I expected to catch hell from Paul for not coming in with Green.

"Testing, testing, can you hear me Paul?"

"Yeah. Why aren't you on that helicopter?" he barked.

"I wanted to finish the hike."

"Yeah, right. You're up to something. What are you doing out there?"

"I'm camping."

Big sigh.

"Your GPS signal's gone Cass. I know you. You attract trouble like a bug zapper attracts bugs, and I don't want to see you get zapped. If something happens to you, I won't know where you are."

"Tomorrow morning I'll be where you last picked me up. After that, I'll be on the trail to Elk Meadows. Michaels can pick me up the day after tomorrow. I'd say tomorrow night, but that's pushing it and I don't want to push it. If I happen to get there early, I'll just set up camp. There's a water stop two miles before Elk Meadows so I should be fine."

I would hear basically the same things from Michaels, but I figured I better call him before he talked to Green. Since the house relied on cell phones I knew there should be some kind of signal in the area. I flipped through my phone book, brought up his number and pushed the call button.

"Hello?"

"Hey, there. It's me. Did you hear the news?"

"I heard you found Kelly. Where are you?"

"I'm about seven miles from Elk Meadows."

"Why didn't you come out with search and rescue?"

"I didn't need rescuing."

"What are you doing back there?"

"I have some unanswered questions. I'm going to go back and do some poking around."

"What kind of poking around?"

"Observation."

"Surveillance?"

"What's the difference?"

"You know what the difference is."

Sigh. "I'm going to walk around an area and make a map of it. Then I'm going to write down all the license plate numbers I see. I'm going to sit in the woods and watch a house to note how many people there are and what they do. Then I'll try to figure out how the people actually got here, because this house shouldn't exist. After that I'm hiking to Elk Meadows. Can you pick me up the day after tomorrow?"

"You know I'll be there. But I want you to turn your back on all this and hike out in the morning."

"I'll stay out of sight."

"What is this place that you are going to poke around in?"

"Can't say yet."

"You know something or you wouldn't go back."

Time to change the subject. "Are you going to see Green?"

"In the morning. I figure he'll spend most of the night in ER or surgery."

"He'll be fine. He's a tough one."

"I haven't heard much. How bad was it?"

"He broke both legs and I suspect there's some broken ribs. He took a tumble down a cliff. I'm not a doctor but I suspect there could be some internal damage from dehydration, if not from the fall. And he was shot twice. Upper torso. He seemed to be as alert as you could expect a guy to be under the circumstances. He joked about his family.

"You can expect to get chewed out for sending me out by myself, but I assured him that you tried your best not to. Look, I don't want to run out of juice. I'll radio the station when I am headed for Elk Meadows so you'll know I'm not kidnapped again, and then I'll just hike straight through until dark and be there as soon as I can the next day. If I get there early, I'll pop up my tent as a marker. At this time of year, and during this part of the week, it should be the only one there."

"Okay. Take care."

"You, too. Tell Green I said 'Hi'".

"Will do."

I got back to the farm bright and early. I wanted to see the place come alive in the morning. I circled the entire property. Behind the fields, I discovered two small cabins where the workers slept. I waited in the woods for the men to appear. First out was Raphael. Kids just don't know how to sleep in. I never did when I was a kid. He came out the door and stretched, his long hair was loose. Amelia followed sleepily. Raphael walked to the edge of the field and glanced up at the sky. It looked like a storm might be brewing. Gray thunderheads loomed over the mountain peak.

The two went back inside and, after some prep time, emerged again with bowls of cereal. They ate standing up, Raphael pacing the clearing in front of the cabin. He rinsed their bowls at an outdoor faucet and brought them back inside.

I sat down and drew a layout of the farm as I recalled it on top of the topo markings on the map. I shaded in the pot fields and drew boxes for the house, two cabins and outbuilding. I marked the ATV and motorcycle paths as I remembered them, and was prepared to change them later if needed.

Raphael walked around the cabin and returned with the blue dirt bike. He picked up Amelia and balanced her on the front of the seat, then climbed on behind her. He kept a protective arm around his daughter as they slowly rode off in the direction of the house. He was careful not to bounce and jar the bike and she seemed to enjoy the ride.

Two men, speaking quickly in Spanish, emerged from the second cabin. They were laughing as they went about their morning routine. A piece of paper was handed back and forth between them. One man pointed at the paper and then off to the side. Then he looked at the other man and pointed to the paper again. It looked like they were making plans for the day. They shrugged into daypacks, straddled identical blue dirt bikes, and motored off.

With the cabins hiding me from view I removed my boots to leave less of a track. I then crept up to the dark and grimy windows. From what I could see there was nobody inside. I followed the wall around the back, away from the field, carefully placing my feet where they would leave as little imprint as possible. I crossed to the other cabin. It also appeared to be empty. The men clearly were not concerned about others coming in because they left their front doors open. I entered, briefly taken aback by the squalor. The cabins had a rudimentary kitchen. A small refrigerator stood in one corner with a filthy sink next to it smelling of rotten food. The floor was littered with clothing, food wrappers, pine needles, and dirt and grime from the dawn of civilization. I noticed very few toys. Clearly, Amelia spent most of her time outdoors. I searched the cabin quickly, looking for something that would tell me what these people did up here. Buried on the table, I found a sheet of notebook paper with a list of abbreviations on it and what looked like dates. I folded the paper and pushed it into a pocket of my cargo pants, making sure it lay flat against my leg. If I was caught and frisked I didn't want it to draw attention. I didn't want to stick around any longer than necessary. I flattened myself against the wall and listened before exiting, my hand on my gun, just in case. I crouched and quickly crossed to the other cabin.

This one was in better shape. Same kitchen, bunk beds against one wall. A doorway led to a small room or closet. On the shelf next to the sink there were some basic household goods and a stack of books. I turned the books over to read their backs. One was a spiral bound notebook. I opened it and dust flaked off, settling to the bare wood floor. There were notes similar to the ones in my pocket. I tore out several pages for later comparison and slipped them into the same pocket. Then I arranged the books as I had originally found them. I glanced around, hoping for more, but I had been here long enough. My heart was pounding with the thought that someone would walk in on me. Again I listened at the door, then quietly slipped out into the forest. I found my boots again and picked them up, carrying them as I went on my way.

I circled around to the outbuilding, staying well hidden in the woods. I could hear voices now and I hid, waiting. The three men were in a group, and orders were given. The two with daypacks got on dirt bikes and rode away. Raphael puttered around the farm, checking the fields, repairing things. He entered the outbuilding and then left to do something else. Raphael seemed to be the only one I had to worry about at this point so I approached the back of the outbuilding and peeked in a window. Although not sure of exactly what I was seeing, I knew the police would know, so I took two pictures of the single room's contents.

Since Raphael's dirt bike was standing nearby, I slipped my hand into a pocket and, without removing the paper, scratched the license plate number onto the paper with the stub of a pencil I used to make the map.

Next was the house. I entered the woods and circled the property until I reached the front of the house. I found a comfortable hiding place that couldn't be seen from the trails, sat down, and sketched the house. When I had a rough drawing I closed in a bit, still careful to remain out of sight from the house and the area where I had last seen Raphael. I looked for a way to see inside the house. I wanted to know who these people were and how they had managed to live undiscovered in the woods. Lights were on inside. How did they get electricity up here? Around the back of the house I found a large propane tank and climbed on top of it. From here I could see a sparkling tiled kitchen. Everything was decorated in sandy earth tones. The kitchen was immaculate. I guess if you live in a house in the woods and can't be seen by outsiders, you do a lot of cleaning. The person turned and it was a woman. She was carrying something to a place I couldn't see off to the side. Cooking smells wafted from the kitchen making my mouth water. It felt like ages since I'd eaten real food. Breakfast that morning had been rehydrated chicken and rice dust.

This was the only window that was going to reveal anything to me and I felt very vulnerable lying on top of the tank. If anybody looked out the window, I'd be in plain sight. Sliding down I made my way to the outer perimeter of the property. There had to be a road into this place. You can't build a house with things brought in on a dirt bike. I followed the ATV path away from the house. At first it appeared hopeful, but then it petered away as it went further from the house. There was a grassy area next to the road that brought to mind an airstrip. However I convinced myself that it was too short and bound to be full of burrows and rocks. Open fields are seldom as flat as they appear to be.

I was disappointed with my little fact-finding excursion, not having found much useful information. Hopefully the papers in my pocket would shed some light on the goings on. I entered the forest and followed the trail to the outskirts of the property then down the bank to the trail. Putting on my boots, I got ready for a long fast hike to Elk Meadows believing I could make it all the way in one afternoon, but my real goal was just to reach the water source.

I was making good time, enjoying the coolness of the overcast sky when the clouds released a deluge that soaked me to the skin. I looked through my pack, but couldn't find the rain poncho. It had either been left at home to cut down on weight or had been lost when the bear went through my pack. Either way, I was in for a wet hike. At least I wasn't going to overheat. Hiking in a rain poncho is pretty damp going anyway. This was actually very good news, I told myself. I'd be able to find water now. Sandy water, but water, nonetheless.

The trail left the meadowlands and turned into the forest again. It turned a little bend and suddenly I was at the Pacific Crest Trail. This was one of the iffy water sources that Paul had mentioned, so I left the trail and looked around for a little stream. I thought it was funny that I was looking for water while I was soaked clean through. The stream was a muddy trickle and the spring was only three miles away. I decided it wasn't worth the bother to collect and filter the muck in the stream.

Thunder cracked and echoed off the neighboring peaks as I ducked my head and started down the trail once more. I was listening to the sound of the storm and trying to keep the rain out of my eyes when a blue dirt bike roared into view. I quickly stepped aside to let it pass, my heart in my throat. The driver pulled up. He was wearing a helmet so I couldn't see any facial features. I decided to play the dumb hiker card.

"Can you tell me how far it is to Elk Meadows?" I yelled over the storm and engine noise.

"Hold on," he yelled back. No Spanish. Maybe it was a freak coincidence. He turned off the bike engine and hopped off. He took out a radio and spoke into it.

"Never mind, I'll just keep going," I shouted.

I turned and hiked off down the trail. Distance, that was my goal here. If I could get some distance between us I could duck into the woods. The engine started again and I heard the dirt bike heading towards me. I unsnapped the flap on my holster. I turned.

"My boss says you should come back to the house with me. He said you should not be hiking in such weather. You can stay until the storm is over."

"I can't." I lied, "I bet a friend that I could hike from Piney Point Campground to Elk Meadows in 3 days, and I am going to do it."

"A bet? It isn't worth a bet to die of pneumonia. Besides, my boss is not someone who can be refused."

"I'm sorry, but I do refuse," I said, drawing my gun. "I don't want to use this, but I will if you insist. First, I will take out your tire. It's a long wet walk to anywhere from here, so you don't want me to do that. After that, if you push, you are fair game."

Most people don't take me seriously when I have a gun in my hand. I don't know why that is. Probably because I look like I wouldn't know which end is which. But I do. I was tired and battered and sore and soaked and I sure didn't want to get into more trouble when I was so close to the end of the trail. He pulled a rifle from the side of the dirt bike.

"This is no game," he said.

What could I do? I was standing in the middle of the trail like a sitting duck. Take away his advantage, a voice in my head said. Taking careful aim I shot out his tire. One thing I can usually count on is that guys hesitate to shoot girls. I probably should have shot him first, and then worried about the tire, but a part of me thought he still considered this a game. I took aim again and backed away. Cover, I needed cover. Once I was in the woods I could lose him. I needed time and distance. That rifle could take me down from half a mile away. All those things I needed seemed like a real tall order at the time. I was backing, backing and he stood with the rifle in his hands. I'm sure he had shot lots of things up here in the woods, lots of things smaller and faster than me, maybe things bigger and stronger too. Maybe Green.

A large tree appeared to my right. I backed towards it. He raised the rifle and I jumped behind the tree. Splinters scattered from his shot, stinging my arm. Okay, now I knew, he was playing with me. I was pretty sure he could have killed me if it had been his intention. He still thought he had to bring me back, so he would eventually get serious about this stand off. But maybe, just maybe, he didn't really want to kill me. Maybe he was supposed to bring me back alive. I knew though, that to let myself be brought in was to die. I knew too much for them to let me get away.

I stole a glance. He was still on the trail and seemed reluctant to venture off it. I chose a direction that offered plenty of cover and left room to maneuver, and took off running, zig-zagging in and out around trees. I knew from experience that it's harder to hit a moving target, so I dashed off, deeper into the woods. He cursed and followed. A game trail wound down a hillside and I followed it knowing that game trails could vanish into thick brush. This is what I was counting on. I ran on and on, no thick brush. What's wrong with this forest anyway?

I stopped behind a tree to catch my breath and took a look behind me. This guy didn't appear to be very smart. He was tromping slowly through the forest, clearly out in the open. He might be a hunter, but he was no stalker. Now was my chance, if I wanted it, but, no, I didn't want it. I didn't want to shoot him. It wasn't that bad a situation yet. Not now that I had my distance and I had a feel for the kind of woodsman I was dealing with. I switched into a different way of thinking. I made for the shale mountain, hiding my tracks and staying behind trees. I hid, took stock the situation, chose the next hiding place, crouched and ran for it, hid, took stock of the situation... It was a more efficient way to travel because it allowed for short rests, and also allowed me to keep my head. I kept a tree between us at all times and when I finally found a thick patch of brush I crawled directly under it, rested, drank some water and continued. I was gaining.

I took off on another sprint, following the terrain, and found myself back on the trail again. I put some speed on while I had good footing. As the trail turned behind a rock, a bullet ricocheted off, startling me. I crossed to the other side of the trail and entered the woods again. I looked around to locate the enemy. He was closing in. Shit, I needed distance if I was going to cross that mountain.

The presence of boulders along the trail marked the start of the shale mountain. The trail would go up the side of the mountain, level off, and continue for a mile and a half, fully exposed. To skip the trail clearly meant a different route. The bottom of the mountain curved away from Elk Meadows. So there was a choice before me - the shale mountain and Elk Meadows or shelter and wilderness. Every moment I stopped to think brought him closer to me.

I hated the spot I found myself in. I hated the rain making everything slippery. The shale mountain was the worst place to face this kind of attack, but I had to get to Elk Meadows. I hated myself for even being capable of this, but it was time to better my odds. I squared off, took careful aim and fired. I watched as the man jerked backwards and fell. I hit where I had aimed. It wasn't a life-threatening wound, but he'd have a hard time shooting right handed anymore. I sprinted up the trail.

I kept thinking, Cass, you jog a mile and a half at the gym, you jog a mile and a half around town. You can do this. But jogging a mile in the gym is not the same thing as jogging with a backpack at an elevation of five thousand feet with sharp, wet rocks underfoot. I wouldn't advise anybody to run over the shale mountain, but when it came right down to it, I'd rather tumble off the mountain than get shot, then tumble off the mountain, so running gained precedence. I'd have to talk to the people at the gym, have them add rocks to the treadmills. Not that they'd stay. I almost laughed at the absurdity of it. It's funny what pops into my mind sometimes.

My lungs were burning and my legs were aching. I almost ditched my pack but I really wanted to see the face of the guy at the sporting goods store when I tried to take advantage of its lifetime warranty. Okay, so it probably doesn't cover bear mauling or falls off cliffs. I'd be willing to buy another one just to be able to show them the old one. I also thought that a shot in the back was a possibility and the pack might offer some meager protection from a bullet.

A glance back showed my stalker trudging down the trail. I think I'd made him mad. I was expecting a shot right about now, but then he sat down on the trail. I worried that possibly I'd hit him far worse than I had originally thought, but then I saw him set the rifle on a rock, grasp the gun with his left hand, and ease the trigger. I took off. I varied my speed, trying to be unpredictable. A shot echoed off the wall in front of me. He wasn't doing too bad, even left-handed. How many shots had that been?

I ducked behind a rock outcropping. There was a crack in the mountain about three feet wide. I ducked further in and, bracing my hands and feet against both sides of the rock, ascended the crack chimney style. About ten feet up, I braced myself, back against the rock, knees locked so I could get a real rest. I aimed the gun downward. If I was lucky he would pass me and not look up.

Slowly I got my wind back. I looked at the sky. It was late afternoon. I should be calling Paul. In fact I should have called him before I took off. He thought I was still at the farm. I couldn't call now. Silence was my best friend at this point.

As I was sitting up in the crack in the rock, I heard a noise. It rumbled up the trail and echoed off the shale mountain. I recognized that sound. It was a dirt bike. Reinforcements.

I climbed up the crack until I came to a ledge on the mountain. I decided my best bet was to just wait and watch. From here, I could see a good-sized chunk of trail. If I let them pass me, then I would be stalking them; a distinct advantage. But I also wanted to see what these two had in mind. I was in a very defendable position if I was spotted, but for the most part people don't look up much. They expected to find me on the ground.

I explored my ledge a little and found that it continued around the side of the mountain and sloped down to almost trail height. I looked at the terrain in the distance. The shale mountain came to an abrupt end and a little band of trees separated it from the meadowlands I was aiming for. The tall pale grass waved in the wind, beckoning to me. I knew I could hide forever in that waving grass.

One problem I had was that I wanted this to end before I got to Elk Meadows. I didn't want Michaels to walk into this situation. I watched the pair below. One man slowly walked down the trail while the other rode back and forth, up and down the trail on his dirt bike. They knew they had lost me at the shale mountain and they seemed to be guarding the boundary between the mountain and the meadow. At last the man on foot, the one I'd shot, slumped back on the side of the trail, clearly exhausted. He set the rifle across his knees. His head slumped. He was just waiting now, his attention no longer on the trail. A dark stain covered the right shoulder of his shirt. The other man continued to prowl back and forth on the dirt bike. What did they expect? Did they think I fell off the mountain? If so they were looking in the wrong place. Nobody would be getting back to the trail from down there.

As dusk settled, I knew it was time to make my move. If they gave up on me, they'd head for Elk Meadows and wait for me there. I didn't want them to reach Elk Meadows, and I had my eye on that dirt bike. Following the ledge down to where it overhung the trail, I lowered myself to the ground and crouched in the brush, waiting. There was a tree nearby and I tied my climbing rope firmly around it. I waited until the dirt bike was headed back towards the mountain. I let it pass, gave it a minute to put some distance between us. I made sure the other man was still there, head on knees, and I silently crossed the trail, laying my rope down as I went. I raised the rope to about wheel height, tying it around another tree. I slid into the grass behind and crawled on my belly until I was past the resting man, then I aimed my gun in the air and fired. Instantly, the sitting man was on his feet facing me and then the neurotic buzz of the dirt bike zoomed up the trail. The bike hit the rope, catapulting it into the air. The front fender snapped off, sailing into the woods. The rider flew off the bike and into the wounded man who howled with pain. I leaped onto the trail stalking towards them, gun drawn.

"Don't move!" I shouted in my most authoritative voice. It worked for dogs. I hadn't had much practice with men. "I want to see your hands. Put your hands up! Your gun!" I demanded stepping forward to take it. "Give me your gun or I'll shoot!" The wounded man tossed his gun aside. I picked it up and threw it over my shoulder keeping my gun trained on the more dangerous one. "You too! Give me your rifle!" He didn't have it. It was still slung on the dirt bike. "Your radio! Give me your radio!" They handed them over and I threw one deep into the woods and clipped the other to my belt. I looked them both up and down. No room for more weapons except maybe a knife. I backed towards the dirt bike, gun trained on my captives. I pulled the bike upright and one of the men made a dash for me. I shot instinctively and sloppily but it was enough to stop him. I straddled the bike and took off, leaving them in a cloud of dust.

Night was upon me when I got to Elk Meadows, but I just kept riding up the dirt road that circled Elk Mountain and met with the highway linking Joshua Hills to the L.A. area. I wanted to put as much distance as I could between those mountains and me, so I was really sailing along, taking the curves too fast. I was rattled and tense and I was zipping along a downhill straightaway when a highway patrol car pulled out and turned on its lights. I was never so glad to be pulled over in my life. An officer stepped out of the cruiser, saw the rifle strapped to my back and strode forward gun drawn. I put my hands up.

"It's okay," I said, "take it easy." He wasn't taking it easy.

He took the rifle and my pistol and stepped back. "Step off the bike slowly. You know it's illegal to ride this bike on the street?" That seemed like a lame question under the circumstances.

"Yeah," I replied. "There's another rifle strapped to the bike." Please, just haul me away!

"You have a license?"

"No," I replied trying to hurry this along. "The bike and the rifles are stolen." Actually I did have a motorcycle license. We rode dirt bikes a lot on my family's ranch. Everyone was expected to be able to ride motorcycles, horses and drive cars as early as possible.

He talked into the radio clipped to the front of his shirt. I was so exhausted from all I'd been through. I quit caring what happened. All I remember is being cuffed and put in the cruiser. I didn't know what happened to the dirt bike and I didn't care. The rifles, I assumed, were stowed in the trunk.

"Which station are you taking me?"

I didn't recognize the name.

"Can you radio Rusty Michaels at the Joshua Hills station? It's really important. Tell him you're bringing in Cassidy Callahan."

I was cuffed, belted into the seat and uncomfortable, but I didn't care. The toils of the day were too much. I put my head down on the seat and promptly fell asleep.

Chapter 8

The next thing I became aware of were gentle hands, but in my sleep, I barely perceived them. They unlocked and removed the handcuffs. I felt a gentle shaking, a hand on my shoulder.

"Cassidy. Cassidy, wake up." Soft, thundery voices. More gentle shakes. "Cass, come on, it's okay, it's all okay now." I bolted upright banging my head on the roof of the police car, my hand flying to the place where my holster should be. It was gone! I looked around frantically. Michaels had me by the shoulders, keeping me still in a gentle iron grip. Relief flooded through me, not because of my safety but because he was here. He wasn't at Elk Meadows. And I was here. "You okay?"

I wanted to say "Yes," but I numbly shook my head.

The patrolman cleared his throat. "Think I'll go inside and a get a cup of coffee," he mumbled awkwardly.

Michaels crawled in the back of the patrol car and we just sat silently for a minute, hoping for some normality to settle in. Normality seemed elusive and wouldn't be showing up any time soon.

"Did they save my pack?" I finally asked. The silliest things pop into my head. After all I went through, I still wanted to show my pack off at the sporting goods store. We went around to the trunk. Michaels pulled out my pack, the two rifles and my pistol. He looked at it all. The guns were all in plastic bags. I didn't remember them doing that.

"Holy cow, Cass, what happened to you out there?"

"Paul told you about the bear."

"Yeah, but this thing's been thrashed. The braces are snapped…"

"And Green told you about the cliff. That pack probably saved my life."

He took out the contents: my stove, a package of lasagna dust, three Band-Aids, and a small can of pepper spray. I'd forgotten all about the pepper spray. That could have been useful. Where was my water? Surely I had some water left. But there wasn't even a bottle in the pack. The last I remembered having any water was on the ledge on the big shale mountain. The memory gave me a shiver.

We put everything back in the pack and went into the station. Michaels took the guns to a window and checked them in as evidence. We went to his office. It was all so stark after being in the woods. I curled up in one of his chairs, even though technically they were not big enough. It felt safer to be small. Even in the station, with all the officers and protection a person could ask for, I felt vulnerable.

Somebody knocked on the door, making me jump. Michaels gave me a worried glance. He opened the door quietly and stepped out into the hall. I heard quiet voices, and then the person left. He went to his desk and did some writing.

I wanted to say something. All this silence and the stark walls and the business-like atmosphere were grating on my nerves. I wanted to go home. I wanted to get something to eat. I wanted to curl up into a little ball and sleep till September. I wanted to say something, but Michaels was writing and I couldn't figure out whether to call him Michaels or Rusty. Michaels was my detective friend, but I knew the moment I called him Rusty I was sunk. I'd never be able to go back. Emotionally, I was standing on a cliff, looking down. Down into a deep cavern of uncertainty and I was falling, not knowing where I'd land, and before I knew it, I was crying. I didn't want to cry. I didn't know why I was crying, but I couldn't stop. I curled up tighter, hugging my knees to my chest until he came around the desk, uncertain of what to do with me or how to comfort me. He pried my hands loose and tried to pull me up, but I was too scared and feeling so lost. He knelt down handing me a tissue, and brushed aside some dirty, matted hair from my eyes.

I don't know how long we sat there like that; me curled up in a little ball, him kneeling by the chair, just being there, silently comforting me with his presence. Eventually, I relaxed a little and the crying stopped and he finally drew me up out of the chair and wrapped his arms around me. He put his chin on my head.

"I took tomorrow off to go to Elk Meadows. I've written some orders for people to do tomorrow. They'll check out the guns and we'll hear something about the bike. Let's get you home."

I followed him out of the station and into the staff parking lot. We got in the Explorer and drove to my house. I walked up to the door numbly and staring at it realized I didn't have a key. Everything I had left was in the pack and I didn't have a key. Where was my wallet? Where were my keys? My side gate had a lock on it, but I never locked it. It was just to keep people from opening the gate and letting Shadow loose. Michaels gave me a boost up and I removed the lock. We walked around to the sliding glass door. It was locked, too, but the lock was so hokey I thought Michaels must have a tool to push the lever back. He went to his car and returned with a small toolkit. Sure enough, there it was. He slipped the tool through the crack in the door and the lock popped open.

I walked into my own home as if it was a stranger's. Nothing felt familiar. I looked at the clock and alarm bells went off. I hadn't called Paul. Did I even have a radio anymore? It was close to midnight. He was probably going into hysterics.

"Did I come home with the radio?" I asked Michaels.

"I don't think so."

"Shoot." I picked up the telephone book and called the forest service and was given the number for the Piney Point ranger station. Someone I didn't recognize answered the phone. I asked for Paul. He wasn't there they said, could they take a message? I told him to call Paul at home and let him know I was fine, that I was home and to call me the next day, late.

"Will do," he said.

I stumbled to the fridge, but despite my hunger I couldn't make a decision. I needed a shower, that's what I needed. If I felt better, I could think better.

Michaels watched me dejectedly.

"Cassidy, what's wrong?"

"I can't think. I am hungry and I can't think enough to eat anything. I haven't eaten since breakfast and I can't even choose what to eat."

"Why haven't you eaten?" he said, "You need to eat."

"I was…I was too busy."

"Cass, that's not it, why didn't you eat?"

I took a big breath partly to fight back the tears and partly because I could feel the words boiling up and there was going to be a bunch of them. "I lost half my food to the bear and I was conserving what I had left and then I was being chased through the mountains by the guys with the rifles. I only had backpacker food and I couldn't stop to cook and I lost my water so I couldn't cook it even if did have time and, and I better shut up or I'm going to cry again."

He brought me close. "You don't ever have to do that again. I promise I will never ask you to…"

I interrupted him, "Don't say that. You can't make promises like that. I would do it again. I would do it again for you or for Green or for some lost kid. I really would. So don't say you'd never. Some day if you need to, I hope you will." I shuddered, but I had meant it. "I need a shower. Can I take a shower? I'd feel so much better."

"What do you want me to do? It's getting late."

That cliff appeared before me. I stepped off falling, falling, "Will you stay? Please. I can't. I just can't."

"I'll be here when you get out."

I started the water, stepped into the shower, and let the filth and the grime run off down the drain. A week's worth of mountain dirt and sweat. When I thought about it, I wondered how Michaels could hug me, but he didn't seem to mind. I washed my hair, soaped up, shaved my legs, and rinsed off. It was all I had the energy to do. When I stepped out of the bathroom, I realized I'd left my bedroom door open out of habit. I wasn't used to having people in my house. I wrapped the towel around me and closed the door quietly, then dressed in sweat pants and a t-shirt. I brushed my wet hair and fluffed it up a little so it wouldn't dry all flat.

When I stepped into the kitchen, there were sandwiches made and glasses set out.

"What would you like to drink? Looks like we have water or week old soda."

"Water's fine."

He poured some week old soda for himself and water for me. We took the sandwiches to the table.

"Thank you," I said, "That was really nice of you." I looked at the bread thinking it should have been moldy but I guess he had checked ahead of time because it looked okay.

After we ate we moved to the living room.

"I need to go pick up Shadow in the morning."

"Okay, is there anything else you would like to do?"

"What did you have in mind?"

"I didn't. I just thought since we have a whole day we could do something."

"There's something I want to show you, but it takes two days to see it."

"Maybe we can plan that some time."

In the middle of the night, I dreamed I was being chased. I found myself running down an endless deer trail, and there was nowhere to hide, nowhere to hide. It was closing in. It was closing in, and I couldn't run.

Again, the gentle shake and the kind, thundery voice, "Cassidy, it's okay. Wake up, babe, it's just a bad dream."

I woke with a start. I was on the couch, curled up in a ball and he was stretched out on the recliner part of the couch. I'd never gone to bed last night. I got up and stumbled around, thinking I should go to bed. He got up and led me back to the couch.

"Stay here, I'm right here. I won't leave you. Come on, relax. It's okay."

Morning dawned and I slept on. I couldn't get enough sleep. I felt movement and I heard cooking noises. Then I heard washing up noises. I couldn't wake up. The couch was lumpy and uncomfortable, but it was better than the ground, so it was lovely. I heard newspaper reading noises. Rusty.

He must be bored stiff. He came and sat on the floor next to the couch. I woke up mentally before I opened my eyes. I didn't want to be all bleary eyed in front of him.

"How do you feel?" he asked me.

"Better."

"I made eggs. I hope that was okay. I didn't want to take off on you."

"Thanks."

"Would you like me to make you some?"

"No, thanks, I just ate. I spent four days on only two pouches a day, so it'll take me a few days to get back to normal."

"Cassidy, what's it like out there? What does it feel like to be charged by a bear?"

"Is this a trick to get me to talk? Or do you really want to know? You've been out in the woods. I know you have. I remember telling Green that I needed to take you out in the woods, to teach you some tracking so you'd be more comfortable letting me go out, and he laughed at me. He thought it was funny that I thought I could teach you something."

Michaels smiled. "You can teach me anything you want me to know."

"Well, I don't want you to know what it feels like to be charged by a bear. I can tell you that when things like that happen to me, my thinking narrows down to the tools I have at hand and the lay of the land. It's like a puzzle. I fiddle with the puzzle until I find the best solution I can, then I go for it with all my strength."

"I wish I had your strength. Kelly didn't know how you found him. Last thing he remembered was that you were just there. But he thinks you're a keeper."

"I told him briefly how I got there, but he probably doesn't remember much of our conversation. I don't think he should know. Let him think I'm the world famous tracker and not the bumbling idiot who almost got herself killed."

"That reminds me," I said, quickly getting up. I found my camouflaged pants and fished around in the pockets. I brought out the bullet that I'd dug out of the sand, the map, the notebook papers I'd taken from the cabins and my cell phone buried deep in a cargo pocket. I dropped the bullet in his hand. "See if this matches either of those two rifles. Or if it matches the bullets they took out of Kelly. This bullet was shot by a guy named Raphael. I was lucky Raphael is a lousy shot." I unfolded the papers. They were stiff and the ink had run from being soaked in the rain, but the letters were still legible.

I opened the map, better to show him the map than the papers. I wanted some time to myself, to figure those out. I plugged the phone into the charger in case I needed it charged to get to the pictures in it.

I pointed to the map. "These large areas are pot fields, two different kinds, although I don't know anything about the plants. I just noticed the two were slightly different. These two buildings are small cabins. There are three workers at the farm. They are all Hispanic and probably in their early twenties. Raphael lives in this cabin with his daughter. I'm guessing she's three, and she shouldn't be growing up like that. This cabin houses the two other employees. They've got a bare bones kitchen, sink, fridge, a few shelves, and bunk beds along the other wall. This building I took a few pictures of with my phone, because I couldn't tell what it was. I thought you might be able to tell me. These lines are ATV or motorcycle trails. They get around the farm and to the trail by these trails. This is a house; a big fancy house that shouldn't exist in this location. I watched the house for a few hours but didn't learn much. I met the man who lives there, professional looking guy. Latino, Hispanic I couldn't tell. He didn't give me his name. The workers are all scared to get on his bad side. I saw a woman inside this house, but they rarely come out. I only saw her enough to know there's another person in there. I couldn't find any road going in. As far as I can tell, the dirt bikes make runs down the trail to get in and out. Why they go in and out every day, I don't know."

"What made you think to go gather all this information? And how do know what the inside of these cabins are like?"

"I thought there might be some ongoing drug investigation or something, so I thought the information would be useful either for that or to catch the guy that shot Kelly."

"And the cabins?"

"You don't want to know about the cabins. I'll just tell you that I didn't get caught and they won't know I've been there. I didn't leave any tracks."

"Speaking of tracks, Kelly was really surprised you were able to follow him off trail. He spoke very highly of you."

"He was trying to hide his tracks just like I was. I could have tracked him to where he was, if things hadn't turned ugly."

"Do I want to hear this?"

I sighed, "Yes and no." So I told him about hiding in the woods and returning Amelia to her dad. "I guess I did take a bit of a risk doing that, but I couldn't let the kid get lost. And I thought I could use the situation to find out where Green was. I don't want him to know about that though. I don't want him to think about..." I was lost for words because I didn't want Rusty to know how much I was willing to risk either.

"It's okay," he said kindly, "we won't tell him."

"I guess I'd rather he see it the way it happened to him without thinking about the way it could have happened to me."

"If he'd have had an ounce more strength, he would have turned that helicopter around and gone back for you."

I swallowed the lump forming in my throat. I retrieved my cell phone.

I brought up the first picture. "This is one of the workers at the farm. You might ask Kelly if this is the guy that shot him. This is a picture of the big field. The resolution isn't great, but the guys at the station can probably make out that it's marijuana plants. The next two pictures are of the inside of the outbuilding. No, I didn't go in. These were taken through a window."

His eyes narrowed as he looked at the two pictures. He knew what they were but he also saw something I hadn't seen at the time. I'd taken a picture of a man standing inside the building, and he had seen me. I was so focused on getting a picture I hadn't seen him. Now the whole mess with the guys on the dirt bike made sense. I *had* been caught.

"Shit," I said softly, "I'm lucky I made it off the property, and I didn't even know they were after me!"

"How could they not catch you, once they knew you were there?"

"After I took these pictures, I snuck into the woods, then went back to observe the house. I was very careful to stay out of sight and not leave tracks, but I didn't know they were looking for me. I just didn't want to get caught."

"You have got to be the luckiest person I know. You ... I don't even want to think about what could have happened."

I lucked out again because his cell phone rang and he spent some time talking to someone at the station. I used the time to wash up and get dressed. I debated what to wear for a long time. I thought Rusty should see a different side of me. The "me" that kept landing on his doorstep was always bedraggled and distressed. I was determined to put that "me" behind me for the day. On the other hand, I wanted to be prepared for anything. Fashion choices are not my strong suit. I decided to go with a more feminine look. I chose denim Capri's. I liked my khaki ones better, but they were too much like my woodsy look. Then I topped it with a cheerful short sleeved pucker shirt. It clung a little, but not enough to give him the wrong idea. Then, leave it to me to only have tennis shoes, moccasins and hiking boots. I dug around in my closet and finally came up with some flat casual shoes I'd worn to a get-together four years ago. I owned nothing with heels. I figured heels just made it look like I was trying too hard.

I took time to blow dry my hair and put on makeup. It felt good to care about my looks for a change. My shoulder length blond hair had just enough curl to add some body. A little bit of mousse and a blow-drying and I was good for the day.

I entered the living room a whole new person.

"This is the Cassidy I don't get to see often enough," he said smiling.

Then on a more serious note, "That was the station. They said your gun was fired four times and that the rifle you were carrying when you were pulled over was fired four times. The rifle on the bike hadn't been fired at all. Want to tell me about that?"

"Ummm, it sounds right to me?" There was a pause while he waited for me to continue. "My first shot went into the tire of the first dirt bike."

"How close were you?"

"I don't know; fifty feet, maybe?"

"And the second shot?" I blanched. I knew I'd used that shot for my own gain but I'd also acted in self-defense in a way.

"Rusty, I…" I couldn't tell him. I just couldn't, but I knew I had to. He guessed what had happened.

"Cassidy, did you have to shoot someone? I know you wouldn't if you didn't have to. Is that it?"

I nodded.

"Where did you hit him?"

I looked up at him. Gee, I hated him to see me like this. I pointed to his right collarbone.

"How close was he?"

I went to the window to give him a better perspective. "If he were standing on my sidewalk, I was on the roof of that blue house." I said, pointing down the street.

"I'm impressed. Too bad you didn't kill him."

"Don't say that. Please, don't say that. I hit him exactly where I aimed." I faltered. "I needed some insurance. I thought it was the only way I'd survive. And… and I couldn't let them get to Elk Meadows. I was worried about what you might walk into. I had to do something before then, and I only had three miles to do it in." There, I said it. I'd done it to protect him.

"I don't even want to ask about the third shot."

"That one I fired up in the air. They fell for the old climbing rope across the trail trick. That's how I ended up with the bike and the two rifles. I thought if I had the bike, I could make it home before you left for Elk Meadows. You can't believe how glad I was to get arrested."

"And the forth shot?"

"After I had the bike, they tried to charge me one last time, so I fired a warning shot."

"And what about his shots?"

"I can only remember two of them. The first one he hit the tree I was ducking behind. Someone can dig the bullet out of the tree to prove that one. The second one was while I was crossing this mountain where the trail was wide open. The shot hit the rocks in front of me. If he'd had a good right shoulder he would have got me. That bullet is long gone."

"And you don't remember the other two shots?"

"Maybe it was the two shots Raphael fired off the top of the cliff, although I don't think Raphael was the man after me on the trail. Or it could be the two shots that Kelly took. Maybe I ought to go back and find that other gun."

"Very funny. Nope, I'm not letting you out of my sight today."

"It's getting late. Let's leave Shadow at the kennel one more day. What do you do for fun?"

"Kelly and I go rock climbing, but I don't want you back in those mountains any time soon."

"Do you like the beach? We could go to the beach, walk the boardwalk and ride the rinky dink roller coaster."

"Sounds like a safe plan except for the roller coaster part."

"You don't like roller coasters?"

I fished around the house for extra house and car keys, then I dropped the keys to the Roadster in his hand.

"You can't go to the beach and leave the Roadster at home. It's California law that if you have a convertible and you're going to the beach, that's the car you have to take. Why do you think you see so many convertibles at the beach? You don't want to get a ticket for Convertible Neglect do you?"

We took the Roadster. I called Paul before we left and listened to his tirade about me not calling him. He'd been worried, not knowing where I'd been. I apologized and told him that the radio and the GPS system got lost in another mishap. I'd have to settle that later, after Paul had a chance to calm down.

Then he said something that put a crimp in my otherwise joyful day. He said that everyone in town was talking up the lost ranger story and that I was famous up there. Oh, man! That's one thing I did not need.

Chapter 9

We left the top up on the Roadster while we were on the freeway. I liked watching guys drive that car. There was just something about it. It felt powerful and in control. When I drove it, I felt like I was trespassing. I tended to drive it more timidly than my Jeep. We took the 14 to the 5 to the 405 to the 10 and followed that west until it hit the waterfront. It was a glorious day, all sun-shiney and warm. The really hot weather hadn't set in yet and the water would be too cold for swimming, but it was so nice to get out and away from town with no worries. When we neared the coast, we pulled off and put the top down. We drove back and forth along Ocean Avenue looking at all the tourist shops and seafood restaurants. We were going to stop, but I wanted to get down to the water so we drove to the pier.

"Hey look!" I exclaimed excitedly, "You didn't tell me you had a restaurant down here." And there it was, *Rusty's* clearly written in white rope letters on a bright red sign. We ate lunch there, and I bought him a *Rusty's Surf Ranch* polo shirt at the gift shop. We followed the steps down to the beach and I took off my shoes to walk in the soft sand. I pointed at some footprints in the sand. "These were made by a woman, taller than me, probably a hundred and fifty pounds. Look, if we follow her, we'll find out she's a mom. See? Here come the kids." I pointed out a group of footprints coming up to meet the woman's. "She's got three kids and the little one gets tugged around by an older sibling. The bigger kid is more of a loner. See, he's off to the side and the middle kid watches after the baby. These two trails are the younger two. You can tell what's going on because the little one strays and then the older one jerks him back. They join the mom and then head off down the beach. See the older one take off ahead again?"

I found another set of prints. "Now this girl you'd better stay away from. She's wearing a skimpy bathing suit and she's strutting her stuff. See how she reaches out with her toes and comes down on the ball of her foot? She's got long legs…"

"Cassidy, what are you doing?"

"I'm just talking."

"You sound like you are reading the newspaper out loud to me."

I laughed. It was a newspaper of sorts. "I'm sorry. I'll try not to. There is just so much information to be had and people walk around all the time without even seeing it."

"What did you do before you learned how to read tracks?"

"I read them anyway. I just grew up with this hyper awareness of what is going on around me. My curiosity kept me asking questions. Questions about minute things that no one else seemed to notice. So I had to search out the answers for myself. Why did the chicken cross the road? Why are there dogs checking out the ranch every night? Turned out they were coyotes after my sister's lamb. I snuck out late one night and shot one of the coyotes with a BB gun. I got into big trouble for that. I was only six-years-old. How was I to know that my BB gun wouldn't take down a coyote? I bet my dad was more mad at me for going out there with the coyotes than the fact that I shot it, but when he scolded me for it he focused on the gun angle and that now there was a poor wounded coyote out there who would be even hungrier for lamb steaks." I looked up and there was the mom and kids, the little blonde one being tugged along by a little brown-headed girl. I didn't press the issue, but I think Rusty noticed them too.

We wandered down to the water's edge and waded at the edge of the cold surf. The water came up splashing around our feet and we felt the sand suck out from under our toes as the waves flowed back out.

I found another set of tracks and saw a large dog in the distance but these tracks didn't belong to him.

"Here, try, this," I said pointing out the trail at our feet. "Find this dog." He looked around.

"It's right there."

"Are you sure? Follow the tracks and see." So we followed the tracks and they led up to the parking lot where a couple was loading a golden retriever into the back of an SUV.

"You knew ahead of time that it was a different dog."

"The dog you assumed was the right one was too lightly built for this trail. And a retriever moves a lot differently than that greyhound. If you watch the greyhound, you will see that he couldn't possibly have made these tracks."

"I have a question, and I don't want you to take it the wrong way, but why do you do this? What difference does it make which dog made which trail?"

"It doesn't. But studying this easy stuff builds up observation skills that come in handy later. It builds an awareness in you. How do you think I was able to tell Kelly's trail from the other four men at the farm? Kelly is taller and moves differently. The workers moved in worker circles and Kelly was moving in stealth mode. It takes a lot of observation to find the guy in stealth mode in amongst a bunch of tracks of people who aren't."

"Okay, I can see that. Let's go up to the boardwalk where you aren't so tempted to read."

I didn't tell him it wouldn't matter. There was even tracking to do on the boardwalk.

We poked around the tourist shops, wondering why anybody would want a neon two foot long surfboard on their wall or a foam hat of an alligator head. We stood at the rail, watching the people walk by below. There was the couple with a tote bag walking hand in hand. There were two boys kicking a soccer ball between them down the beach. There was a guy in faded black gang banger jeans building a sandcastle with a little girl. My blood ran cold. I turned away from the scene, the color draining from my face. I grabbed Rusty by the hand and pulled him into a nearby shop.

"Cassidy! What's wrong! Stop, hold on. Look at me, look at me and calm down." I stared at my feet waiting for the pounding in my head to settle down.

"I need to buy some sunglasses. Big, dark sunglasses and I don't care what they look like on me." I snatched a pair of sunglasses off a rack and paid for them. I shoved them on my face and warily went back to the rail. I looked out over the people again and quickly turned around. "If I tell you, you have to promise me that you won't act on what I say."

"I can't promise that, Cass, you know that."

"Okay, you need to promise you won't act on it until after you've heard me out."

He paused. "Okay, I think I can manage that."

I still couldn't turn around. "See the guy with the little girl at the water's edge building sandcastles? Baggy black jeans, no shirt, pony tail. The little girl's wearing an old lavender sundress and white shoes with cartoon characters on the side. She has black curly hair. Her name's Amelia. And her dad's name is Raphael. Does that trigger anything for you?"

"The guy who cut your rope. Are you sure?"

"Look at me! Am I sure?"

"Yep, you're sure. Now why don't you want me to shoot him on the spot or walk down there and wring his scrawny little neck?"

"Because it wouldn't do any good. We can use this for a better good if we don't strangle him."

"What's this *we*? I didn't way *we*. I said *I*."

"Listen, we'd be much better off watching and gathering information. Look at it this way. What do those guys do at the farm? They make drugs and they transport them out here. So, what is Raphael doing out here? He's probably making a delivery. And even if he made it already, he has to go somewhere. He didn't ride the dirt bike down here. He'd have gotten stopped. He had to swap it for a car of some kind. If so, where is it? What's the plate number? Who's it registered to? And look at him. There's fingerprints all over that pail. If we could get that pail and match the fingerprints on it to the fingerprints on one of the rifles, we'd be building evidence on him. I know he shot two shots. You have one of the bullets. And if we followed him, he might lead us to bigger things. He might be at the pier to make a delivery. When they ride those dirt bikes out of the trail, they always wear blue and white daypacks. I bet if we stand back out of sight we can watch a hand off. And then we could follow him to wherever he's going. Or follow the guy that picks up the pack."

"You certainly have thought this all out, haven't you? Did you know this was going to happen when we came down here?"

"No! I had no idea. Oh, I had an idea they brought out the drugs in backpacks and probably did hand offs in unsuspecting places, but I had no idea they would be here today. But now that they are, we can check that list of abbreviations and dates I found and see if anything matches up. Is he still there?"

"Yeah, he's still there. Why not just call the police and let them pick him up?"

"Because of all the lost information. If you wait and let him make his move, he reveals more about himself."

"I guess you really do see things as a puzzle. It sure doesn't take you long to piece things together. I think you should be the detective."

"So, what are we going to do? How important are the fingerprints on the pail? They link him to the Santa Monica Pier. Then if we watch him do a pick up or a drop off, that links him to the drug trade. And if we follow him, we see a link back to the next step in the chain."

"We are *not* going after that pail."

"Why not? It would be easy, just buy a blue and orange sand pail walk past, fake a stumble and pick up the wrong pail."

"Now I see why you get into so much trouble. You're not getting any closer to this situation than you are right now. I'll call in someone to tail him and I'm taking you somewhere far away from here."

"Or we could buy a disposable camera and pretend to take pictures of each other and accidentally take pictures of him."

"Slow down. I need to make a phone call."

He stepped a few feet away and pushed some buttons. I didn't listen. Police stuff wasn't meant to be overheard. I saw the concern in his eyes that I'd run off and do something stupid. The trouble was, I couldn't see the stupidity in it. All the things I'd suggested could work. My mind wasn't slowing down. I was standing with my back to the beach thinking furiously when suddenly Rusty stepped in front of me. Then Raphael shuffled down the boardwalk, a white muscle shirt loosely thrown on and a blue and white pack drooping off his shoulders. He slowed down, allowing Amelia a chance to get her footing on the rough railroad tie boards, and found a place on the railing. He took off the pack setting it down next to him, then picked Amelia up, setting her on top of the rail. He pointed out things to her below, keeping her occupied while they waited. Wanting to run around, she struggled to get down but he gently nudged her to further distractions, asking her to have patience. They would go in a minute.

"Come on," Rusty said, "Let's go see that shop with the t-shirts again." It was just an excuse, a way to blend in. He didn't really want to look at t-shirts. I was afraid to speak, knowing Raphael had clearly heard my voice at the farm, so I felt my sunglasses to make sure they were still there and then followed Rusty away. A car clunked down the boardwalk and stopped in front of us. The men in the vehicle exchanged a few words with Rusty and we continued on our way.

We drove around for a while with the top up on the car. It felt more concealing that way, and even when we were miles from Santa Monica I had the feeling that a blue dirt bike would go buzzing by. In my mind, I knew that dirt bike was still up in the mountains and I wouldn't recognize the car Raphael was driving, but I could still hear dirt bikes off in the distance.

We hadn't gone far when we pulled into a parking garage and stopped. I looked around. Nothing seemed familiar. I unbuckled my seatbelt and started to get out of the car, but I felt bad about the whole beach thing so I sat back down.

"I'm sorry I ruined our day at the beach. I should have just kept my mouth shut and we could have enjoyed the rest of the day."

"You didn't ruin it. I enjoy every minute that I spend with you. Besides, I need your eyes. I can't see the things you see. There's no way I can recognize these guys, and if you hadn't pointed him out to me, something far worse could have happened."

"I'm sorry I freaked. It just took me so totally by surprise."

"You have every right to be freaked out. I'd be more worried about you if you weren't. Speaking of which, I think what's in this building will cheer you up a bit."

We left the car and found an elevator. The elevator rose for a long time and opened on to a lobby.

"We're going to see Kelly?"

"Is that okay?"

"Yeah, sure. It just surprises me, that's all."

We spoke to a lady at a desk and she gave us key cards. We entered another elevator. I always get lost in hospitals. Drop me in the middle of the

Rocky Mountains and I can walk home, but put me in a hospital and I can't find the elevator, don't know what floor I'm on, and lose all sense of direction. The walls were all beige, but there were cheerful pictures on the walls and occasionally there was a mural on a wall that looked like a classroom full of third graders had painted it. I followed down one hallway after another and then we came to the key card reader and big double doors. We slid our cards and were buzzed through. I was beginning to think this was an ICU, with all the high tech equipment sitting around.

"Rusty, stop! Wait a second. I need to know how bad it is first. All this high tech stuff. You said he was able to have visitors. I just need to know what to expect."

"He's doing great. Don't worry."

"Where are we?"

"I don't know. I get all turned around in these hallways. But I know I'm headed in the right direction or the key cards wouldn't have worked."

We came to a nurse's station and then he seemed to know where we were, because he entered the second door down on the right.

Kelly brightened immediately when we walked into the room.

"The great tracker returns from the wild!" he beamed. "I've been sitting here for days with nothing to do but plan how I'm going to get back at you for abandoning me in that helicopter. Those guys tortured me!"

"They did nothing of the sort. They only did what they needed to."

"How did you get them to leave you there? They wouldn't leave me there. I took one look at them and asked to go back but they wouldn't let me. If I had to choose between three burly paramedics or eating stroganoff pudding with you in the woods, I wanted to go back."

"Stroganoff pudding?" Michaels looked at me.

I answered defensively, "It was backpacker food that had been crushed in a fall. It was the only food I had to offer him. Mac and cheese or stroganoff or something else. He asked for something with meat in it, so I did what I could with the stroganoff."

"Yeah, mac and cheese is for kids."

Rusty was getting a kick out of our joking around.

"So, how did you get them to leave you out there?"

"I told them I had unfinished business to attend to. The guy looked like he was going to toss me over his shoulder and haul me out, so I strapped on my pack, unsnapped the strap on my holster, and walked off. He didn't want to mess with me anymore."

This amused him. "I can just imagine that. He was cussing up a storm when he got back up there. Then there was a moment of stunned silence when we realized where you'd been left."

"Yeah. Well, it all worked out."

"I'm still pretty amazed that you tracked me off trail. I did everything by the book."

"When I really don't want to be found, I wear moccasins or go stocking footed. That way you don't leave sharp edges to your track and you also eliminate the creases between the toes problem of going barefoot. Not to mention it still offers you some protection from sharp rocks and twigs. Then you probably missed the part in the book about not touching the ground. If you don't want me to find you, just don't touch the ground."

"I think I'll keep my shoes on and my feet on the ground."

"And avoid confrontations with drug dealers deep in the woods. How did you find out about the farm in the first place? I could tell you were looking for something. You must have heard something before you headed out."

"It was just gossip in town. I thought it might link up to the motorcycle problem. My goal was to find out about the motorcycles, and then the farm got thrown in the mix as a curiosity."

"That was when your trail started getting interesting. When you started leaving the trail and turning around and coming back, I knew you had to be looking for something and it was intriguing. I thought we were both going to end up dead when you led me through the booby traps."

That got Rusty's attention. Kelly looked really worried when I reminded him of that. "You followed me through all that?"

"I had to. It was the only way to find you. For a little while I was afraid of what I might discover. Some of them were just to warn the workers that people were approaching but others were really dangerous."

"How did you know that?" Rusty asked.

"Well, the fish hooks hanging in the trees were obviously meant to hurt someone. I only avoided those because I was crouched down, staying out of sight. If I had stood up I'd have been in a mess. Later, I followed a trip wire to see what was at the end of it and it turned out just to be a noisemaker. So I was tracking Kelly, watching for drug dealers and booby traps and trip wires. It got a little tense."

"A little tense? Do you know what could have happened to you? Lord, I don't even want to think about it. I didn't even want you to go when I thought it was a hike in the woods. To think I sent you into a booby trapped drug farm…" Rusty said in frustration.

"It's okay, you didn't know. And I'd have gone even if you'd told me all that was up there."

We had a long visit and Kelly never seemed to tire, but eventually we had to go home. As we were leaving, he called me back. "Cassidy, the docs all tell me it was real close. I don't think they gave me another day out there."

"I'm sorry," I said, "I got there when I could…"

"No, no, no. I meant 'Thanks'. Thanks for coming when you did. Rusty told me some of what you went through on the way."

"It's okay, a normal day in my life."

"See ya around?"

"Yeah. Take care."

Out in the hall, Rusty waited. "He thinks the world of you, and you'll never have a better friend."

"I already do."

"I hope we can find the garage again."

"Me, too."

The drive home was quiet. I think we were both mulling over the events of the day, and what they might mean in the long term. I was still worried about the future, but I was content that the past was right. I'd done something right, and the rewards felt wonderful.

We pulled up to the curb at my house and there was an awkward moment where he didn't know if he was dropping me off or staying.

"Want me to check out the house for you? I'd feel better if I did."

"Sure. It looks quiet though."

I walked up to the front door and waited as he locked the car. I saw a small white box sitting on my doorstep and picked it up, dropping it in my pocket. I didn't like the sound of the object in that box, but I didn't want to alarm Rusty. To me it sounded exactly like a bullet. A single bullet in a cardboard box, probably meant to scare me. It probably had my name written on it or something.

Otherwise, the house looked clean. I missed Shadow. I really needed to pick him up in the morning. The house seemed empty without him.

We sat on the couch looking at each other, "Well, the house is still standing. The neighborhood's quiet. What about you? Are you okay with all this?"

"Yeah, I think I am. Only one thing bothers me, and I can't hide from it forever."

"What's that?"

"When I talked to Paul, after he got through scolding me for not calling him from the trail, he was telling me about the talk in town and how everyone was celebrating the fact that Kelly was found."

"That's to be expected. You're a hero to them."

"Yeah, right, well, what bothers me is that I'm not too popular with certain people up there, and if they wanted to know where to find me, all they would have to do is act friendly and talk to a ranger. With all the hoopla, people are handing out information left and right. Just enough information to point the drug dealers right to me. Am I being paranoid? Is this something I should be concerned about?"

"No, you're not paranoid. I think you are very wise. So, do you think you shouldn't stay here? Do you have some place else to go?"

"I don't want to run. I have two places I can run to, but I don't want to do that." A sad thought occurred to me, so I got out my wallet, pulled out a small stack of business cards and shuffled through them until I found the right one. I pressed it into Rusty's hand and he read it.

"Wayne Gordon. Quarter Horses? What's this?"

"That's how you can contact my parents if... if it ever becomes necessary. My dad's Wayne, although nobody calls him that, and my mom is Betty. Her real name is Elizabeth, but that was too cultured for ranch life so she shortened it."

"What do people call your dad?"

"Everybody, even close friends and the people in town call him Mr. Gordon. If you ever meet him, you'll understand why. It's not that he isn't friendly. He's just that kind of a guy. Mom's the only one who gets away with calling him by his first name."

He flipped the card with his fingers, the sound reminding me of a kid dragging a baseball card across a picket fence. "Cass, you wouldn't be doing this unless you were really worried. What are you thinking?"

"I think this is going to get a whole lot worse before it gets better."

"Okay, let's go to my place and pick up a few things. I need to go to work in the morning, so I'll need some fresh clothes and toiletries."

We got into his Explorer and drove across town. His street had condos on one side and single-family homes on the other; a green and shady street compared to most of the city. He pulled in at a condo. A tiny postage stamp yard was out front, green and carefully landscaped as were all the others. I don't know what I had expected his house to be like. I always imagined bachelor pads to be cluttered and tacky. His was neither, but it didn't really feel like a home either. Everything was in its place, the hardwood floor was recently swept and the furnishings were old yet comfortable. I stood in the living room and waited for him. It looked like he had a bedroom and office upstairs and living room/dinette area and kitchen downstairs. I soon got tired of waiting, and sat on his brown corduroy couch. A coffee table separated the couch from the TV set which sat inside an oak entertainment center. A bookcase on one wall was filled with books that hadn't been read in months.

A clock ticked noisily from the kitchen. One long wall displayed outdoor travel posters, but all in all it looked like Rusty hadn't had much time or inclination to decorate.

He came down the stairs with a sports coat slung over his shoulder and a duffle bag in the other hand. He was trying to hold onto a thick binder with papers sticking out of it so I got up to take it from him.

"I hope you made yourself at home," he said, and we walked out the door and got into the Explorer again.

We stopped on the way home and picked up some fast food. The house seemed quiet and peaceful, which left me thinking it was silly to make him stay. Having Shadow here would help. I wouldn't be entirely alone if Shadow was here. His bold black and white presence seemed to fill the house with activity.

It was late after a long day when we went to bed. I showed him his options and he chose the guest room. I had set it up as a place for my parents to stay if they visited, but they rarely did. The third bedroom was sort of an office, although I didn't really have need of one. I paid bills and wrote letters in there. I had a computer, but I only checked email, and the only email I ever got was Spam and an occasional note from my mom or sister. My sister always sent news about her boys and what was going on at the ranch. She had married one of the ranch hands, so in a way she'd never left home. Her family lived in a small house on the edge of the ranch property. Ironically my sister's name was Jesse and she had married a James. My dad was an old west buff, so the match had appealed to him.

I closed my bedroom door and changed into PJ pants and a loose t-shirt. I threw my clothes into the hamper next to the bed. I reopened the door and climbed into my queen-sized pillow-topped bed. It felt like it had been too long since I'd slept in my own bed. I'd slept on the ground more often lately. How long had it been? I fell into a fitful sleep, enjoying the familiarity and trying to listen to Rusty's breathing in the next room.

PART 3

TROUBLE TARGET

I don't know how long I slept before the nightmares came. I was at the hideout noticing a dim glow at the top of the canyon. I watched as it intensified and then ran in horror as a wildfire raced down the canyon. I crawled into the hideout trying to gather up my things and then I couldn't get out. I could hear the fire approaching. It roared down the canyon. The branches on top of the tarp were crackling in the fire and the tarp was melting. The heat was searing and I was crawling, trying to find the flap to get out, but everything was noise and sensation. I coughed and coughed, whether in my dream or for real, I couldn't tell. Nothing was real any more and it all grew fuzzy, so fuzzy… and then nothing. I felt nothing.

Chapter 10

How can you describe nothingness? If you give it a color or a feeling, it goes away and becomes something. I didn't know how to describe it, but there sure was a lot of it. A lot of it. Little things tried to make their way through the nothingness and I'd grasp at them. Mentally? Physically? I couldn't tell. They faded and time stood still. How long? How long will the nothingness last? Where is sensation? Sometimes I thought the nothingness felt dizzy. I reached for the dizzy feeling hoping it would materialize into something I could recognize, but it was elusive.

The first sensation that came back to me was touch. I could feel softness at my fingertips. I twitched my fingers trying to grasp the softness. Fabric. I stroked the fabric, but the only thing that would move were my fingertips, and I faded away again. The next sensation was hard. My fingers twitched over the hardness. And it was smooth. Hard and smooth. And linear. Anything familiar I reached for, but the reach always left me drifting, drifting until another sensation came to me.

The fabric was back. I twitched my fingers and there was more movement. I stroked the fabric letting the sensation flow into me, but then the fabric was gone and there was something else. It moved and I would have jumped if I could, but instead I drifted again. No! No more drifting. I grasped at the feeling. Tried feeling it with my other hand. The fabric, then again the movement, the new texture. I calmed with the touch. Skin, the movement was called skin. I stroked the skin. A hand maybe?

In the haze I could hear sounds, but I couldn't make any sense out of them. Sometimes the fabric was there, sometimes the hand. There was more something than nothing, but I couldn't reach it. Sounds were a jumble and the only thing I could see through my closed eyes was dark or light, but most of the time it was just dim. I tried to open my eyes, but they didn't seem to work. The hand in my hand moved and I heard something. Something nice, but I couldn't tell what.

The fabric was back. I could stroke it with both hands. My hands could move! I tried to open my eyes. What was I seeing? My eyes tried to close. I fought back the feeling. I opened them again, not trying to focus, just allowing them to be open, and it was easier. I blinked and someone was there. I stroked the fabric looking for the hand. It was there. A face swam into view but I couldn't focus on it. A voice I couldn't understand. A calming voice. Things were making more sense, but not fast enough for me. I wanted to touch and hear and feel it all. Too much nothingness. I was all through with it. Come back, whoever you are, I need your sensations.

The next time I opened my eyes the hand came back, the voice, that calm voice said, "Hey, there. Don't talk. You can't talk yet."
I struggled. I wanted to ask the voice to stay. "It's okay! Shhhh, babe, it's okay. Quiet." He stroked my arm, my whole arm and I could feel it. I could see and I could focus. Tubes. And machines. And sounds, beeping sounds. Mechanical sounds. And dryness. My mouth was so dry. I tried to swallow, but I couldn't, something was in the way.
"Hon, be still. Just let it come and it'll come."
A woman came in, a nurse; I could see a nurse and she looked at me. She touched my wrist, said something and then walked away. She came back with a glass of water and dabbed some water on my dry mouth. I tried to swallow, to move the water around, but I had to just accept the parts that it hit. It was better. I tried to pick out the noises around the room. There was a *beep* of a heart monitor and a *blip hiss* that sounded like a respirator. And there was a clattering noise that sounded like a food cart. I fell asleep. Not the nothingness, not quite.

I awoke, but my eyes didn't want to open yet. How much time had gone by? I stroked the fabric and the voice came again. No, not the same voice. It was a different one, a woman. The nurse? No, this was a different woman. And the tube was gone. I could swallow.
"Rest honey. It's okay, you're back with us, that's all that counts. Wayne, call Rusty and tell him Cassidy's awake." My parents. Both. They were here.
A doctor came in. "Well, look who's back from the dead! I'm Doctor Ron." He held out his hand and when I couldn't take it he reached down and shook mine anyway. "You have given these people quite a scare, but I think we are out of the woods."
Out of the woods! We sure as hell were. The woods were peaceful and welcoming. No harsh mechanical noises and beeps. He spoke to me as if I could understand what he was saying, but I could only wrap my mind around the familiar.
My mom swam into view again and said, "I've been going through your room. You're going to need all new clothes and bedding. They are all smoke

damaged." Smoke damaged? "We can go shopping just as soon as you get well. I'll go get some things for you to wear like you had in your closet and you can choose some more later." Her jabber faded and my dad looked on grimly from the sidelines.

"I think she is sleeping again," my mother said, "but the doctor came in and said she was doing well. He spoke to her, but I don't know how much sunk in. We're going to go get something to eat."

"Thank you, Mr. and Mrs. Gordon."

I struggled. Opening my eyes was getting easier, but I still had to think to do it. "It's me," Rusty said, "don't fight it. It'll be easy some day. Relax. Cassidy, you're not relaxing." I wanted so bad to see him. I tried to relax. "There you go, relax." Gentle arm strokes. "Okay, now try again."

Think, eyes open, eyes open. I pulled up with my eyelids and there was a little movement. And there he was. I wanted to cry, but I didn't know how. What happened? What made me like this?

"Shhhh, just be here with me. That's all you need to do. Just be here. Can you see me? I can see you."

I struggled to get his name out but my voice wouldn't work. I tried a whisper, "Rusty."

"There you go. You're back. Thank God you're back."

"Don't go."

"I won't, where would I go?"

"What happened?"

"Shhh, you aren't ready for that yet. We'll talk about it when you're ready. It was a fire. But it's okay, as long as you're here, it's okay."

"It wasn't a fire."

"W-what was it?"

I was fading and I had to say it. I mumbled, "It was a bullet in a little box."

"Huh? Cass, wait! What did you say?"

"Just a sec."

I rested a bit, but I couldn't come back. I tried, and then his calm hands let me know it was okay. Okay to rest. I slept again.

When I woke up again, he was still there. He said he wouldn't go, and he was still there. He was sleeping, his head on the mattress, his hand touching mine. I stroked his hand. I wanted every second I could grasp.

"R-rusty?"

He stirred.

"It's coming back."

Caring eyes, little laugh lines.

"What's coming back?"

"Every time I wake up, I can feel a little more coming back."

"What can you feel? Tell me."

"I can feel my hands and my eyes and my thoughts and my words. I can feel touches."

"What about your feet, can you feel your feet?"

I hadn't thought of that yet. I moved my feet and the fabric slid over them.

"I can feel my feet."

"Are you going to stick around for a bit? Can you tell me about the bullet in the box?"

"When we got home, there was a little box on my doorstep. I didn't open it because I didn't want to worry you. It felt and sounded like a bullet in a box."

"Why didn't you want to worry me? Cass, I need to know these things."

"I thought it would just be a bullet in a box. I thought someone left it there to scare me, but I never opened it. I forgot about it in my pocket and I threw it in the dirty clothes before I went to bed... I have to slow down. Don't let me fade. I hate that feeling." I was mumbling again. Quiet. Rest. I closed my eyes. "I'm still here," I whispered. "I'm listening. Tell me something happy."

He told me a story, a funny story about something dumb he did as a kid. It felt good to laugh, and I rested while I listened.

"When did my folks get here?"

"The next morning. The first several hours were the worst. Cass, I didn't think you were going to make it. I heard you coughing."

"My dream. I was coughing in my dream."

"Maybe, but you were really coughing. Your room was full of smoke. I couldn't see a fire, but there was smoke everywhere. All I could think of was to get you out, and by the time the rescue squad got there you weren't breathing."

"Stop," I whispered. "Rusty, stop. That's not happy. Just be here with me. How long have I been here?"

"Two days. The two longest days of my life."

"How long will I have to stay?"

"As long as it takes. Don't worry about it. This wasn't an ordinary fire. Cass, someone was trying to kill you and they damn near did it. The investigators said it was a chemical fire. Whatever was in that bullet was ignited from an outside source, and the chemicals in the smoke were designed to kill you." He paused. I couldn't tell if he was gearing up for something else, or if he was just tired. "Would you consider going home with your mom and dad when they leave? Just until you recover? Your mom says there's plenty of room and lots of things you can do to regain your strength. She says it's the safest place you could be, with all those protective ranch hands all over the place."

"I'll think about it. I don't want to. Right now I'd say no, but I'll have to see how strong I am when they let me out of here."

"I think it might be more up to your dad. I do see now, why people call him Mr. Gordon." He laughed. I hoped my dad hadn't been too rough on him. "You better rest up. I don't want to wear you out so you can't talk to them when they get here. They stuck to you pretty close the first day, but now they seem to be more focused on getting things ready for your release. Your mom's been going through your room and your dad has been pacing."

"Shadow, where's Shadow?"

"He's at home. Your dad needs something to train, so he takes him outside and runs him through your obstacle course. I guess he trains horses at the ranch?"

"Yeah, although he should leave it to the hands. One of these days he's going to kill himself."

"That sounds familiar. Now rest. They will be here pretty soon."

I could hear them before they came in the room. Typical Mom and Dad discussion.

"Wayne, now I don't want to hear you telling Cassidy what she has to do. You know she's just like you and if you go demanding that she do something that'll just as sure turn her against it. This is her decision and you need to let it be her decision. If you're smart, and I know you can be at times, you will tell her why you think she should or shouldn't do something, but you will *not* tell her what to do." Smart mom. She knows us well.

"Hey," I said as they came through the door. "What's going on in the real world?"

"We have a new colt at the ranch," Daddy beamed. "Looks real promising."

"What color is he? You know I always want to know what color they are."

"He's a bay with the prettiest little white blaze. You'll love him."

"I love all the horses, Dad. How's Shasta doing?" When I went home, Shasta was my horse, and when I was away, they kept him working on the ranch so he'd be well trained when I returned.

"Shasta's doing great. He's a real looker. Always has been with that fine dapple-gray coat. He's a fine horse. You made a good choice when you chose him. I taught you real good how to choose a good horse."

"Thank you for working Shadow while I've been gone. I had him kenneled for a week before this happened, so he needs the work."

"Oh really?" interjected my mom. "Where did you go?"

Hoo, boy! How much did they already know? "I just went for a hike in the woods. I took four days to hike from one campground to another."

"You are always having such great adventures. Who did you go with?"

"Nobody, I just went by myself. I do that a lot."

"And just how far did you hike in four days?"

"I guess it was about twenty miles." Minus two or three miles by dirt bike.

"Cassidy, what are you thinking? A girl your age taking off by herself in the woods! What if you ran into trouble out there? You know how you always run into trouble. What would you do?"

"Oh, I always think of something."

"Well, I'm talking to Rusty about that. He shouldn't let you go off like that, especially now."

"Mom, Rusty doesn't tell me what to do and what not to do. He knows me too well for that. And he already told me that you were going to ask me to go home with you, but I'm not ready to make that decision. I promise I'll think about it."

"That's a nice young man you met. Real polite." Coming from my dad, this was high praise. "Real smart too. You should listen to him. He's onto something with this case and he'll have it solved in no time." The eternal optimist.

And mom added, "And a real looker, too."

The next morning I was transferred to a normal room. I called my mom and asked her to bring me some pajamas or exercise clothes, something I could be seen wearing as I walked the halls. I wasn't going anywhere with this half gown on. The goal, I was told, was to flush out the poisons and gain enough strength to walk to the end of the hallway and back. The IV would do one but I had to do the other. I was glad no one was around on my first try. Just standing up made me sick and dizzy. This was going to be harder than I expected.

A nurse appeared in the doorway and said, "Miss Callahan, you have a visitor."

I arranged the covers on the bed and sat up. When a strange man walked in I instantly buzzed for the nurse.

"I wanted to meet you in person," he said calmly. His presence felt like ice in my veins. He was playing games with me and I didn't like it. "Anybody who can cause this much chaos down below and still remain alive deserves respect. How do you do it? How many times must I kill you?" I buzzed the nurse again. "You took out two of my men. I lost several valuable deliveries. I don't understand how a little girl such as you manages to elude me. My men are usually efficient, yet you managed to escape both of them."

"They underestimated me." I buzzed the nurse again.

"I won't underestimate you anymore."

"Who are you?" I demanded. I buzzed the nurse again.

He stepped forward extending his hand. "I'm Mario Peccati, and you are Cassidy Gordon Callahan. A pleasure to meet you." He turned and walked out the door. I buzzed the nurse.

A nurse popped her head in. "Yes? Oh my! Child, what is wrong with you? You were doing so good and now look at you. You are white as a sheet."

"Please, please don't let anyone in here except my parents and Detective Michaels. That man tried to kill me. I need a piece of paper. I need to write down a name. I don't have anything here."

She took a note pad from the drawer and I wrote his name down. Mario Peccati. I had to remember that name. I tore off the page and held it in my hand until Rusty arrived. The encounter was so exhausting that I slept the rest of the morning.

When I woke up, I tried standing up again. I had to get out of here. The dizziness came in a wave and I clutched the IV pole. Okay, Cass, you can do this. I walked two steps, two extremely shaky steps and I was about to turn around and take two shaky steps back when Rusty walked in. I locked my knees to keep from falling over. He scooped me up, depositing me back onto the bed.

"You're trying too hard," he said arranging the blankets around me. "Don't try walking without a nurse in the room."

"I have to get out of here. I can't stay here."

"Everybody feels that way about hospitals, but it's what's best for you. By the way, what's with the key card? I had to check in to get up here."

I was shivering. I hunkered down in the blanket.

"I h-had a visitor today. I asked them to limit my visitors." I handed him the note page. "I didn't trust my memory."

Rusty read the note, smoothed out the wrinkles, and put it in his shirt pocket. Why was it so cold in here? I didn't mean to fall asleep on him. I wanted to visit, but I was so cold and all my energy left me. The next thing I knew, it was dark. Three days. That made three days.

I thought after sleeping most of the day I'd have enough energy to try walking again, so I buzzed the nurse. She got out a walker. I clutched it like a life ring and walked five shaky steps. It was an improvement. I walked the five shaky steps back and slept until morning. Even if I had been able to walk the hallway to be discharged, I still wasn't ready to take on Peccati. The ranch was looking better and better.

When I saw my mom and dad again, my mom exclaimed, "You sleep so much! You didn't sleep this much when you were in a coma!"

"I'm sorry, Mom, I've been trying to walk. I'm getting better. It just wears me out. I'm anxious to get out of here, so I walk whenever I can. Did you two pay for this private room? I know this isn't a normal room." She didn't need to answer. I knew they did.

When the IV came out on the fourth day, walking became easier. The fifth day, I walked in the hall and was nearing my goal. On day six, the doctors came in, explaining that everything was looking good. I was as healthy as a horse except for the need to build up my strength, which they believed could be done at home so they released me. I was wheeled out to my parent's rental car, and they drove me home. Before I got out of the car, I asked my dad to go in and restrain Shadow. One leap from him and I'd be back in the hospital. I shuffled up the walk and upon entering the living room collapsed wearily onto the couch. Shadow, a black and white blur of motion, bounded into the room and landed on my lap. My mom brought out bags of purchases and held them up for my inspection.

"I couldn't find any clothes like you had in your closet. How old were they? The fashions have changed so much since you bought those clothes. And I didn't know where you shopped so I hope these will do." I didn't tell her I did half my shopping at the army surplus store.

I thanked her for the clothes, and then went to see my bedroom. Everything had been replaced, curtains, bedding, clothing. The carpet had been professionally cleaned. I sat down, stunned. I didn't have the energy to go through all the thanks again, so I climbed into bed.

That evening, Rusty shook me awake. "Think you could eat something? We've got dinner on."

He helped me get up. I brushed my hair and shuffled shakily out to the dining room. Everyone was there waiting, so I took my place at the table. The food looked great, and I tried to eat, but I just couldn't. The talk flowed around me and everybody was so cheerful.

"How's Kelly doing?" I asked Rusty.

"Driving his wife nuts." So he was home. That was good news.

"Well," I announced, "I've decided the best thing for me to do would be to go home to the ranch. Mom and Dad, I can't ask you to stick around here, and I can't ask Rusty to babysit, so I think the wise thing for me is to go home with you. I'll go on two conditions: I don't want to fly, and I want to take Shadow. You can rent a SUV or a van or whatever, and I'll stay a week or two. Working with the horses and with Shadow will get me out and about. I think if I stayed home, all I would to is putter around here. It isn't safe to putter around here. My house is a death trap until we catch this guy." After that long a speech, I was ready to go back to bed.

After dinner, Rusty carried a chair in and set it by the bed. "I think you are doing the smart thing. It'll be safer there."

"You have the address and telephone number on the card."

"And I'll sure use it. I'll call."

"I really, really don't want to go."

"I know, but I'm glad you made the right choice."

Chapter 11

Driving to the ranch was an all day trip. The drive itself was four hours, and once you add loading and stopping for meals, it took almost an entire day. We drove by the police station on our way out of town so I could say good-bye to Rusty. He came out to the parking lot to save me the trip inside. I almost backed out, but he assured me going to the ranch was the right thing to do.

The trip was shorter for us because, after an hour or two on the road, I fell asleep. I wouldn't wake up for meals, so my folks ate fast food on the road and we made good time.

I don't remember arriving at the ranch. I just recall waking up in my old bedroom. I lay there, exhausted. How could I be so tired after all that sleep? I was determined to work on my stamina. I walked along the hall and looked down the stairs. I knew I hadn't climbed these last night. I looked at the stairs again. I'd never make it. I thunked down them one step at a time. After several steps, I sat down. I had to rest. My mom found me there, and sat beside me. I tried a few more steps. When I reached the bottom landing, I collapsed onto a chair in the entry way and fell asleep. I heard voices around me. They came and left. Ranch business. I woke to find Randy, one of the ranch hands, sitting on the floor in front of me.

"Cassidy, it's good to have you home again. I heard you were here and I had to come round and say 'Hi'. Your mama told me not to bother you. Am I bothering you?"

"Hi, Randy." Randy had lived on the ranch since he was fourteen and he was two years younger than me. He worked at the ranch, and had been raised in the bunkhouse. Randy always had a fondness for me, and tended to tag along after me like a puppy. I hadn't forgotten about him, but hadn't considered this aspect of coming up here either.

"Can I do anything for you, Cass? You name it, I'm here. You know me, always needing a job to do." Especially for me, I thought. He had plenty of work to do. I unfolded myself from the chair.

"Point me to the kitchen."

We walked slowly to the big ranch kitchen and Martha, my mom's helper, was there. She ran over and gave me a big hug, nearly bowling me over. She sat me down in a chair at the long table where everyone at the ranch gathered for meals. She bustled about the kitchen and always kept things immaculately clean. After a bit, I realized she was overdoing it. I couldn't possibly eat whatever it was she was concocting, and I was right. She set down a big plate of chicken fried steak and eggs, with mashed potatoes, biscuits and gravy. I thanked her anyway, and ate as much as I could. I gave her a hug on my way out. Randy took my chair and finished off the food on my plate. He could eat anything.

I stepped out onto the porch and slept in the big bench swing overlooking the corrals. It was one of my favorite places on the ranch. I could see most of the corrals, the big barn and the good solid oak trees that dotted the land around. I heard the dogs barking and the busyness of everyday life. I wondered where Shadow was, but I knew he was around. He wasn't a stranger here and he would get fed with the other dogs. That was one reason why I'd brought him. He'd be well taken care of here.

My dad jiggled the porch swing. "Hey, Trouble, can I show you something?"

"How far is it?"

"Just around the porch and across the driveway."

"I'll try." So I followed him across the porch, balked at the stairs, and made it down. He led me to the corral fence. I thought he was going to show me the new colt, but it turned out to be an agility course set up just for me. Tears welled up in my eyes. He'd done this just for me, to get me outdoors because he knew it would get me moving. I gave him a hug, something I hadn't done in years. You just don't go hugging Wayne Gordon. But he hugged me back.

"Thank you, Daddy," I said, "Thanks so much."

He left me there, standing at the fence. I didn't tell him I hadn't the strength to walk back. Still, I'd made it down the stairs, to the kitchen, out to the porch, and all the way to the corral. I considered it a milestone. I was walking along the corral, using the fence for support, when a group of the guys walked by, all in plaid western shirts, Levis, boots and armed with western style pistols. Big silver belt buckles gleamed on their hand-tooled belts. I thought how odd they would look back home. I didn't remember them carrying guns before.

I stared at the front door with the swing beside it. It looked a mile away. I started across the expanse and my knees buckled. I landed face first in the dust. Steve and Zack ran up, helping me to my feet. They gave me worried looks.

"Where to, Cassidy?" Steve asked.

"The swing, or my room."

Steve scooped me up, and before I knew it I was back in my bed. I slept through dinner again. My mom brought me a plate after I woke up.

"You have to eat something or you'll never get well."

"I know, Mom. I'll try. Light stuff works better for me right now. Just little bits of light stuff. I don't have any appetite, but I will eat. These big plates are so intimidating."

"You did good today. You got down the stairs and outside under your own power."

"Yeah, and then made a fool of myself."

"No, you didn't. The boys all know what you've been through. They are all rooting for you."

"How could they know?"

"Your father told them. He had a big meeting."

"But not even Daddy knows. He doesn't know the half of it. The fire was just the latest thing. You wouldn't even know about that except for Rusty."

"Rusty called today. I gave him the run down of what happened since we took off."

"Why didn't you come get me?" I asked.

"You were sleeping on the swing. It was good for you to be out there. He didn't want to wake you."

Something seemed to be missing around the ranch. I finally put my finger on it. Jesse wasn't here. If she were home, she would be here. She was always helping out. I asked mom about it.

"James, Jesse and the kids went back east to look over breeding stock. They had several stops to make and they were going to take the boys to Disney World. I called and left a message when we heard about the fire. Then in all the travel and hospital visits, it took a day or two for us to connect and get to talk. She asked if she should come home, but by then you were getting better so I told her to stay."

The next day I showered, dressed, rested, and made it all the way down the stairs in one try. Martha put a small bowl of fruit in front of me and a bowl of homemade rolls and butter. This was much better.

"What can I make for you to perk you up?" She asked.

I thought about it. There wasn't much I didn't like. "Cheesecake," I said. "I haven't had cheesecake in the longest time. I'm going into cheesecake withdrawal."

"You got it, hon. I'll have cheesecake for dessert tonight."

Randy trotted up when I walked out the door.

"Walk with me to the barn, will you Randy? I might need some help."

"Why sure, Cassidy. You know I'll do anything."

I made it after stopping for breath a few times. Shasta was looking silky and ready for work. I fished a carrot out of my pocket.

"I brush him every day," Randy said.

"You take good care of him."

"I could put a saddle on him for you."

"No," I said, "Think about it, Randy. If I can't lift a saddle, I'm not strong enough to ride. When I ride, I'll saddle him myself. But thanks for the offer."

Over the next few days I got out more and more. I sent Randy to find Shadow, and I tried out the agility course working slowly, one obstacle at a time. There were even some obstacles here that I didn't have at home, so I worked with Shadow on how to do the dog walk and the broad jumps. It was good to work in a different atmosphere with him. On the ranch, he had to deal with the distractions of other dogs, people, and animals. At home, it was just the two of us.

Rusty called, and we had long talks.

I was awake more and slept less. My mom took me into town for clothes shopping and I had my hair cut.

Finally, I asked Old Frank to send me a helper, and I saddled up Shasta. Randy came in and saddled up his horse.

"Check the girth. I don't know if I was able to tighten it enough."

He checked it and I hauled myself up onto the broad strong back.

"You're riding English today?"

"The saddle was lighter and I'm only going to the corral. If this works, maybe I'll try a trail ride tomorrow."

I found out I had balance issues, and the English saddle didn't help much, perching me high atop the horse. I walked Shasta around the arena and then tried varying the gait. He had a smooth comfortable trot, and I hardly had to post. Randy started out right next to me so he could grab Shasta's bridle if he needed to, but after a while he backed off and let me go, riding on the other side of the corral from me. Steve, Old Frank and Zack came to the rail.

"Oh, no!" One of them shouted. "Trouble's on the loose again!" It felt good to be alive.

I talked to Rusty that night. Things were going good here, I told him. I was feeling better.

"I can tell," he said. "Did you know your mom has been emailing me pictures? I get three or four pictures a day at work. It's great. I didn't have any pictures of you before. She says when you catch her at, it she'll know you're back to your old self."

"You're kidding. She does that?"

"Yep. The first day she only sent two pictures. One was of you sitting halfway up the stairs. The other showed you sleeping in a swing. I can see you getting better and better in each of the pictures. I like the one of you training Shadow in the agility course and there's a really nice one of you with a gray horse in the barn. Do I need to worry about that cowboy that's in all the pictures?"

"No, that's Randy. He's just a little too eager to help."

The next day I put the western saddle on Shasta. It took several tries to get it up on his back, but I finally managed. I bridled him and spent time talking to him, telling him we were going to take an easy ride. I pulled up into the saddle and walked him out of the barn and over to the corral. I put him through a walk, trot, and canter cycle to make sure he was listening to me and then headed out the gate, following a dirt road out into the hills. A minute later, Randy came tearing up the road after me. I thought something was wrong until he settled into a walk beside me and rode along quietly.

"Don't tell me. Daddy sent you to watch out for me."

"Well, yes and no. He told all of us you weren't to leave the ranch alone and I was just the lucky guy who saddled up first."

"What if I want to do something by myself for a change?"

"Depends on what you're up to."

"I was going to go see if there are still deer in the flats. And if I found some, I was hoping to stalk them. It's just something I like to do. If you won't let me do that, then I might as well go home. I can't sneak up on a deer with a guy in clumpy cowboy boots tagging along."

"We'll look for the deer and if we find some, I'll keep watch on the sidelines while you go out."

"You have to keep still. If they keep looking up at you, I'll never make any progress." That being agreed on we rode to the flats.

The country around the ranch is rolling hills dotted with hundred-year-old oak trees. Yellow knee-high grass blankets the hills. Occasionally there is open land, and there are plenty of deer out in the hills. The place I called the deer flats was just an open area where deer frequently grazed. I wanted to see if my old stomping grounds were still there, or if the area had become built up. If it had, the deer probably took off for other parts of the country.

The day was sunny and the wind was a light breeze, something I'd have to keep in mind while I was stalking. I saw deer in the brush, but it wasn't the setting I was looking for. These deer were already on the move and following them wouldn't do any good. Randy didn't see them or he would have pointed them out to me excitedly.

The flats felt further away than when I went there as a kid. I thought things were supposed to become smaller when you grew up. Maybe I was just so full of mischief I didn't know how far I'd come as a kid.

"How much further is it? I haven't been here in a long time."

"It's at the base of that hill over there," he said pointing.

I eased Shasta into a canter to eat up some ground. This was an easy gait for him, and a comfortable gait to ride in. We pulled up before we got to the flats. No use scaring the deer before I even dismounted.

We tied the horses to a tree and advanced on foot, slowly and quietly. Sure enough, there were deer in the flats. I counted ten, but knew there were probably more that I couldn't see. We found a spot in the trees and made sure the wind was blowing our scent away from the herd. Randy started to talk, probably outlining his duties while I was doing my thing, but I shushed him, pointing at the deer. He gave me an "Oh, yeah, right" look. I gave him a "Stay put" look and walked into the flats.

I had to walk a ways before I was within stalking range. The effort wore me out, but I was determined to at least try. As I got closer, I became more careful. While the deer grazed, I crept closer. Usually one deer was always looking up, but when they were all looking down I gained a few steps. Up, stop. Down, step, step. They knew I was there now, trying to decide if I were friend or foe. Now was the time to stop and wait. Let them get used to me and see me as part of their normal day. I knelt down on the ground where the waiting was easier. When I got up, I crouched down, placing my hands on my knees for stability. Step, step, stop. Wait. Heads down. Crouching step. It took me an hour to get into the herd, but when I did, I was thrilled to have deer all around me. I chose a doe that seemed close and calmer than the others, and crept her way. Step, step, freeze. I got down on my hands and knees. Stretching out, I lay beneath the grass and stilled my breathing. I peeked over the grass to make sure she was still there. I started the crouch walk again. Twenty feet. Head down. Step, step, step freeze. I got to within ten feet and figured that was as close as I was going to get. I lay in the grass, thinking about all the deer around me and feeling their movements.

I stilled my breathing again feeling something close to me. It was the doe. She'd wandered closer, just grazing, like she accepted me here. I lay rock-still, trying to become part of the earth, hoping she would step right over me. I knew that was an impossible wish, but it kept the experience alive. Finally, I decided I'd better get back to the ranch. I sat up quietly, not wanting to startle the deer.

"Thank you, deer," I said softly, whispering it in the noise of the wind. The heads all came up. I could feel tension in the air as the deer stared off to one side. Dang that Randy. He knew to stay put! Then *BAM*! A single shot, and the doe fell in front of me, a bullet through her head.

The rest of the herd took off, leaping across the flats straight towards the spot I left Randy. I stood, trying not to get trampled, and suddenly Randy was galloping up, holding Shasta's reins for me. I heaved myself into the saddle and we took off. I was cursing him a mile a minute, even though something didn't quite add up.

I pulled Shasta up to slow him down, and Randy came back for me.

"Cass, you okay? Keep going."

"You idiot!" I yelled, "What were you thinking? Those deer weren't going to hurt me. And it's not deer season! Do you want to be arrested for poaching? And it wasn't even a buck. You, of all people, should know not to shoot a doe! You bring in a buck for the ranch every year. So what's the deal shooting the doe?"

He was taken aback, ashamed I'd blame him. His face was as red as the plaid on his shirt. He pulled his hat down because the wind had pushed it back on his head.

"I didn't shoot the doe, Cass. The deer wouldn't have run toward me if I'd shot at them. They were running from someone on the other side of the flats. See, here's my gun, no shots fired."

I looked back the way we came and put my heels to my horse and we got the hell out of there.

After a while, we slowed the horses and let them rest. When we pulled into the ranch yard, nothing looked out of order except that I was splattered with blood.

"Randy, can you take the horses? I need to get out of these clothes before Dad sees me. And don't tell him what happened. If you feel the need to blab to somebody, talk to Old Frank. He knows when to keep quiet and he knows how to get through to my dad. If Dad asks you directly, just tell him we had a good ride, I handled the horse okay, stuff he wants to hear."

I stalked my way to my room, hiding when there were people around and quickly walking to the next spot frantically nonchalant. I bet I didn't fool anybody. They had eagle eyes for me right now, and I didn't have the energy to try too hard. I climbed the stairs, not even thinking about them, and closed the door behind me when I got to my room.

I was feeling almost back to normal, so I took Shadow out to the agility course. My stamina wasn't great, no long backpacking trips were in my near future, but I could do normal activities with little discomfort. I led Shadow slowly through the obstacles, and then thought what was good for the dog might be good for the master. I walked around looking at all the equipment.

The A-frame was made of good solid two-by-fours and three-quarter-inch plywood. The dog walk was built the same, but since it was a long thin expanse, I would probably bow it in the middle. The tunnels were straightforward. I took a good long run and bolted up the A-frame. I hadn't thought of how to come down the other side, and I slipped down, bashing my head against the top. Shadow ran up barking at me and people headed for the corral to see what Trouble was up to.

"Someone go get ice."

"It's okay, Mrs. Gordon, it's just a precaution."

My mom made *tsk tsk* noises and went back to the kitchen. An ice pack was pressed into my hand. Zack started taking bets on how long it would be until we needed another ice pack. The longest bet I heard was three days; the shortest, two hours. Two hours later I was at it again, except taking it easier. I went at the A-frame like the walls in boot camp, scrambling over, then running across the dog walk, stepping lightly in the middle so it wouldn't bow. I jumped over the tunnels and came back to the start. So far, so good.

Since I was running the dog walk okay, I tried the rafters in the barn. I borrowed an old rope from the tack room and tied it to a rafter. I climbed the rope, ran around the rafters, and jumped into the hay pile. At first, rope climbing was hard. My arms were not used to pulling, but after a while I got the hang of it. When that was easy, I began timing myself. I borrowed a stopwatch from Old Frank and hung it around my neck. I climbed the rope, ran the rafters, jumped down, and clicked the button as I arrived back at the rope. Steve walked in, so I asked him to time me. I climbed the rope and ran down the rafters. A quick *thunk* startled me, splinters few, and I slipped. Down into a stall I flew, startling a horse who began rearing and dancing in his stall. I backed into a corner, avoiding the flying hooves. Steve flung the gate open and urged the frightened horse out. Two men ran up and clipped a lead on him, steadying the horse while he calmed down. Steve ran into the stall to assess the damages. I had a gash on the side of my head and bruises up and down my side where I'd hit the stall wall.

"Somebody get some ice." He yelled. He checked his watch. "Whoever guessed closest to thirty hours wins the pot." He gave me a hand up. "You okay?"

I was okay. I was more than okay. I was mad.

"Let me borrow your pocketknife." All cowboys had pocketknives. It was Cowboy Law that you couldn't leave the house without your pocketknife.

"I'll cut it down, Cass, you don't need to worry about it."

"It's not the rope I'm worried about. I still plan to use that rope."

He pressed his 4-inch Buck knife into my hand. I slid it into my pocket and climbed the rope again. I walked the rafter until I was at my falling off point and lay down, examining the wood. Definite splintering. I dug around in the wood until I found what I was looking for. I slid out the knife, pried the thing loose, and stuck it in my pocket. Then I lay on the rafter looking about. Who could see me up here from outside? And then I saw, down the path of the bullet and through an open stall door, the hillside beyond. I was willing to bet I'd find a casing on that hill. I walked the rafter, jumped down into the hay pile, and returned the knife to Steve.

"We need to talk."

I took him to the stall door the bullet had come through. I dropped the bullet in his hand. "See that hill, the one with the big crooked tree?"

"Gotcha."

"Don't go out there now. Just bring the casing back if it's found and give it to me. I'll pass it along to Rusty."

"You think this isn't going to get back to your dad?"

"Did the first one?"

"This isn't the first time?"

"I need to go clean up."

"Nope, you're not going anywhere till I hear the truth out of you."

"When I went riding the other day, I went to the flats where the deer hang out. I wanted to go stalking. I was out in the field with the deer and someone shot the doe I was sitting next to. I know they weren't trying to shoot me. They shot the doe with a nice clean headshot. She dropped instantly. If they were trying to kill me, I'd be dead. It's just something to keep in mind."

"Yeah, right, that's all. And now here you are skinned up from head to toe because of another crazy shot."

"I gotta go clean up."

Someone pressed an ice pack into my hand.

I thought I was making progress on the recovery front. I thought I might even be able to surpass the shape I was in before the fire. I found out the bunkhouse had a punching bag and asked that it be hung in the barn. I punched at that bag for hours. I pretended it was Peccati and creamed it. Randy just looked at me and shook his head. He thought I'd gone off the deep end.

I started running the racetrack, first along the smooth outer track and then through the deep sand in the middle that the horses had churned up. It was rough and pitted and deep, but I ran it anyway. No shale mountain was going to beat me again. I'd be ready next time. After I ran the track in the center, I put on a full daypack and ran with that.

I was progressing. I could walk, run, and climb almost normally, but I still felt something was off in the balance department. I saddled up Shasta and walked him out to the corral. I put the reins on the horn of the saddle and carefully stood on the saddle. I picked up the reins and flicked them. He didn't budge. I tried talking to him and he still wouldn't budge.

"Zack," I called. "Can you call Shasta? He won't move."

Steve looked up. "That's because he's smarter than you. Get down from there! You're going to break your neck."

I sat in the saddle, gave him a gentle kick, and he started forward. I brought him around the edge of the corral, like we were going to do pace work, but while he was walking I slipped my feet out of the stirrups and brought my feet up under me. I got onto my knees, carefully straightened up and balanced as he slowly walked the length of the fence. Cowboy surfing. I laughed at the notion. I flicked the reins and he picked up his pace a little.

We were almost at the end of the fence when there was a loud *Bang!* and Shasta took off. I slipped from the saddle and fell against the fence. The rein got wrapped around my hand and I was jerked to the ground. He took off through the gate and down the road with me dragging along beside him. In the distance I could hear someone yell, "Cass! Let go!" But I couldn't. I was bumping and rolling around and rocks were gouging and sand was in my eyes. I grabbed the rein with my good hand until I had the tangle in front of me. I unwound the leather that was trapping my hand and let go. I slid to a stop and watched my horse gallop off, followed soon after by two riders. One of them broke off and circled around back to me. I got to my feet. I wasn't going to be carried back like some broken ragdoll. I was going to walk back of my own accord. I was mad enough to walk back and tear the hide off of Peccati. Randy rode up, shock clearly visible on his face. I kept walking and when he tried to stop me I ran. I ran until I got to the fence and I jumped up on it, searching the hills. I tried to identify the hill I heard the shot from, but they all looked just as likely as any other. Steve gave me a knowing look.

Chapter 12

The sun was streaming in my window and the world seemed different. I was stiff, sore and didn't want to move, so I was late getting up.

People were looking at me strangely. I wondered if word had gotten out about why all these "accidents" were occurring. I assumed Randy and Steve were the only ones who knew anything because my father hadn't called me on the carpet about it yet. I showered and dressed in jeans, t-shirt and moccasins, and then ate breakfast. I couldn't get over the feeling that something was different today. I went down to the barn to look in on Shasta. He seemed none the worse for wear, but I was sure his mouth must have been hurting him. Just keeping a tight rein on a horse can hurt their mouth with the wrong bit, and he had dragged me, pulling on the bit the whole way. Lifting each hoof, I checked him over. The guys had already done this, but I felt better after doing it myself. I vowed to give him a rest or only ride him with a halter. I didn't blame him for the accident, but I talked to Randy about getting him used to gunfire. It was a project Randy was glad to take on.

I went back to my room and changed into black spandex running pants and tennis shoes. When I looked in the mirror all I saw were scabs and bruises. Not a pretty picture. This guy was not going to beat me. Bruises and scratches would heal, but my attitude was not going to heal until I had control of my life again. Peccati had better watch out because I was mad. He had ticked off the wrong person. I went to the barn and attacked the punching bag with a vengeance. I went to the track and ran it as hard as I could. I walked it to cool off but nothing worked. I climbed the rope to the rafters and just lay there, letting the solid wood support me. I had to do something about Peccati or I'd go nuts. What was he trying to do? Goad me into doing something stupid? Play with me? Slowly kill me? Guess the quick way didn't work. Damn, but I was mad.

Afternoon came and I was still stewing. I ran the track twice, as hard as I could, feet churning, sand flying. Mentally, I was on the mountain again. That big, bald mountain. Completely open. And I had to outrun the bullets. I pushed myself hard, but it was no use. The frustration was still there. The punching bag never saw so much use. I climbed the rope and ran the rafters several times without stopping, and attacked the punching bag one more time. I ran the obstacle course and I was just fixing to head out to the hills to track down the shooter when a new track stopped me short. It was a track I'd never seen at the ranch, and it was a track that meant more to me than anything. It was a wheelchair track! And behind the wheelchair track were Rusty's, now familiar, footprints in the sand. Beside the two men's tracks I could see Mom's canvas tennis shoe prints. I ran up to the house and burst in the front door but everybody looked normal. I searched the down stairs but only found Martha busy in the kitchen. Okay, I thought, I'm a tracker. I'll just track you down.

I returned to the wheelchair track and looked at the prints. Wheelchair, men's casual shoes, and Mom's canvas tennis shoes. They had gone around the side of the wrap-around porch and then down to the land overlooking the track. I imagined them talking, and… and what? What were they doing? The footprints showed the organized randomness that goes with a conversation, but they were all facing the same direction. They were watching me. I followed the tracks from the racetrack to the side of the barn. Again they just stood around, the open stall doors giving them a view inside without being too obvious. They had wandered around the back of the house to the backside of the obstacle course. They had barely paused there. I was so absorbed in the tracks that I walked right past them, sitting in the gazebo beside the house. I followed the track back towards the house and there they were, sitting and talking and watching me with amused faces, Rusty and Kelly and Mom. I leaped up the gazebo steps and I crushed Rusty in a big bear hug. I was so stunned. I couldn't believe it. He was here. I couldn't let go. If I let go, he would disappear and I couldn't stand that. And Kelly was here. Okay, I thought, time to let go. I stood back and gave Kelly a hug too. They were beaming.

"How long have you been here? How long can you stay? Why didn't someone come tell me?"

"Cass," he said quietly, "remember when I took you to see Kelly at the hospital, and you were afraid to go in? Afraid that your hopes and reality wouldn't match up?" A short pause while he let this information sink in. He continued, "I just had to see for myself. I had to see you were really okay before I saw you face to face, and I am thrilled. I can't believe it. You've come so far."

I was momentarily speechless.

"How long can you stay?" Forever?

"We can stay tomorrow, but we have to be back the next day."

"So, we have a day?"

My mom looked at me weird. "Cassidy, you still don't know, do you?"

"Know what? What should I know?"

"Honey, today's your birthday!"

"It is? I don't even know what day of the week it is. I haven't seen a calendar since before the fire. How can today be my birthday and me not know it?"

"That's what everybody else has been wondering," she said.

So that's why everybody was looking at me weird. They all knew.

Rusty, Kelly and I laughed and talked while walking the ranch. Kelly was able to get out of the wheelchair briefly by using crutches until his aching ribs drove him back to a sitting position. My mom caught up with us as we approached the house.

"Why don't you run upstairs and get dressed for dinner?"

"Dressed for dinner? Mom, we never get dressed for dinner. I was going to change before dinner. I don't want to wear these grungy running clothes."

"Wear that pretty dress we bought at the mall," she hinted.

"Is this why you made me buy that dress? You didn't plan anything, did you?"

"Honey, we got that dress because it was made for you. When you find a dress that is just made for you, you have to buy it. It's in the Shopper's Law. Section one, code six hundred and forty two."

I excused myself and went upstairs to get ready. If Mom said to dress for dinner I better *dress for dinner*.

I showered and blow dried my hair and then dressed quickly. I ran downstairs to borrow a curling iron and mousse from Martha. She winked at me as she handed them over. I ran upstairs again, put a little mousse in my hair, then brushed and curled my hair carefully making sure my bangs looked nice and feminine. This was a very feminine dress, not usually my style. Mom was right, though, it was made for me. When I saw the dress at the store, I thought, nope, no way is this going to look right on me. Mom insisted I try it on and it fit like a glove. It accentuated all the right places. Slipping this dress over my head turned me into a princess.

I put on make-up, trying to hide the slight bruising. There wasn't much I could do about the gash over my left eye. It had to heal on its own. There was no forcing that, but mascara and a little eyeliner did a lot to draw attention away from it. A tiny bit of eye shadow helped, too. When at last I was convinced it was as good as it was going to get, I put on hose and a slip and slid the dress over my head. It fell into place like it belonged there. Now I loved the light, almost crinkly fabric with the subtle little beads running up and down it. Without the inside layer there would be nothing to it, I might as well go out there naked. But it had a matching inside liner that gave the fabric depth and helped it cling and move just right. I slipped on the matching pumps. It was all the heel my mom could talk me into. I twirled around in front of the mirror. I felt good, but in reality I was a mess. When you get dragged through a corral and down a road the rocks are not kind. They bite and gouge and the marks they leave are not a pretty sight. The sleeveless dress didn't do much to hide the fact that I'd been run through the mill.

My mom poked her head in the door.

"Come in, Mom," I said. I twirled around. "I can't wear this. Look at me."

"Cassidy." she said in her gentlest voice. "You're a beautiful girl. All you have to wear out there is a big smile and you'll melt every heart in the room. Here, I have a present for you."

She reached into her apron pocket and pulled out a small box. She opened it and eased the chain of a necklace loose from its velvety card. She stood behind me and clipped the ends together, then let it gently fall. It was a gold heart with inlaid diamonds. The chain followed the lines of the dress and the heart settled just over the swell of my breasts. She handed me the box and inside were delicate gold earrings that dangled a little and sparkled when they moved. I'd gotten my ears pierced as a teenager on a dare, but I rarely wore earrings. They went with the dress perfectly. I put them on and I moved in front of the mirror all sparkly and curly and feminine. Who was this person?

"Thank you so much," I said sincerely. I gave her a big hug. "Did you tell Rusty it was my birthday?"

"No, he called me. But I was going to invite him up here anyway. Did I tell you Jesse's back in town? She said she would try and make it in time for your birthday. Her and James and the kids will be here in a little while. Now," she said matter-of-factly, "you wait up here for just a little bit and then you walk slowly down those stairs and I promise you that you'll be able to read every face in that room."

I opened my bedroom door letting the sounds filter up from the entryway. All the guys were coming in one or two at a time. The sounds were joyful in a masculine sort of way. My father was downstairs, his booming voice echoing off the stairway. Martha was down there making sure there was room for everyone. In a house this massive there was bound to be room for everybody. I used to wonder why we had a bunkhouse, but as I grew up I came to realize why the hands needed their own space. As a kid, I would invade it occasionally to play poker and lose my spare change to them, or challenge one of them to a game of pool. I was listening at the door when Rusty walked by on his way downstairs. His room was just past mine. He was dressed in a tailored black suit with a red silk tie, and looked very dashing and formal. I ducked into my room. Kelly was already downstairs where the wheelchair was easier to use.

My stomach did a little flip flop. Why was it I could manage almost anything except trying to look pretty? Put a dress on me and I became a nervous wreck.

I gave Rusty enough time to get downstairs and, if needed, help Kelly get settled in with the crowd below. How many people were down there? Four ranch hands, Mom, Dad, Rusty, Kelly, Martha, Jesse and family, thirteen. Thirteen wonderful people. Time to go down.

I walked down the hall and stood anxiously at the top of the stairs. I hated being the center of attention, but I knew I could count on the people down there to lighten up the occasion. I took the first step and descended slowly, watching, like Mom said. Randy was in the far corner of the room. He let out a whoop and yelled, "Here comes Trouble!" I laughed uncomfortably. Everybody else looked up and all the ranch guys applauded and called out, "Hey Cassidy!" and "Way to go girl!" They were all dressed up in their finest clothes, all freshly pressed. Their boots were all black and polished. Their ties coordinated with their colorful shirts. Mom and Dad beamed, while Old Frank and Martha looked like a proud aunt and uncle. And Rusty? Rusty melted. He was clapping with the guys but he swallowed a lump in his throat and his eyes laughed and his smile brightened up every corner of the room. Kelly was laughing and whacked Rusty on the back, pointing at me. I found the smile that my mom mentioned and joined the party.

Martha came up offering me something to drink. I took a glass of sweet white wine. I knew it had been carefully chosen from a local winery. They dotted the hillsides all over this part California. She knew what I liked. People began breaking into smaller groups and I wandered around the room thanking them for coming. Zack tried to give me the fifty dollars he won on the ice pack bet but I didn't let him. I knew he needed it more than I did.

Steve raised his glass, "A quarter of a century of trouble! Happy Birthday, Cass!" I thanked him and clinked glasses.

The front door then opened and Jesse, squealing with delight, ran across the room, clasping me in a long-lost-sister hug. James entered and shook my hand. Then the boys came up shyly. They were dressed up in black jeans, pinstriped white shirts with bright red and blue string ties. They didn't know me very well since I lived far away and they were still young. Patrick was four and Wyatt was three. Patrick walked up and hugged me stiffly and said, "Happy Birthday, Aunt Castidy."

Wyatt gave me a high five and a down low. Jesse, always the happy homemaker, went to the kitchen to see if Martha needed any help. Growing up, she was all girl while I was all boy. She had glorious, long, honey brown hair and hung out with her groupie friends. They went shopping just for the fun of it and Jesse did handicrafts in her spare time. Her house was decorated, with each room having a theme. The boys had western murals painted on their walls. I was the loner. I tracked, camped, stalked deer, hunted with the guys, and trained the horses and dogs. I'd climb up on green-broke horses, rescue baby birds and adopt lost puppies. Growing up, we had been worlds apart. But since we've both been married we have something in common and we got along great.

Now that everybody was here it was time to make introductions, but it didn't take long for Jesse to pick out Rusty and Kelly. She hurried back to me. "My god, Cassidy, who's the hot hunk in the black suit? He's not from around here. If he was, I'd sure know it!"

"Come on, I'll introduce you to him." I took Jesse over to where Rusty and Kelly were talking separately from the ranch groups.

Rusty saw me coming and picked me up at the waist and twirled me around, setting me lightly on the floor with a look of admiration. Jesse almost fainted. This was not the sisterly introduction she had expected. "Cass, you just broke every heart in the room coming down those stairs. Those poor guys."

I blushed. Jesse was the one who broke hearts. I was the one they made bets over how soon I would need the next ice pack.

"Jesse, this is Rusty Michaels and Kelly Green."

"Hey," she chimed in, "my den is painted in Kelly green!"

Kelly smiled. I guess he was used to this.

"Is it dark or light?"

"It's dark. Why? Is that different?"

"That's my brother, Hunter. He's the dark one. I'm Green lite." He had that right. There wasn't a serious bone in his body.

Rusty said, "I'm pleased to meet you, Jesse."

Martha came to my rescue by sending everybody into the dining room for dinner. We wheeled Kelly in and he eased into a dining room chair.

The table was packed. It was a big table often surrounded with large groups, and we filled it. Martha brought out steaming platters of turkey, pot roast and venison, bowls of mashed potatoes, side dishes and salad. Wine was poured and the conversation flowed until all the food had been served. Daddy rose from the table and said, "I'd like to thank y'all for coming tonight and bein' here to celebrate Cassidy's birthday. This is a birthday we thought we might not see. An' I'd like to thank Rusty Michaels for giving my daughter back to me. If it weren't for Rusty, we wouldn't have our little bit o' trouble."

It was the first time I'd seen my dad choked up. And he'd called me his daughter. I'd never heard him do that either.

Everyone clapped and raised their glasses and then silence reigned while everybody ate. Martha could always tell when her cooking was good and the ranch was running well by how quiet the table got. If the ranch was having problems it was dinner where they spilled over, where everyone was gathered at once and they could discuss it in a group. This wasn't one of those meals though. We were all enjoying the evening, the food and the company. I was just soaking it all in. That smile that mom talked about came quickly and frequently.

When dinner was over we moved to the living room to talk. After a while the storytelling began. I had to sit through all the old stories of my major catastrophes. Everybody seemed to have a favorite story that involved them. By the end of the evening Rusty had heard my whole life story. Randy added a new one to the list, telling about the deer at the flats. He didn't mention the shot, but instead just said something had scared the deer. Patrick's eyes got big and he asked, "How do you stalk a deer?"

"Well," I began, "you have to have a lot of patience and be really sneaky because deer are scared of people. What you do is, you quietly come up on a herd of deer grazing. When the deer have their heads down, you sneak as quietly as possible, and when they sense you coming, they will all bring their heads up and that's when you freeze. You have to not move as long as their heads are up. Even if it's for an hour, you freeze. Even if your nose itches, you can't move. Then they put their heads down again, and you sneak some more. When you get close to the deer and you think it is risky to walk, you lean over in a crouch so hardly any of you is showing above the grass. When you get really, really close, you lay on the ground and let the deer get used to you being there, but invisible, and then you crawl closer and closer, without making a sound, until you are close as you can get."

"Have you ever touched a deer? I mean, not in a zoo. In the wild?"

"Only once, but I've gotten real close many times, and sometimes it is more fun just to lay on the ground and let the deer graze around you."

"When I tell Ricky Mallory about the things you do, he never believes me. Can you tell him that I'm not fibbing?"

"Sure."

Jesse piped up. "I want to hear how you met Rusty and Kelly."

I looked up, shocked. They didn't know. I'd never told them because I didn't want them to worry, and now Jesse wanted me to tell them everything. I looked at Rusty and he glanced back. I grabbed Rusty by the hand and rushed him out onto the porch.

"What do I do?" I almost shrieked. "I can't tell them I was carjacked and kidnapped and shot at. What'll they think?"

"It'll give Patrick a great story to tell his little friend."

"Very funny."

"Do you really not want them to know? You can't hide these things from them forever. They can tell you have secrets. You can't go through what you went through and not be changed. They see the change. Hearing how it came about might be good for them. Your mom was really puzzled by your running and rope climbing and punching bag murdering, but I wasn't. I could see what you were doing. I think they should know."

"Well, I can't do it. I guess, I don't mind if you tell them, but I just can't. I'll field questions later."

"Kelly can tell them how he met you. He tells a good story."

And so we went back in and Rusty told the whole story about how we met. It was nice for me to hear it from his point of view. Patrick gave me the wide-eyed look again, thinking about how his Aunt Castidy tracked down a real live bank robber and murderer. I filled in about how Shadow had distracted Silva and Shadow got an extra dog biscuit for his part in my escape.

Rusty turned the story over to Kelly, and Kelly said, "Well, I was lying at the bottom of a cliff, all broken up from a fall and being shot at. And when I came to, there was this girl pulling a top down over her head. And I thought…"

"Hey wait a minute!" I interrupted, "It wasn't like that."

"Yes it was. That's what you were doing the first time I met you."

"Okay, back up a bit. Kelly's a forest ranger and he was out doing his forest ranger duties and he ran across these drug dealers who shot him and dropped him over a cliff. That's how he broke his legs and his ribs. He was stuck out there at the bottom of the cliff and Rusty called me because he remembered that I had tracked down the bank robber. He thought maybe, just maybe I could find Kelly, too. So I set out down the trail to track Kelly, and his trail led me to the drug dealers too, only they didn't shoot me. They showed me where Kelly was, and when I tried to rappel down to where he was, they cut my rope. And, since I was supposed to be dead at the bottom of this cliff, I changed clothes and arranged the clothes they last saw me in to look like me dead on the ground. That's when Kelly came to. Okay, now you can tell it."

"No, I can't. You just did. Cassidy brought me food and water then called the helicopter, and paramedics took me to the hospital in L.A."

"Yup, that's about it."

Then Rusty threw in, "You can ask her later how she got attacked by a bear, tricked two drug dealers out of their dirt bike and two rifles, and escaped to tell about it."

I shot him a dirty look. Randy picked up on the look. "Oh, man, you are so dead!"

I looked around the group. My mom was staring open mouthed. My dad had fallen asleep halfway though the story telling. Yes! Miracles do happen! The guys were just shaking their heads, thinking Rusty was nuts to be interested in me. Jesse looked a lot like Mom. And Patrick had a new hero.

Rusty wasn't finished with me yet, though. "I brought you a present." From behind the couch he pulled out my old backpack and then he pulled out a new one. Same size, same model, but an updated design. I looked at him dumbfounded.

My mom was shocked "Cassidy! My god! What happened to it?"

"Well, this is where the bear got it." I said sticking my hand through the foot long gashes. I twisted the frame "And this is from falling on it down the cliff." I looked it over. I was in deep enough, but what the hell. "Hey!" I said, "No bullet holes!"

I turned to the new one. This wasn't just a new pack he'd given me. It was affirmation. It meant he believed in me, and believed I was capable, and that I could do it again.

"Thank you," I said with tears in my eyes. "You don't know how much this means to me."

Martha set out dessert for everyone and served coffee. We were too full from dinner to eat much more, and no one would budge, so we ate in the living room. Martha made cheesecake, apple pie and birthday cake.

I'd never forget this day. I wanted it to never end, but finally the guys started wandering back to the bunkhouse and Jesse, James, and the kids went home, promising to be back the next day.

Chapter 13

That night I had nightmares again. In the dream we were back at the party, all standing around laughing and talking. Kelly had just finished telling a joke and the room was teeming with smiling faces when the doorbell rang. My mother went to answer it and when the door opened in waltzed Mario Pecatti, all smug and proud of himself.

"I heard we were having a party," he said. Anger boiled up inside of me and I started to launch myself at him when I awoke frightened. I bolted upright in bed. It was just a dream, I told myself, it never really happened.

I tried to go back to sleep but I couldn't. I was too tense and alert. I slipped from my bed, padded next door, and cracked open the door to Rusty's room. He was still there, sleeping peacefully and soundly. I closed the door silently and padded around the house nervously. Everything was still and peaceful but I couldn't shake the feeling that something was wrong.

I put on a light jacket and went downstairs. I stepped outside for some fresh air and was momentarily startled when the motion sensor turned on the porch light. I stepped across the porch and went down to the gazebo to sit, think, and watch the horses under the dim moonlight. The porch light switched off.

I knew Mario Pecatti was here somewhere. No one else would take all these cruel jabs at me. Where was he staying? Why was he hanging around? Why didn't he just finish me off? Was there another house and another drug lab in every out-of-the-way corner of California? It was very tempting to just go after him, but I had a feeling that's exactly what he wanted me to do. I'd be walking into a trap. So the trick to it was tracking him down before the trap was set. No, that wouldn't work. I'd never get off the ranch alone and I wasn't going to drag anybody else into this mess. At the very least I needed to do some detective work first, find out if he did have a house nearby. If he had a house, he had a car here too. What kind was it? Would the police search his house if I could prove Peccati was a danger to me? If so, what would they be looking for? I remembered the notebook pages I took from the cabin. If only I had those here. They might give me some clues, but I'd forgotten about them. Waterlogged notebook pages were not high on my list when I packed to come to the ranch. Looking back, I doubted I had packed at all. Mom probably did it.

I stretched and yawned. What was that noise? It sounded like a car pulling into the drive. The driveway to the ranch went through fields of fenced pastureland so there was plenty of time to see a car coming towards the ranch but I didn't see one. Still, the sound was unmistakable. I shrunk back into the shadows. "When in doubt, be invisible" was my motto. I slipped off the light blue jacket so it wouldn't draw attention in the moonlight. I crouched low in the gazebo keeping below the level of the seats. As I watched, a Mercedes Benz SUV drove quietly up the driveway with its lights off. It paused, the driver unsure of the roads on the ranch. The car then turned heading down to the barns. What to do? If I ran upstairs and woke Rusty up it could be gone. I needed to find out what this car was doing here. Cursing the motion sensor, I ran inside the house. The closest gun rack I knew of was in my dad's study just off the entryway. I grabbed the first rifle in the rack and hurried back out the door. I jogged down to the barns, keeping to the shadows. The SUV was parked at the barn and a shadowy figure moved ahead of me. The white license plate was easy to read in the moonlight. I scratched the number in the sand next to the barn.

The man was doing something to the barn door. Trying to open it? It wasn't difficult to open. Was it locked? Surely not. In the event of a fire, they needed to get the horses out quickly. So what was he doing? Whatever it was, he was up to no good. I cocked the rifle. The man froze instantly. I stepped out of the shadows.

"Ah, Cassidy Callahan," he said, "I can always count on you keeping things interesting."

"All I have to do is fire one shot and this whole ranch is going to come down here and tear you limb from limb. They are on to what you are doing. It seems kind of childish to me. Why don't you pick on someone your own size? Do you enjoy picking on me?"

"Why, yes, I do," he said calmly in a mocking tone of voice. "Did you enjoy picking on my men when you had a chance?"

"I didn't pick on them. They were going to kill me. They got what they deserved. I haven't done anything to you. I've only tried to protect myself and the ones I love."

"How noble of you. How noble will you feel when they have to bury you? Perhaps misfortune will befall someone else this time, your horse or some young cowboy who comes to the barn in the morning."

He was trying to trick me, I knew. He wanted me to go to the barn door but I wasn't falling for it. I fired the rifle into the air. He looked around nervously.

"It's not noble." I said, "It's necessary, with creeps like you around. It shouldn't be necessary to constantly defend myself from people like you. Why don't you go open the barn door? Maybe some misfortune will befall you." I motioned with the rifle for him to walk to the door, but he didn't move.

I cocked the rifle again and heard an empty click. There had only been one bullet in the chambers. He smiled. Anger flared. I hated this guy. Here was the punching bag in real life, the real face of Mario Peccati. I wanted to attack him; I wanted to hurt him like he'd hurt me. I wanted to keep him from hurting others.

He made a dash for the vehicle and I tackled him. We struggled until he managed to stand up. "You aren't getting away that easy." I yelled. "You ruin the lives of hundreds of people selling them drugs." I grabbed him and turned him towards me. I socked him in the jaw, surprised that he staggered back. "You send your goons to take out some girl in the woods just because she was trying to help a friend." I stomped on his foot and punched him in the side. He tried an upper cut but I jumped back. I kicked him in the leg. "You send little deadly gifts to poison people in their own homes." I heard footsteps and he did the only quick thing he could think of, which was to pick me up and throw me at the crowd approaching. I hit the dirt with a hard thump that knocked the air out of me. He jumped in his SUV and scattered gravel on the way out. Steve jumped into a ranch truck and sped after him.

Gasping for breath, I crawled towards the barn. "Don't touch the barn door!" I cried in raspy voice. "Don't touch the barn door!" I heaved myself to a standing position. My stomach turned over. I staggered over and blocked the way. I was tempted to open it myself. The punching bag really needed a workout. But I knew there was something wrong with this door. It was booby trapped in some way. "Take the horses out the back door and put them in a pasture."

Randy, always the thinking one, said, "But some of these horses don't get along."

"Then put them in two pastures! Just don't touch this door. Somebody call the police." I doubled over. Rusty came running up, wrapping me in his warmth, trying to steer me away. I pulled back. "No," I said. "Gotta keep people away from this door."

"It's okay, everyone knows about the door. Come on. Zack will guard the door, won't you Zack?"

"It's booby trapped or bombed or something. Shit! I wanted to kill that guy coming in here like this. He thinks he's so smart picking on us. I wasn't through with him yet. I'm too tense to slow down. I need to do something. Stupid punching bag. Why does it have to hang by the booby trapped door?"

I went on like that and Rusty kept to me. I kicked stones and punched at fence posts and tried to go back to the barn but he blocked me, gently steering me, dirty and angry, to a place where I could stop and calm down. Calmness was a long time coming and dawn found us back in the gazebo. I'd never calmed down enough to go back to bed.

An officer approached. Rusty got up, showed them his badge and talked to them until they got the information they needed. He'd get the report from me. He asked a few quiet questions and the officer went back to the barn.

He sat down again. "How did you know?"

"I woke up with nightmares and I couldn't get back to sleep so I came out here. I was just sitting here, almost like this, and I heard a car drive up. I couldn't see it because its lights were off. I knew that a normal car would have lights on so this car felt out of place. When it turned to go down to the barn, I ran in the house and grabbed the first gun I could find. I didn't want to run upstairs and wake everybody because they'd get away, so I just grabbed my dad's rifle."

I told him what happened, remembering the license plate number scrawled in the dirt.

"Somehow," he said, "you have got to stop taking these things on by yourself."

"I know. That's why I fired the first shot. I thought I had him. I thought I could just hold him there until help arrived. I didn't know there was only one stinking bullet in the gun. And then I just got mad. He tried to get away and I wasn't going to let him, and I just got mad."

"Have you known he was up here?"

"I suspected. He'd never shown himself after the hospital visit, so I couldn't be sure. You heard the story last night about the deer?"

"Yeah, great story. I wish I could have been there. I'd love to see you do that."

"The thing that scared the deer was a single shot. It felled the deer I was laying next to. Randy left that out so Daddy wouldn't know. And when I got thrown and dragged? A single shot scared Shasta and he bolted. And the time I fell off the rafters into Satan's stall? A single shot hit the rafter two inches below my foot. It startled me or I wouldn't have fallen. All these accidents have not been the accidents people think. Randy knows about the shot at the deer and Steve knows about the shot in the barn. We have just been trying to stay vigilant. The shots always come from the surrounding hills, from a high-powered rifle. They are never meant to hit me, but they are always meant to hurt me."

"Well, the barn door was meant to hurt somebody. You were right, it was rigged to blow when the door opened."

"Did Steve get back yet? He took off after the SUV. I hope he's okay."

"He's okay, but I don't think he had much luck."

"Would you like to go see if the deer are in the flats?"

"Aren't you worried about being followed?"

"No, I think Peccati had a rough night. He'll stay away for a day or two."

"What about you? Do you need some sleep this morning?"

"No way. I'm too wired and I don't want to miss a minute of today. It's our only day to ourselves. Do you know how to ride a horse?"

"I haven't ridden since I was a kid."

"Would you like to try? We have plenty of reliable horses around here. We can take it slow or, if you are comfortable, we can get out there quick and have more time later. We'll put you through some practice laps in the corral before we take off. What do you think?"

"OK. Let's do it," Rusty agreed.

I chose Buck and Shasta for the ride out. All the horses were general ranch horses except for a few of the racers. Steve had trained Buck well and Buck was used to working around the ranch. He listened to his rider. I put a halter on Shasta, still afraid of causing him pain. He was used to neck reigning so I'd only have trouble if he bolted.

I looked at Rusty seriously, "Shasta doesn't have a bit, which means if he bolts I might have a little trouble stopping him. As long as I'm in the saddle, I'm fine. You have to remember that. Don't go after me if he bolts. If you don't know what to do, just tell Buck 'let's go home' and make him go the speed you want. I don't expect trouble but I don't want you to worry either. All those movie scenes showing runaway horses going under trees and poor helpless girls being dragged off at the last minute are really hokey. All I have to do is stay on the horse and keep my head down. Eventually he will get to a place where he feels safe or he'll get tired and stop."

We rode to the corral and walked the horses around a bit, letting Rusty get used to the movement.

"Now the next gait is bumpy, so if you don't like the bumpiness of it push down with your feet and use your knees as shock absorbers. Most people don't like to trot, but it is comfortable for the horse, and they can trot for a long time."

I could see Rusty was like most people. He didn't like the trot.

"Are you ready for a little speed?"

We cantered around a little and he seemed to be doing well. He moved comfortably with the horse, and took to the reining and stopping easily.

"We won't gallop at all unless something comes up. If that were to happen, it is actually smoother than the canter. Just keep your head and Buck will follow Shasta. What do you think? Are you sore yet?"

"Let's give it a try."

We left the horses and went up to the house for some lunch to take along. I packed it into saddlebags and we set off. Randy chased us down but I sent him back.

"Your dad will kill me if I let you ride off alone."

"I'm not alone. I'm with Rusty. Daddy trusts Rusty. If it makes you feel better I'll wear your gun. You do keep it loaded don't you?"

"Sure Cass, it's loaded. Steve checks all the guns every day before we start our duties."

"Tell him to add Daddy's guns to his list."

I strapped on Randy's pistol and he walked dejectedly back to the ranch. I'd probably get the riot act from my dad tonight, but I had a bone to pick with him too.

Rusty and I worked our way back up through the gaits. I preferred a canter. It is comfortable and eats up a lot of ground. We didn't have far to go so the horses would not get overly tired. They would have a long rest once we got there, too.

We had to look around to find the deer. They weren't in the same area that I had found them before. We followed a game trail across an arroyo and they were on the other side.

I looked at the plants around. I couldn't see any sign of a breeze but wind can be fickle and so can deer. I licked my finger and held it up. A very slight breeze was coming out of the west like usual. We brought the horses to the east side of the clearing and I staked them out.

"Do you remember what I told Patrick?" I asked softly.

"Yeah, go when the deer look down. Freeze when they look up."

"Watch me and do what I do."

"Okay. When do I get to watch you and do what I'd like to do?"

I blushed and went on with the instruction, ignoring the play, "This is easier to do without guns, but I don't want to leave the guns with the horses. And it's easier to do alone, so don't get your hopes up."

"Okay"

"Ready? Move smooth and quiet."

We walked into the clearing. The deer were skittish. They became alert almost right away and it was a long, slow stalk. A quarter mile closed to a hundred yards very slowly. Rusty showed extreme patience as we stayed frozen for long periods of time. He showed skill in his movements. I'd have to teach him how to walk better, but I couldn't speak now. It would frighten the deer. I inched closer to Rusty to give him a visual cue. Pointing with my eyes said, "Go for the doe lying down." An almost imperceptible nod said, "Okay".

I entered a crouch, hands on knees. Rusty did the same. I crouched lower. He was still taller than the grass. He crouched lower. It was the best we could hope for. The doe looked agitated. Freeze. If she got frightened she would stand and we'd know to stop. Crouch steps. Freeze. Crouch steps. Stop. Wait, wait. Half an hour later we had only gained a few yards. We weren't very close but I thought it was time to get lower. I had a hunch something was bothering the deer. When their heads came up some of the deer looked at us and some of them looked in another direction. What was in that direction? I stretched out in the grass and Rusty tried to copy me. It wasn't a natural movement to him, so it wasn't smooth. The grass crunched.

What were the deer watching? I wasn't used to stalking competition. If it was predators, I wasn't worried. Predators were after deer. If it was people they were worried about, then I was worried too. This position would be hard for Rusty to maintain quietly. I decided to call off the stalk, at least until we could figure out if we were in danger.

I gave Rusty a stay signal and crouched lower than the grass. I stalked over to him and stretched out again.

"We aren't very close, but I think we need to quit."

"Why?"

"The deer are acting strangely. I think something else is out there. Our goal right now is to figure out what they are scared of that's not us. Look at the deer and look where they look. If you can make it out, tell me quietly. This is going to take some time. We are safe as long as we are low."

We lay in the clearing, the deer in the close distance. When the deer looked up we followed their gaze, heads barely over the grass. I was praying it had nothing to do with the horses. We didn't want to walk home from here.

Suddenly the deer tensed up. The doe we had been stalking stood at attention. The deer milled around nervously. The herd turned as one and leaped away, a few stragglers bounding behind. A tawny shape moved through the grass. Coyotes. I pointed them out to Rusty with a huge sigh of relief. If the coyotes were out, there were no people abroad. Lying in the grass, we were free to talk. The deer were gone and our voices would send the coyotes packing.

"I'm sorry I called it off. When I come out here I get so tuned in to the deer. They are smarter than me. They know when to worry, and when they worry, I worry. I didn't want to get trapped out here by some lunatic with a rifle trained on us. At least we got to see coyotes too. I know a better place to do this, but it is back home."

"How long will you stay up here?" Rusty asked.

"I don't know. I was hoping you could help me decide. Physically, I am fine. I'd jump in the car and go home with you and Kelly tomorrow. But if Peccati is up here, I'd like to help bring him in. What can we do to bring that about? How can we find out if he has a home up here?"

"Actually, I brought something I was going to show you. I thought a little mental gymnastics might be good for you too. It's a notebook we picked up in the raid. I didn't bring the actual notebook but I copied a bunch of pages, hoping you might see something in it that I don't. You're good with patterns so something might jump out at you."

"Why are we lying in a field whispering at each other?" I asked.

"Because it's more fun than sitting around the ranch."

"Did you like stalking or did it drive you nuts?"

"I thought it was great. We'll have to try it again some time," Rusty replied.

"Most people don't have the patience for it and this was a particularly boring stalk. We actually did really well for your first time. It takes a lot of practice."

"How far did you get the first time you tried it?"

"When I was a kid I stalked everything. Old Frank used to haul me into the house and ask my mom to tie me up because I'd pop out of nowhere and make him jump. Shadow knows how to stalk too. I have a signal that he knows means to hide. He crouches, finds a shadowy spot, and lies still until I give him the okay to move. Only thing is, he thinks the deer are sheep and they don't herd very well."

"You didn't answer my question."

"I got a little closer than this. But I was alone and I had stalked rabbits, horses, cows, dogs and people. I used to practice going places without being seen and not leaving footprints. I've tracked deer, foxes and bears. Moving around in the outdoors is what I do best."

He smiled. "We should be getting back. I'd love to lie out here all day and talk, but I bet people will start worrying."

"And the horses are probably ready to move around again."

"Oh, joy. The horses."

"Unless you'd rather walk. Horses know how to walk too, you know."

"It's a long ways. I think the horses are a better bet, but don't be surprised if I'm a little bow-legged when we get back," Rusty responded.

"How about if we break up the trip a little. There's something I want to check out on the way back."

The horses were glad to be on the road again, but we weren't going far. I led Rusty back to the first clearing. I dismounted, standing in the middle of the field. I wanted a look at those hills. Rusty dismounted and brought the horses over. The fallen deer had been removed. Randy had called in the poaching and somebody had removed the carcass.

"It was one of those hills," I said pointing. "It had to be. The deer was standing right there and she fell right here at my feet, so the bullet had to come from that way."

I climbed into the saddle and we loped off to the first of two hills. Halfway up the side I dismounted. I wanted to examine the area on foot. Nothing looked out of place. I lay on the hill trying to get the shooter's perspective. No, this wasn't the hill. The view wasn't right.

I walked to the second hill and everything clicked. This hill was a little taller and had a trail coming up the back. Footprints covered a small area and a flattened area showed where the shooter had lain. The sharp indentations of a tripod marked where the end of the gun had been supported. I walked down the hill towards the deer flats and looked back up. Invisible. I couldn't see the spot at all. Bingo.

I climbed the hill again and explained my findings to Rusty. He'd figured most of it out on his own.

"Let's go for a walk." I said.

I followed the trail down the back of the hill. That was a no brainer. Then I was in tracking mode. The trail was faint but ran through the tall grass. The grass beside the trail had sprung back up since Peccati walked through, so his footprints were buried beneath the thick growth. Still, I could make out a slight bend to the grasses. I looked at the thin reeds. Yes, there was definitely a little leaning. I bent the grasses aside. A faint mark of a man's shoe. These shoes were not meant for hiking. Hopefully they gave him a little trouble on the way in. That would provide more clues for me to follow.

Examining the grass each time and parting it to find the prints was tedious, but I had a feeling this man had not walked far. He wasn't a hiker. He was a trickster, and I suspected I'd find a lazy trickster at the end of this game. He wasn't going to follow along stalking me through the woods. He saw me head out and followed the easy way. But what was the easy way? Rusty followed, riding Buck, patiently leading Shasta so I could work. This was not easy reading, and I was hoping he was gaining a little appreciation for what I was capable of doing. I knew my actions made sense to him, but I also knew it was unlikely he saw anything to follow down there on the ground at all.

We'd come perhaps a quarter of a mile, me tediously examining the grasses, bending them aside and choosing a direction when Rusty stopped.

"Cassidy, mount up. I can see where we're going."

I put my foot in the stirrup and hoisted myself up. I was still too short so I stood in the stirrups. There was a road. Yes! But where did it come from. It wasn't here when I was growing up.

We angled the horses up a short rise and came out on a dirt road that followed the base of the hills and disappeared off into the distance.

"We need to get back, but we need to remember this road," I said.

I dismounted and did a quick inspection. No footprints going up and down the road. No footprints climbing the bank on the far side. He had parked and hiked in. He had an idea where I'd been going and knew an easier way to get there. And he'd probably been watching me the whole time. It gave me the creeps.

We walked the horses on the way back, eating sandwiches in the saddle. I'd point out rabbits as they bounded away. I pointed out a few crouching under bushes, but Rusty only saw them when they bolted. Rabbits had been fun to stalk when I was a kid. Once I learned to see them, I took advantage of their tendency to freeze until pursued. The rabbit would see me coming and just stay in place and I'd thought I was making remarkable progress. Even though I never actually caught one, I came close enough to give joy to the hunt. That encouraged me to try other things. I'd have to start Patrick out on rabbits. They could be found close to home and would take his mind off the deer.

We crumpled up the sandwich wrappings and stuffed them in a saddlebag, then took out dessert. It was melted and squashed, but it still tasted like cheesecake. Once satisfied that we'd survive until dinner, we continued to walk, letting our food settle. Soon, though, the need to get back drove us to let the horses go and they broke into a smooth lope for home. There was no need to steer them. The barn was calling and they were ready to go. Horses are like homing pigeons. No matter where you take them, they always know where home is. They have Barn Radar or something.

When we got back to the barn, Randy took the horses and looked at Rusty accusingly. "That was a long ride," he said.

I folded the belt and handed back his gun. "Thanks Randy, no lunatics lurking in the hills. No shots fired. The deer were farther away than they were last time. Then I got curious, so we looked around and found the hill the shot came from. I followed the tracks to a road. Did you know there is a road back there less than a mile from the flats?"

"Sure, Cass. We ate the dust from that road construction for months. Tony Macaluso bought a place back in the hills and is going to start a vineyard back there. Your dad told him if he wanted to be well known he'd have to be more visible, but he likes it back there."

"How old is the road?"

"I'm guessing about two years, although if I say two years it's probably more. I always guess short."

"Do you want me to take care of the horses?"

"Naw, I can do it. Did Shasta handle okay with the halter?"

"Yeah, he did great. I'm going to leave it up to you to decide when to use a bit again. You know him better than I do."

We walked up to the house and I refrained from laughing at Rusty. He *was* walking a bit bowlegged.

"Do you really have to go home in the morning?"

"It depends, I don't want to make Kelly stay if he needs to get home. Let's take a look at those papers I brought. They might convince me to stay and work with the authorities up here."

As we walked in the house, Patrick ran to greet us. "Mommy has a birthday present for you and Grandpa wants to talk to you."

"Thanks, Patrick."

We took our lunch leftovers to the kitchen and threw away all the wrappers. Jesse found me as I was leaving the kitchen. Leave it to Patrick to be the little messenger boy. Kelly crutched his way into the living room and settled on the couch.

"I'm sorry we were gone so long." I said. "Were you bored out of your mind?"

"Hell, no," He replied a mischievous look in his eye. "I've been telling Patrick all the tall tales about your adventures in the woods."

"That couldn't have lasted too long. You've only known me a few weeks."

"It can take a while to tell a story. You have to build it up."

"Well, don't build it up too much. He's only four and I think he might take after me."

Jesse brought out a box and sat down, placing it beside me. "I had to finish it after I got back."

I opened the box and inside was a photo album. I opened the cover. The first page held my senior class picture. There I was in a sapphire blue floor-length gown, blue eyes sparkling. I remembered the dress had brought out my eyes. It was another one of those dresses that fit and looked just right and mom had to buy it. Code 642. Overlapping the sweet little high school girl photo was one of me in my dress uniform, standing in front of a United States flag. What a contrast. Did she really accept both of those people as the same person I am today?

"Now, the next few pages are really scary. You don't have to look if you don't want to."

I didn't want to. I knew what they were just from her description.

"When you were hurt I was back east. I had to know what was going on and I asked mom to send me pictures. I was trapped in hotel rooms with lots of time on my hands, so I started this book as a comfort to me. And then, when everything turned out okay, I decided it should be yours so you could see that nothing is impossible for you."

I decided I should look at the pictures. I needed to know what Mom, Dad and Rusty had been through. I turned the page. Rusty grew still, turned, and walked out the door. In a moment, we could hear the powerful *thump, thump, thump* of the punching bag.

There I was, sleeping in a hospital bed. No, not sleeping. I hadn't known about the machines. I remembered feeling the tube in my barely conscience state. I could feel the smooth roundness. I saw in the picture that the one comforting tube I felt beneath my fingers an age ago was just one of many.

The pictures progressed. Me awake. Me talking. Me smiling, with tousled hair in my eyes. Me walking just a few steps. How weak I'd been. Kelly watched for a few more pages over my shoulder, and then followed Rusty out. A friend in need was out there.

Mom had written my sister letters about it all and Jesse had printed out portions of them as captions and titles to the pages. Since it was the only thing she knew, she decorated all the pages with a cowboy theme using rope borders, little saddle stickers and horses with fences and barns. It was a beautiful work of art, telling a story and it hit home. I didn't know if I could open it again, but I was grateful for the thought and work that went into it. I thanked my sister with a heavy heart.

"Do you think I should go out there?" I asked.

"Not yet. I bet Kelly will help more than you could. He'll be back when he's come to grips with it."

"Kelly didn't know much about what happened. He was still in the hospital."

"He's married, though. He knows what he would feel like if that were his wife. He's good for Rusty."

Chapter 14

My father called me into his office. Being called into his office was never a good thing. If he just wanted to talk or if he was in a good mood, he would find me and talk to me there. When he was angry or had something of a serious nature to talk about, then the dreaded call to the office would happen. Just like in school, it was like being sent to my doom. I never meant to land in the principal's office but I tended to get carried away. At school when I was called in, it had never been for intentionally breaking the rules or being unkind to people. I'd just lose focus and before I realized it I'd be way out of bounds. One time a dogfight started on the playground before school began. At first recess I happened on some tracks which led to the scene of a fight. I became so engrossed with the trail and finding out the end of the story that I followed the dog's tracks off campus and down the road. I was at some lady's house with a picket fence watching a husky dog nurse a cut on his leg when it dawned on me that I was supposed to be at school. I hurried back, but recess had ended. When I walked into class I was handed the little yellow slip of paper that spelled DOOM.

It was always things like that that landed me in trouble at school, and I suppose in a way that's exactly what happened this time, too. I walked into my dad's office and sat down in *the chair*. He walked around calmly then sat behind his desk; that big, wide desk that seemed like a gulf between us. I knew the cues by now. The distance meant stress. As the issue was resolved, the further he'd ventured from behind the desk.

"Cassidy," he began, "I want to know what the hell you were doing out and about in the middle of the night. What made you go down to the barn of all places, and why at that time? That situation could have turned very ugly. You could have been killed."

"Dad, I know it looks bad from your point of view. But I was really only doing what I had to do. I couldn't sleep. I went out to the gazebo to get some fresh air and when the car came in with its lights off, I knew it was up to no good. If I'd have waked you or Rusty to come help me, he'd have been long gone and we would never have known about the barn door. I ran in here and grabbed the only weapon I could lay my hands on quickly."

"Why didn't you wake the boys? Steve and Randy have been through training specifically to protect the people of this ranch. They are all armed."

"That's the point. If I had rushed into the bunkhouse, I'd have gotten shot. Daddy, with all the things that have been happening around here, everybody's on pins and needles. This office and that rifle were my only options at the time."

"Maybe you should tell me about some of these things that have been happening."

So I told him about how the accidents I'd been having were a little more planned than how they may have appeared to him. He looked stunned, not only that they had occurred, but that all this had happened without his knowledge.

"You mean there's some kook out there taking pot shots at you?"

"Yeah, I guess you could put it that way. Dad, if I was armed I would have had that guy at the barn, but I grabbed your rifle and there was only one bullet in it. If you have guns around this place, we have to be able to trust them! I fired the one bullet to call help and I was going to use the next one to hold him there, but there wasn't a next one. Then, when he bolted, I knew people were coming so I tackled him. I wasn't going to let him get away. I did the best I could and if I hadn't done what I did, then somebody would have gotten hurt a lot worse. Issue me a pistol and I'll wear it out and about. I won't wear it indoors. I know how Mom feels about that. I just feel like I need some insurance when I'm outdoors and away from the ranch."

It was a long speech and it was borderline treason to stand up to my dad, but I thought my points were valid.

He sighed, ran his fingers through his hair and I knew we were closer to a truce. He didn't allow himself any signs of backing down unless he was really willing to do just that. It was time to put in a word for the guys.

"Daddy, you can't blame the guys for not telling you about these things. When they happened, it took a while to make the connections. They all thought I was just living up to my old name. It wasn't until I pried the bullet out of the barn rafter that Steve knew anything was happening. When Shasta bolted, everything happened too fast. Everybody just jumped on horses to try and stop Shasta. Everybody's looking out for me and the shots just got lost in the background of all the activity."

He stood, an indication that the discussion was concluding.

"Take this rifle," he said handing it over to me. "Clean all the dirt out of it. Fix it up good as new. Put bullets in it and lock it in my gun cabinet. Then go talk to Steve and we'll see about getting you armed. You still shoot?"

"Yes. I still practice and I'm still pretty good."

"Okay, get outa here." It was said in a friendly tone, so I knew I was in the clear. It was best to leave him thinking justice had prevailed. He'd done the right thing. That was important to him, and a hug or a handshake would have lessened that feeling for him. He was a take-charge kind of guy, and that didn't include hugs. I walked out of his office with the rifle over my shoulder. Rusty was waiting outside the door. As I came out, he went in. I almost stopped him, but he had to learn just what kind of a guy he was dealing with.

I walked down to the barn office. I checked and made sure the rifle wasn't loaded. I would really kick myself if I'd have found a bullet in there but I hadn't. I inspected the bore and went through all the working parts of the rifle, making sure they moved correctly and seemed to be in good shape. I put solvent on a brush and ran it through the bore to remove any rust or grime that might have accumulated. I ran a dry patch through and checked it for rust or lead deposits.

Rusty found me in the office and watched as I worked.

"You've done this before."

"Since I was twelve. I used to take rifles out rabbit hunting when I was young. At first I shot the rabbits, but then as I became more adept in the woods I quit and began snaring them. It was more of a challenge, and I could track the rabbits at the same time, so it had a double bonus for me. My mom didn't like to see me come home with rabbits because she hated cooking them."

The patch had rust on it so I ran the brush through it again. Dad always made his employees meticulously clean their firearms but it didn't look like he was as conscientious himself. Cleaning the rifle to Dad's specifications was tedious, but I had tossed it carelessly into the corral and I needed to know it was truly clean. Rusty watched as I disassembled the gun and cleaned all the parts with solvent and brushes and cloths.

"What happened when you talked to Dad?" I asked him. I couldn't help it. I had to know if DOOM really hit if you just walked through that door.

"Nothing. We talked. I told him you were right, that you needed to be able to protect yourself. And I told him he was right in what he was doing around the ranch. I urged him to hire a security guard at night or someone to check cars as they enter through the gate. We talked about the problem of shots coming from the hills. As long as you leave him thinking he's still in charge, he's really a nice guy."

"You learn fast. It took me years to figure that out."

"Maybe it's a guy thing."

I reassembled all the parts, checked the action, and visually inspected the bore one more time. I thought this little exercise was good for Rusty to see, too. He should know I didn't take these things lightly, that I was capable and knowledgeable about something besides following people around in the hills. I loaded the gun and took it back to my father's office and locked it away like he had asked. I didn't need to show it to him, knowing he would check it when I was not looking. He would inspect the gun, and if I wasn't called back to the office it was his sign of a job well done.

"Let's see about those papers you brought up here." I was anxious to see them. I'd been sorry I left behind the ones I'd taken from the cabins. Rusty went up to his room and came down with a folder. Kelly joined us and we spread out several pages.

"This one we figured out from past experience."

He handed me a sheet of paper. The lines were labeled AF then a number that looked like a date and then letters like LBM and SMP and SW. This page made sense, especially after running into Raphael at Santa Monica Pier. AF was Angeles Forest. LBM was probably Long Beach Marina. SW was Stearns Wharf. Others I had to guess at. DT might have meant downtown. It was always DT and then a letter that stood for a city name. I was guessing DTP was downtown Pasadena because Pasadena had a busy downtown area full of young people just like Santa Monica Pier. All the places that I could connect to the abbreviations were busy, touristy places where a hand-off would go unnoticed.

Rusty handed me a new page. These lines all started with NWR. The destinations were places like DTPR, DTAT, DTSLO, DTMB, DTCBS, and CRMNT.

Still another page had the abbreviation AC followed by dates and the destinations of FW, DTSAC, DTSJ, and DTOK.

All the starting places were AF, NWR or AC. Those were the ones to focus on. Those were where Peccati could be found. All the others were hand-off spots. But if we could identify the hand-off spots, they could point to a nearby central location.

The AF abbreviation stood for a broad area, so I assumed the other ones would only identify an area, and not a specific place. The one abbreviation that jumped out at me first was SLO – San Luis Obispo. Many people up here just called it SLO. It didn't quite fit the profile of the L.A. hand-off spots, but this part of the country was not L.A. If we assumed SLO was San Luis Obispo, then it wasn't too far a stretch to say PR was Paso Robles, AT was Atascadero and MB would be Morro Bay. But what was NWR? The first thing that sprang to mind was North West Railroad, but I knew that couldn't be it.

With these few clues, I thought it was time to get out a map. I went to the office. "Knock, knock," I said quietly. "Can I ask a question?" It was never a good idea to go barging into Dad's office. He motioned me in. "Do you still have that big map of California with all the tiny towns on it? And can we use it for a little while?"

He went over to a bookcase where there was a section of maps. He took out several and handed them to me.

"What are you doing?"

"We're trying to crack Rusty's case and there's a bunch of abbreviations of places, so we are trying to match them up with real places."

He followed me out. No big surprise. He loved maps and puzzles.

I spread out the map. "Okay, here's Paso Robles, Atascadero and San Luis Obispo. Morro Bay is over here on the coast. So the other two will also be within a couple hours drive of NWR."

I was beginning to think this map had too many little bitty towns. It had a dot for every farmhouse, it seemed. I looked for one that said Gordon Ranch, but apparently each dot represented a population of more than 10. I followed the likely routes out of the known area. Highway 101 led to Soledad and Salinas. But Highway 1 led to Monterey and Carmel-by-the-Sea.

"That's it!" I exclaimed pointing. "MNT is Monterey and CBS is Carmel by the Sea. The CR next to MNT is Cannery Row. That's a big area, though. It doesn't seem like it would be worth all the travel to take drugs to these little peaceful communities."

"Have you priced drugs recently?" Rusty asked.

"Well, no, of course not."

"It's worth it."

"But it seems like the San Francisco area would be the place to focus. There's thousands of drop-off areas within the city."

"Maybe Peccati likes his mountaintop getaways. Now where is NWR?"

I drew a circle around the identified areas with Monterey to the north and San Luis Obispo to the south. It was somewhere in that circle. And so were we.

Everyone was sitting there mulling it over when Dad, barely audible said, "I got it. It's Nit Wit Ridge."

I gasped. He was right. Nit Wit Ridge was in the circle and the small mountain community fit the type of place Peccati would pick.

"Let's take a drive over to Cambria."

Rusty, Kelly and I piled into the Explorer. The drive was easy and pleasant through rolling hills. The oak trees gave way to pine, and things felt more foresty as we neared the town. Cambria was nestled in the hills along Highway 1 overlooking the Pacific Ocean. I was wishing we were here just for the fun of it, but we had work to do. We drove the narrow winding streets of Cambria looking for a silver Mercedes SUV. It's funny how you don't notice something until you look for it. Suddenly, it seemed like I saw a Mercedes on every street corner. The fact that this area of California was expensive to live in had something to do with it. Still, the silver SUV was nowhere to be seen. I pointed out Nit Wit Ridge to Rusty and Kelly, explaining how it was a historical landmark built from junk and local materials. We noted the abalone dotting the walls and pillars of the old house. It stood out from the other homes like a creaky old man in a beauty pageant. We didn't have time to take a tour, but I'd often wondered what the inside was like.

Since Rusty was the detective here, I let him do what he did best. We stopped by the police station and he went in to update the authorities on Peccati's latest activities, and then came out with a picture. I was the only one who had seen him up close and in good light. I was glad to have something to show everybody back home so they would know who to watch for. As busy as the ranch was, Mario Peccati could drive right in and act interested in a horse and everybody would talk to him.

We ate dinner at a little café that looked as if locals dined there. Many of the restaurants catered to tourists, but we wanted to get a feel for the locals. Kelly helped. It seems you can't go anywhere wearing a cast without telling the story of how you got it.

"Wow. What happened to you?" Exclaimed our waitress.

"Slight accident," Kelly said. "I'm lookin' for the guy who broke my paw. He drives a silver SUV, lives around here."

"There's a lot of SUVs around here and a lot of silver cars, but I can't recall a silver SUV. Course I'm not much of a car person."

Rusty showed her the picture. "The guy looks like this."

"We see all kinds in here. People drive up and down Highway 1 from all over the world, and many of them stop here. Unless he is a year round resident I don't know him."

Rusty circled the cell phone number on his card and handed it to her.

"If you happen to see him would you give me a call?"

We all ordered. I was feeling adventurous and ordered something I'd never heard of. Rusty ordered a smothered steak and Kelly ordered shrimp kabobs. The less sawing he had to do, the better.

"You know, this guy's house could be as remote here as it was back home." I said.

"I don't think so, though. Not if he's driving a Mercedes in and out of it."

"They switched over to cars for their deliveries in the L.A. area."

"How did you know that?"

"Actually, I didn't. I just assumed it since they couldn't ride dirt bikes into L.A. without getting pulled over. It doesn't take long to get pulled over riding a dirt bike on the street. I was very happy to find that out."

"By the way," Rusty said, "do you know why I wouldn't follow Raphael when we saw him in Santa Monica?"

"No, I just assumed it was to keep me out of trouble."

"That, and I didn't want your car to become marked. If they figured out we were following them in a blue BMW Roadster, you would have been marked for elimination until you got rid of the car."

Kelly looked at me like I'd been holding out on him. I laughed, "You can drive it when you get your casts off."

Kelly said to Rusty, "You're not ready to go back tomorrow, are you?"

The waitress brought our food.

"What's that?" they both asked when my plate was set in front of me.

"I don't know. But I'm going to find out," I answered taking a bite. It was delicious. The wine and cream sauce almost covered a seafoody flavor, but I couldn't quite figure out what it was.

"Don't eat like that when you're camping," Kelly quipped.

By the end of the meal, I still didn't know what it was.

"Well, we didn't accomplish much on this little trip." I said dejectedly.

"We did more than you think. This is a small town. Word will get around. People will talk. If it gets around too much, Peccati will catch it and that will make him nervous. Hopefully he'll do something stupid and draw attention to himself."

When we got back to the ranch Steve approached me and asked me to come down to the office in the barn. He took out a variety of handguns and I tried them for a good fit. They were all too big for my hands, but I chose one that I could work with. We loaded it, flipped the safety on and found the holster for it. I strapped it on and went up to the house. My mom looked at me with disapproval when I came in the door. She would talk to my father and it would all be settled behind my back. I would try to be careful not to remind mom about the gun, and we'd all be fine.

Rusty and Kelly disappeared to discuss their plans for the next day. Would they stay another day? I doubted Peccati would be caught in a day or two. This was going to take some detective work. But that's what Rusty did, right? So maybe he'd stay. Kelly couldn't stay indefinitely, although both men were welcome. The rooms were available and Martha always cooked too much anyway. The extra security was welcomed by everyone except Randy, who adopted a sullen attitude when Rusty was around.

It had been a long and wonderfully uneventful day. Walking down to the barn to check in on Shasta I was thinking I could use more days like this one. I said "Hi" to Buck and thanked him for being easy on Rusty. I've always talked to the horses. I didn't care if they understood or not. They seemed to appreciate hearing a kind voice. I climbed up on Shasta's back and laid my head on his strong neck. It brought back memories of lazy summer days when we would ride bareback through the oaks, just rambling, enjoying the day and finding critters to stalk. He was a good horse.

The barn door creaked and I tensed. I slid behind Shasta's back, keeping the big horse between the door and myself. I sensed movement, slid into the next stall and then out of the barn through Buck's open stall door. It opened into a little paddock. I kept to the fence, stalking around to the front of the barn again where I could get a good look at whoever had entered.

"Cass?" he called. It was Rusty. A wave of relief flooded through me. I holstered my gun, unaware that I had even drawn it. He heard the gun settle in the holster and spun around.

"Don't sneak up on me like that," I said.

"How'd you get over there? I just saw you with Shasta when I walked in."

"You startled me, so I snuck around where I had a better vantage point."

"I'm glad to see you're so vigilant."

We walked up to the house to sit in the gazebo. I was waiting for the bomb to fall but we just sat for a long time.

"It's so peaceful when you're here." I said "I didn't even have one catastrophe today. Did you know the guys have an ongoing bet on how long it will be until I need another icepack?"

"I talked to Schroeder and Kelly. I'm going to take Kelly home tomorrow, tie up some loose ends, and come back. Kelly's willing to stay if I do, but there are some things back home that I need in order to work up here, so I might as well take him home. I talked to your dad and he's okay with it."

I sighed. "Okay, how long will you be gone?"

"A day or two. It depends on how much has gotten done while I was away."

"Can you pick up something at my house on the way back? It's a manila envelope on the dining room table. It has some papers in it that I took from the cabins when I was there. They may have some clues on them that weren't in the notebooks you found."

"Sure. Anything else you need?"

I thought. Oh, shoot! My bills. I had completely forgotten about my bills.

"Can you collect my mail and bring the envelopes from the basket on my breakfast bar? I completely forgot about my bills."

"Okay."

"I wish I could go with you but I can't leave everybody up here in this mess I've created."

"Hey, look at me," he said sternly. "None of this is your fault. You can't blame yourself for the actions of others."

"I know, but if I weren't here, then everything would be fine. There wouldn't be a lunatic out in the hills shooting at the ranch. But since there is, I feel like I should stay and see this through. If I go home, Peccati won't know I've gone. He'll still be out there looking for ways to provoke me. I don't think I should leave."

"Don't let him provoke you. It gives him an edge."

"He's going to be real mad after his failed barn bomb attempt."

"Don't give him any chances. The reason things are quiet when I'm here is because *you* are quiet when I'm here. You don't do as much to attract his attention. That's why he tried the barn stunt."

A shadowy figure crossed the driveway walking towards the barns.

"Who's that?"

"Desmond Carr. Your dad hired him as night security. I talked to him. I showed him Peccati's picture and gave him a description of the SUV. He's on top of things. He'll be here from 8:00 p.m. to 8:00 a.m., and I think he'll do a good job."

"My dad really likes you if he's willing to take your advice. Most people know better than to try and advise him on anything. He likes to take credit for everything. I was even surprised that he thanked you at dinner for saving me from the fire. Did you know that was the first time I ever heard him call me his daughter?"

"Really? Well, I can tell you are his daughter. He doesn't have to tell me that."

"Dad never wanted kids. If he had kids, he wanted boys. Boys could grow up and run this ranch. I was first, so I was the son he never had. I loved learning all the things a boy would know. I went hunting with the guys, learned all I could about training horses, fighting and guns. I took to it. Maybe it's in my blood. I don't really know how tracking came to fascinate me. I only know it came naturally, and that I had all the right people around me to encourage it. It just felt like what I was born to do. So I was my dad's son and Jesse was allowed to be his daughter. She really does make a better daughter."

"I have to disagree. You make the perfect daughter."

After almost no sleep in the past two days, I dropped off into a deep and dreamless sleep. When I woke to light streaming in my window I was worried that I'd slept the morning away. However after I'd showered and dressed I came out to a peaceful and quiet start to the day. Work starts early on a ranch. I found Martha busy in the kitchen preparing a huge breakfast. I grabbed a quick bite and headed for the barn.

In the barn I found the tack I needed and put a saddle on Shasta. I wasn't going pleasure riding this time. I wanted to run, so I chose a racing saddle. I cinched it up and bridled him. As far as quarter horses go, Shasta wasn't very fast, but he was plenty of horse for me. I walked him down to the track talking to him on the way, psyching him up for a run. I don't know if it worked for Shasta, but it worked for me. I was ready. Shasta was always up for a good run. He liked to stretch out but I didn't let him do it very often.

It was a cool, pleasant morning with mist hanging over the hills. We worked our way up through the gaits to warm up, then I put my heels to him, leaned forward and he took off. I loved to feel the power beneath me in a good run. The wind whipped my hair around while Shasta eased into a steady gallop. I let him choose the part of the track he wanted so his footing would be sure. I might prefer the deep loose sand of the track for training, but this wasn't training. This was just for fun. I gave him more encouragement and could feel his muscles tensing and reaching beneath me. Oh, this was glorious. I listened to his breathing to be sure he wasn't being pushed too hard. After a little while I pulled gently on the reins, letting him know he could slow down. Still nervous about hurting his mouth, I didn't want to rein him in. I gave him a cue then waited until he was ready to obey. As we slowed down, I noticed people along the rail. The ranch was awake.

I walked Shasta to slowly cool him down then took him to the barn. After wiping him down and brushing him until he was dry again, I took the bridle off and hung it on a peg, then hurried back to the house to see who was up for breakfast.

I sat down at the big table and listened to the conversation flow. Most of it centered on the horses and the day's activities.

"What are you up to today?" somebody asked me.

"It depends on when Rusty and Kelly are taking off. If I have time this afternoon, I was going to see if I could take the truck to the lumberyard. I think I need a project to keep me busy for a few days."

This little announcement turned a few heads. "What is Trouble up to next?" they all seemed to be thinking. I had my eye on a tree next to Jesse's house and I thought her boys could use a tree house. If they didn't want a tree house, then maybe I'd build a playhouse. Well, not a playhouse, for boys it would be a fort or a cabin or a hideout. At any rate, I had in mind to build something.

"Do you know how to build a tree house?" my mom asked.

"A simple one. I imagine it's about the same as building agility equipment. If I had to build a roof that would be another matter, but who says a tree house has to have a roof? An attractive looking box up in a tree ought to be enough to keep two boys busy."

"Okay, boys, what do you think?" Zack said. "Head or hands first?" Oh no, the old icepack bet. The conversation changed to all the ways they thought I could hurt myself building a tree house.

"First time she tries to put the floor in, wham! It'll dump her out of the tree."

"Or fall on her head."

"I'm glad to see you have so much faith in me." I said sarcastically.

"Aw, Cass, it's not that we think you can't do it. We know you can. It just might be a learning experience for you."

"And who said learning is a bad thing?"

Rusty entered the room. "I'll take you to the lumberyard this morning and then Kelly and I will take off."

"Are you sure that's how you want to spend your morning?"

"Why not? At least we will be doing something."

"Okay."

"You're only eating toast for breakfast?" my mom asked.

"This is my second breakfast. I've been up a while. I took Shasta for a run this morning."

We gathered downstairs for the trip to the lumberyard. We took the pickup since it was wider and more beat up than Rusty's Explorer. Kelly sat sideways on the backseat of the double crew cab.

As we walked around the lumberyard and I chose the plywood, Rusty suddenly asked, "You weren't really going to do all this by yourself were you?"

"Sure, I don't mind doing it myself. You're lucky you're not Randy or Zack or you'd find yourself out in the truck just for thinking I needed help."

Kelly laughed.

I chose plywood, two-by-fours, nails, screws and brackets then went back for a couple of two-by-twos. I held the nails and screws up to the two-by-fours to make sure they were long enough. Since I was there I also bought about twenty feet of thick cotton rope to hang off the side of the tree house. I had the lumberyard cut some of the plywood into three-foot sections for the walls. I left the floor a full sheet.

"I'm glad you found something to do while I'm gone." Rusty said. "I'll feel better knowing you are working on this instead of riding the hills."

"Is this your substitute punching bag, Cass?" quipped Kelly. "Hitting nails?"

"I like to work with my hands. I was building something at home when Rusty called me to look for you."

We drove home and Jesse came out to see what the racket was as we stacked the lumber next to her house.

"Mom says you are building the boys a tree house?"

"If you don't mind. I thought if you didn't want a tree house then the boys might like a hideout, but I've never built a roof before so the tree house idea seemed more doable."

"Sounds good to me."

"You'll have to pick out paint. I didn't know what color to buy."

Goodbyes are never easy for me, and were especially awkward with Rusty. Saying goodbye was like watching a part of me leave, but when he returned I would feel whole and warm, yet guilty for having felt that way. It would help if we knew where we stood with each other, but neither of us was sure. I felt an emerging bond growing between us, but what that bond consisted of was a completely different story. Why a guy like him wasn't already attached was a mystery to me. It made me wonder if he had some deep dark secret. I knew he wasn't gay. He'd made that perfectly clear and I sensed he was interested in me. But why? And how long would he wait for me to be guilt-free? I didn't encourage or discourage him. I thought in time we would find our way, but was that stringing him along? Was I being unfair to him? This is why goodbyes were rather awkward, and our goodbye that day was no exception. It left me feeling bummed out and needing to work it off.

Chapter 15

One good thing about living on a ranch is that you always have a multitude of tools available. I dragged three ladders down to the tree and set them in the spaces between three strong branches which would support the tree house. I propped a ladder at an angle and draped a packing blanket over it to make a skid. Working alone, I needed all the help I could get to move the bulky plywood into position. I pushed the heavy sheet of plywood up the skid and into the crook of the tree. I set a corner of the sheet into a rung on a ladder and moved each corner up or down, one rung at a time, until it stood in a spot that looked good and sturdy. Then I drew notches in the plywood where the branches would be and hauled it down. Using a jigsaw I cut notches smaller than needed and hauled the sheet back up, settling the sheet into the tree with the branches fitted into the notches. This was the tedious part of the whole process. It took four trips up and down the tree with that plywood before I was satisfied with the fit. Once the floor had been set for the last time with a solid hold on the tree, I cut small two-by-two pieces of board and secured them to the tree underneath the notches. Trees move and although this was a large, slow growing tree I knew I had to allow for some movement due to the wind and gradual growth. Once the floor was secure I climbed up on it and jumped around. It didn't budge, and not even Randy and Zack jumping on the floor were able to jar it loose. They all shook their heads in wonder that I accomplished so much. So far so good, and no icepacks were needed.

I continued my work the next day. Framing the walls was easy. It was just like building the A-frame of my agility course. I kept the old motto of measure twice, cut once, in mind. The hard part of the walls was the sawing, but I chose to do that by hand instead of hauling all the boards over to the power saw in the shed. I wasn't rope climbing any more so I thought the sawing would be a good substitute. Patrick came out and asked to help saw the wood. I let him have a try but he almost bent the saw when it jammed in a tight spot. I showed him how to move the saw smoothly and consistently through the wood. After I framed the walls, I brought up the four-by-three-foot panels and marked them for cutting. I eventually gave up trying to cut the panels by hand and took them over to the power saw, measuring all the outside panels and cutting them in one trip.

Jesse came out of the house and said she was going to town.

"Are you going to the hardware store?" I asked. "You can pick out paint if you want. Just make sure it is outdoor and weather resistant."

"Okay, I'll get some while I am down there. I don't like to go to town too often, so I do all my shopping at once. Are you going to put a rail around the top? I think it would look more finished that way."

"I don't have the wood for it, but if you get some I'll add it. The walls are almost six inches wide, so you will need to get about twenty-four feet of board at least six inches wide. If it's a few feet short it won't hurt, because I don't need it across the doorway. I'll pay you back when you get home."

She piled the kids into the big ranch truck and took off.

I nailed the panels to the outside of the walls and then stood up to stretch. Hearing the sound of wheels crunch on gravel, I turned around. The silver SUV was barreling down the drive. There were two loud *pops* followed by two hollow *thuds* as a pair of bullets ripped through wood. I dropped to the floor of the tree house, thinking this had better be another cruel joke because I was a sitting duck up there. Gravel crunched again and I peeked over the rail in time to see the SUV tear out onto the road and disappear.

I heard footsteps as several of the men ran towards me. Someone peeked into the doorway of the tree house. It was Randy.

"He's gone Cass. You okay?"

"Yeah, I'm just peachy," I said angrily. I jumped down and looked at the damage. At least the bullets had gone in fairly clean. I could fill the holes with putty and paint over them or Patrick could have quite a conversation piece. I decided a true hideout in a tree could use a few bullet holes.

The guys dispersed, except for Steve. I paced back and forth like a caged lion ready for some action, but the SUV was long gone.

I called Jesse on her cell phone.

"Hello?"

"Hi, Jess. Can you pick up a small can of dark brown paint too? The tree house just took a couple of shots and I thought I'd make them look like they are supposed to be there."

"Are you okay?"

"If I was not okay, do you think I'd be calling you about paint?"

"Good point. Maybe you should call it a day."

"He's gone now so I'll get as much done as I can. I doubt you'll have to worry about the boys playing up here since this guy seems to be after me."

The inside panels of the walls were a bit tougher to fit because they were smaller than the outside ones. I measured and drew lines on the panels and measured again. I was getting low on wood now, so I didn't want to mess up. I took the panels to the shed and made the two cuts to each panel so they would fit the walls. Then I cut two small triangles to use as corner shelves in the tree house. Nailing and fitting all the pieces together like a puzzle, I finished the basic construction.

Later that evening when Jesse came home I measured and cut the boards she'd bought for railings. It was nice wood and I didn't want to paint over it. Maybe it would be better varnished. I was sure there was enough varnish around the ranch to do one railing. I tried to pay her for the paint and the boards but she refused, saying that I was putting in the work and the least she could do was chip in a little paint and wood.

Patrick came in carrying a rock in his hand and handed it to his mother.

"What have you got there, Pat?" she asked.

"I think it's a secret message. I found it under a bush in the yard."

He was right. It *was* a secret message with a note attached. Jesse untied it and read the note.

"I think it's for you," she said handing the note to me.

I opened it, pressing out the wrinkles and read, "Don't be a target. You make this too easy." Turning the note over, I saw there was also faint writing on the back. It was written in pencil, long smudged and dirty. It appeared as if he'd written the note to me an on an old piece of paper that had been floating around his office or car. The writing on the back said, "Meeting Friday @ 2 Tony M." Whatever the meeting was, it had already happened weeks ago. The name Tony M. bugged me because it was familiar and should mean something. Where had I met a Tony M.? I stuffed the note in my pocket and mulled it over.

In the morning I got up early because I wanted to finish the tree house. I ran down the road to Jesse's house with plans to lightly sand and varnished the rail. Afterwards I sanded, dusted and painted the main part of the tree house. Jesse had chosen a colonial blue paint which matched the trim on her own home. I switched back and forth between the rail varnishing and the painting until each shone with fresh coats and had no bare spots. I nailed a ladder together from the remaining two-by-fours and painted it to match.

I went back to the house to get something to eat and left everything to dry. The name Tony M. refused to leave my mind. I knew that name from somewhere.

I was sitting in the kitchen eating lunch and willing the paint to dry when a group of the guys walked in talking about the ranch.

"Did you look at the shoes on Mac and Chet?" one of them asked.

"I looked at them. I'll get the farrier out to take care of it. You know how Chet is about his feet."

"He needs work to do. We got too many horses and too little work for them around here."

Their discussion went on like that but I didn't pay much attention. I cleaned up my lunch and wiped down the counter, then wandered back to Jesse's house. I checked the paint on the ladder and it was dry, so I climbed up to check the paint on the tree house. It was almost dry. I slid down the rope and realized the varnish on the rail was still a little bit tacky. I didn't have all day because Rusty could be back at any time, and I had hoped the tree house would be finished by then. I used dark brown paint inside the bullet holes and made little splintery-looking lines around the outside. I wondered if I was tampering with a crime scene but decided the tree house shooting was small change compared to everything else that had happened.

Tired of waiting for the paint to dry, I went down to the shed and dragged out a ladder. Who said you had to stand in a tree house to put rails on it? I'd just do it from the outside.

I stood the ladder next to the shortest side so I could handle the easy pieces first and then the bigger pieces would be drier when I got to them. I chose a rail and carried it up the ladder and laid it on top of the wall. I borrowed the cordless drill and drilled a hole through the rail and into the wood below. I bolted the rail down securely and looked at the color combination. Colonial blue, deep reddish brown grain, the colors reminded me of fancy sailboats. A nautical, western tree house. Oh, well. I continued working my way around the tree house, fitting, drilling and bolting down the rails. When at last it was finished, I stood back and looked at it from a distance. "Not bad," I thought. "That oughta show the guys a thing or two. Maybe we should break a bottle of champagne on the bow and christen her."

I gathered all the tools and returned them to their various offices and sheds. I put the sawhorses away and stacked the useable wood in an on-going pile behind the barn. All the while, the name Tony M. jangled around in my head. Tony M. Mac and Chet. Needing shoes. Tony Mac. That's it! I hadn't met Tony M. He was the new neighbor down the road. Tony Macaluso. Of course, there could be a hundred Tony M.s in the area, but this was a start. Maybe it was about time I met this new neighbor. Maybe I should ride down the road and introduce myself, and see if Tony had seen any silver SUVs on his road.

I checked my handgun to make certain that I would be ready in case things took a turn for the worse. Then I saddled up Shasta and rode out towards the back of the ranch. Within minutes Randy was beside me. We rode silently. I knew he had to be there and he knew I only accepted it. I put Shasta into a lope and headed for the deer flats. When I got there I didn't see deer, which is just as well because I wasn't stopping to stalk them today. I cut into the hills and continued west until I hit the road. It was a dry and dusty road that day, and little puff clouds drifted up with each of Shasta's steps. We slowed, giving the horses a chance to cool down.

"Cass, where are we going?" Randy asked.

I glanced over, relieved to note that he too was armed. "I just want to see what's down this road. And I haven't met the new neighbors, so I thought I'd stop by and introduce myself. It's been so long since I've explored the area that I thought I'd see what's back here. I also got a clue about Peccati and it mentioned a Tony M. I thought I'd go meet Tony Macaluso, just for a friendly chat, and see if there might be a link."

If I remembered correctly, the house was about three miles down this road. If Randy had meant three miles from the ranch, we didn't have far to go.

It was a pleasant day to ride. The sun was warm and the road was open. A steady trot brought us to a turn-off lined with palm trees and hedges. White board fences lined the road which led to a Tuscan-styled villa, appropriate for a future vineyard. The grounds were unfinished, and it was obvious the house was not entirely completed, but would be impressive when the work was done. We rode back and forth in front of the house and I noticed a drive circling around back. We followed it until we came to a short handsome man dressed in carpenter's pants and a sweat stained t-shirt. He was well-muscled and tanned from working in the sun. His hair was receding, but his eyes gave him an instantly friendly look.

"Hello!" I said in greeting. "I'm looking for Tony Macaluso."

"You've found him," he replied. "Hi, Randy!"

I dismounted and walked forward, extending my hand. "I'm Cassidy Callahan, Wayne Gordon's daughter. I heard we had neighbors back here and thought I'd come introduce myself."

"It's good to meet you, Cassidy," he said, shaking my hand. Glancing at my holstered gun, a slight smile appeared and he continued, "Do you always come to meet new neighbors armed?" He didn't say it in an accusing way, simply an observation.

"We've had a little trouble at the ranch. Someone has been taking pot shots at me from the road and nearby hills. I feel safer this way, but I have no intention of using it."

"What are you doing out and about then?"

"I was wondering if you were having similar problems out here, or if I am just a magnet for trouble."

"You're a magnet for trouble," Randy said. Macaluso ignored him, not yet knowing how true that was.

"It's been nice and quiet out here. I've just been landscaping and the builders are close to completion on the exterior of the house. My wife has been choosing carpet, tile and appliances. We hope to be moved in by the end of summer."

"Have you seen a silver Mercedes SUV going in and out of here?"

"I've noticed silver SUVs in the past, but I didn't think anything of it. Anyone who can afford to build back here can afford whatever car they want. As to how far the road goes, it winds around forever back there. It could go all the way to Cambria or Paso Robles, for all I know. I only use the part that goes behind your dad's ranch."

"Do you know any of your other neighbors? I know everybody's pretty spaced out, but I thought you might have met some of them. How long have you been working on this place?"

"We bought the land three years ago, but you know how it is, building from nothing. There was so much red tape to wade through that we've only really been out here a year. We started out in a motor home but the wife couldn't stand it. She needs more space and a few luxuries the motor home couldn't provide. As far as the neighbors go, there's a guy a few miles down with a place on a lake. Beautiful house. If I'd seen his house first, I might have gone for the same look. He's got a small herd of elk up there, too. Seems California is the place to raise weird critters. Llamas are real popular. Down south a ways I heard there's an ostrich farm. I think I'll stick to grapes. No mucking about or weird diets with grapes."

"Is your wife home? I'd like to meet her too."

"No, she's in town talking to interior decorators. She doesn't come out here much because the house isn't very livable yet. She's here for a few hours, about once a week, to take pictures of the progress."

"It's going to be beautiful when you're finished with it. I'm sure you'll love living back here. Well, I should be going. I don't want to be gone too long. It was nice meeting you."

"Likewise."

I hopped into the saddle, turned Shasta and trotted off down the road. I had picked up on two things in that conversation. One was that Tony had seen a silver SUV, and the other was that this road still held many secrets. All the way to Cambria? I'd have to take a drive down this road and see just what was down here. For now, I had to be content with the little bit of knowledge I'd gained.

I was enjoying the ride. When we got to the end of Tony Macaluso's driveway we continued on down the road. I put my heels to Shasta and he went into a trot, and then into a lope. I still had a little time before we'd have to head back. I didn't expect to learn anything, but the day was pleasant and it was good to just be out riding. We came to a corrugated metal garage and I pulled up. It stood alone and nobody was nearby, so I circled the building. Standing on tiptoes I looked through the small window set in a door. Hard packed earth and cement yielded little information. No vehicles were inside, just a garage with a few automotive tools hung on one wall. I mounted up and we continued. The road wound through grass covered hills and old oak trees. It was pretty country, but it wasn't revealing much to me in the way of information so we turned around to go back.

We had passed the Macaluso place and were halfway back to the ranch when, up ahead, I noticed a dust cloud rising from the road. We scooted over to one side so the car could pass, and then we rode on peacefully. As the car came closer, I was alarmed to see it was the Mercedes.

"Randy, this is bad news," I said nervously. I unclasped the strap on my holster. I couldn't talk myself into using the gun except in self-defense, yet I wondered where the line between safety and danger lay. The SUV moved to our side of the road. I changed to the other side and the SUV followed. The hill beside the road was a little steep to just charge down, but I might have no choice. If I chose that path, I would have to turn my back on Peccati. I took the gun out of the holster and kept it trained on the driver. The gap closed further. I could see Pecatti at the wheel, smiling. He was enjoying this little game of his. I was just heading down the bank, squeezing between the SUV and a tree, when Peccati gunned his engine and blared his horn. Shasta leaped to the side in surprise. He stumbled, trying to get his footing on the uneven slope and lunged for the safety of the road, crushing my knee between the saddle and Peccati's mirror. Shasta lunged ahead, the mirror dragging me from the saddle. I had to release my left foot from the stirrup or be dragged, so I let Shasta go bucking off into the distance. I rolled down the bank to put some distance between myself and Peccati. Randy's horse shied from the ruckus, putting a nice, clean horse-shoe-shaped dent in the passenger's side door and shattering the window. Randy kept to his saddle, moving with the horse like he'd been born there. I rolled to a stop and I held my gun on Peccati. I kept it trained on him as I stood shakily. He hit the gas, spinning gravel in my face as he tore off down the road. Randy took two shots at the retreating vehicle but it continued, dust flying.

Randy offered me a hand up and we took off for the ranch. We knew that when Shasta turned up without me, people would worry.

As we came within view of the ranch I figured I better take stock of the situation before going further.

"Hold up a second," I said sliding down and landing on the good leg. I found a rock and sat down to examine my leg but couldn't get the jeans over my knee because it was too swollen.

"Okay," I said climbing back up, "Drop me off at the barn."

"No," he said, "You need to get that on ice."

Just then Steve came up, concern etched on his face.

"How's Shasta?" I asked.

"Riled. He didn't want anybody near him. He's in the barn calming down."

We all stopped at the stable and dismounted. I went in and Shasta was there, still in his saddle. I started to strip off the saddle and blanket but Steve stopped me.

"I'll do it Cass, you go have that knee looked after."

"He's my horse. It was my stupid mistake that did this to him. I'll do it."

He took the saddle from me and we looked after the horses together. I knew he was just playing the big brother role and was really keeping an eye on me, but I appreciated the fact that he let me do what I thought was right, no matter how bull-headed he thought I was behaving.

The sun was setting as I limped up to the house, checking all the parking areas for the blue Explorer. I discreetly made my own icepack and then went to my room. I took off the gun and hid it away in a drawer. I stripped off my jeans. Tugging them over my swollen knee was painful but necessary because I didn't want to cut them off. I slipped on a pair of shorts and eased into bed with the icepack wrapped around my knee.

After a while my mom poked her head in. I'd missed dinner, so I kind of expected the visit. I pulled the blanket over my knee even though I was already warm.

"You've had a busy day today. You finished the tree house and the boys love it."

"That's good. I hope they didn't go up there while the paint was wet."

"Jesse checked it out first. She had to lift up Wyatt and put him up there. He can't climb the ladder yet."

"That's probably good, too. Patrick is the adventurous one. But he's smart enough to know how to play up there right. He won't fall out."

"You want to tell me about the knee?"

"Something spooked Shasta and he side-stepped me into a tree limb." I lied.

"You don't expect me to believe that, do you? It had to be more than that or you would have just ridden home. I may not know everything, but I know there is one thing that will make all the hands drop everything they are doing and rush off, and that's you. Or, to be more specific, you in trouble."

"Mom, it was nothing. When Shasta got spooked I had to bail out. It all turned out okay in the end."

"You're not telling me everything. If something simple had spooked

Shasta he would have stepped aside and waited for you. He wouldn't have taken off and left you there."

"Okay, so he was a little more spooked than usual."

"How long are you going to be laid up?"

"I'm not laid up. I'm fine."

"That's why you're sitting here on ice and hiding your leg from me."

"Have we heard from Rusty?"

"He's driving up tomorrow. He has to stop by the office, get your mail, and then he'll leave."

Chapter 16

Morning brought stiffness and pain. I showered and that helped a little. I pulled on my blue jeans and decided to wear a little tailored blouse. I then curled my hair and put on make-up, not too much. I just wanted to feel spruced up. Walking down to Jesse's house I took it as a good sign that my knee felt better for the exercise. It had sprinkled during the night and the air was clean and clear. When I arrived Patrick was playing outside, and Wyatt and Jesse were playing indoors as usual.

"Hi Pat!" I said in greeting. "What are you up to today?"

"Nothing much. Can you teach me to stalk deer?"

"Not today. You're not old enough to go out and find deer. You need to stalk something closer to home. Do you see rabbits in your yard? It's good practice to start on smaller animals. See if you can find some rabbit tracks and then follow them until you get to the rabbit. When you see where he's hiding, try and sneak up on him. Just don't leave the yard or your mom will throw a fit. I'm sure you will see rabbits in the yard, especially early in the morning and late in the afternoon."

"Here's another thing you can practice." I said showing him the rope on the tree. "When I got chased by the bear, I had to climb a long rope to get up in the tree where the bear couldn't get me. So I thought it would be a good thing if you knew how to climb a rope. That's why I put one on your tree house. You just grab the rope up high and pull with your arms and then grab it with your feet. Once you are on the rope, you push up with your feet and pull down with your arms until you get to the top. To get down, loosen your grip on the rope so you can still grab it to stop. When your grip is loose enough the gravity will pull you down. It takes a little practice but I'm sure you will learn how to do it real fast."

Jesse came out to invite me in for coffee. Sitting at the table, I added all the cream and sugar my coffee would hold. I was more of a recreational coffee drinker. I usually woke up alert and ready to start the day, so coffee was more of a beverage than a necessity. Therefore, I wanted it to taste pleasant, without the bitter wake-up-call many other people drink.

Jesse was concerned, not just about the problems facing me and the ranch right now, but rather about the big picture.

"What will you do when you go home?" she asked.

"Oh, I don't know. I'll probably go back to what I was doing before. Building obstacles, giving safety speeches at schools, look for a job."

"And what kind of a job would you look for? I can't see you selling ladies clothes or sitting at a desk. "

"I don't know, Jess. I'm just kind of floating right now."

"Because of Jack? Would you know which direction to go if he were here?"

"I haven't been sure of my direction after I left the Marines. It was almost enough just that Jack and I were together, but I still sought something."

"And what was that?"

"Usefulness. I wanted to make a difference somewhere."

"There's a lot you can do. You have many talents. You can find people. You made a big difference to Kelly and to Rusty. You can make a difference to more people, just by following your heart."

"Maybe. I just can't make a living that way."

"Maybe a living doesn't have as much to do with money for you. You're always welcome here to work on the ranch. If you give your name and number to the authorities, they could call you for rescue work and you would have a job here."

"Did Mom talk you into this?"

"No, I'm just bouncing ideas around. I want you to be happy."

"There's no way I can move up here."

"Why?"

Why? I didn't know why, or didn't want to admit it. I loved it here. I belonged here. I would be free to do as I pleased here. I wouldn't be trapped in a lonely house with only a dog. But the ranch lacked one important thing and I didn't think I could turn my back on that one thing.

"What, Cass? What is it?"

I almost couldn't say because it was so hard for me to admit this even to myself.

"I think it's Rusty."

I thanked Jesse for the coffee and left. Now she'd done it. She'd got me all discombobulated. It was a simple question. Why did it have to do this to me, on top of what I was feeling towards Peccati? I was a real mess. I walked back to the house, poked around the stables, but there wasn't anything for me to do. I wasn't going to ride Shasta today, that was obvious. He'd been through enough yesterday. There were no chores for me to do. I had a morning to kill and too many questions bouncing around in my head.

All this business with Peccati had me unnerved. Why didn't he just call it quits? He could have finished me off each time he'd fired on me. It was almost becoming routine to dodge a bullet every few days. This was getting old. Was it getting old for Peccati, too? I had a feeling the standoff would involve something of a game, too. Peccati seemed to enjoy toying with people. When he tired of it, the game would become more serious.

Remembering the search for Kelly, I decided to go into town and look at GPS systems. If it was anything like the Angeles Forest situation, I might find myself a long ways from anywhere and in need of a lift. I had a feeling Peccati wanted to see what I was really made of.

I borrowed the old pickup and drove into town. I stopped at Ron's Sporting Goods and looked at GPS systems there. They only had devices designed to tell me where I was. I wasn't interested in knowing where I was. That wasn't the problem. I needed others to be able to find me.

I noticed at Ron's, though, that when you buy GPS systems you aren't buying a gadget. You are investing in sophisticated technology. They had wrist watch systems for parents to monitor their kids. They had dash-mounted contraptions that would guide you to your destination using a computer transmitted voice. The more information it provided, the higher the price. These systems looked like they were for citified people, cautious parents, or yuppies who had to know where they could find the nearest Starbucks. It would identify a user's location by placing a dot on a small, digital, city map, but what would it do when there weren't any streets? One degree in longitude or latitude covered a lot of ground. I needed a device that would provide my location anywhere to within... hmm. I thought about that. How closely did I need my location to be identified? Judging from the terrain and openness of the woods I gave myself a hundred yards. I wanted to know where I was within a hundred yards. To my technologically limited mind that seemed possible, although I didn't need to know how it actually worked. I wanted the GPS coordinates for that location and needed them displayed in a format that Steve and Rusty could use easily. At least my trip to Ron's started me thinking, so that when I continued my shopping I had a better idea of what I actually needed.

Small towns are not a hotbed for spyware, I decided. If I wanted to have someone tracked and I didn't have a way to do it myself, what would I do? The police wouldn't help with that. Maybe a private investigator? Would a private investigator have tracking devices? Could I hire such a person just to provide information to someone who called for it? There might be lots of rich people around here who needed a little extra insurance. I looked in the phone book under private investigators. Most of the names sounded like motley PIs who chased after people's unfaithful spouses, but one of them jumped out at me: Carr's Private Investigation and Personal Security Specialists. Maybe this was the company Desmond Carr was from. I drove by their offices, which looked clean and professional. That made me wonder how much I was willing to spend for their services. The systems at Ron's ranged anywhere from ninety to six hundred dollars. Well, I decided, it couldn't hurt to ask. I was willing to fork over six hundred dollars if it would help me live to see tomorrow. I found a parking place and went in.

The receptionist was a professional looking woman in a gray skirt and crisp, white blouse. Her hair was styled to within an inch of its life and she was working steadily at a computer when I walked in. She glanced up, smiling.

"May I help you?" she inquired.

"I hope so," I replied. "I'm interested in finding a tracking system or service."

"Okay," she said. "Let me call a representative who can explain what we have available. Just have a seat and someone will be with you momentarily. What is your name?"

"Cassidy Callahan."

"Thank you."

I sat in one of the leather chairs stationed around the reception area. Clearly they didn't have many people waiting in here at any one time, but they did want their customers to wait in style. After a little while, a couple came out of a doorway and a professional looking black man followed. He was dressed in a stylish gray plaid suit, white button-down collared shirt, and a moss-green silk tie. Without acknowledging the receptionist he approached the desk, took a glance at the desktop and then approached me.

"Miss Callahan?"

"Yes," I answered.

"Please follow me."

I followed him down a hallway decorated in muted tones. It looked like a professional decorator had been called in. Berber carpets and cherry wood doors looked stylish and professional. The pictures on the walls were taken by local photographers and framed to match the doors. We turned a corner and entered his office which was decorated similarly but in a more personal way. Photos of his family were proudly displayed on his desk. His cherry wood bookcase held professional volumes scattered with worn novels and well worn binders full of people's secrets.

"My name is Rashawn Carr. Please have a seat. I understand you are interested in a tracking service?"

"Yes, or a device that can be easily used by one person to find another."

"Who is it that you wish to track, if I may ask?"

"Actually, I am the one to be tracked."

"Are you in some kind of danger?"

"May I ask you a question?"

"Certainly."

"My father hired a man for night security at the Gordon Ranch. The man I saw there was named Desmond Carr. Is he by chance associated with your company?"

"Desmond is my brother. He prefers fieldwork. I like the technical aspects," he said with a flourish of his hand. I noted the gadgetry around the office. There was a large flat screen TV on one wall complete with an attached Blu-Ray player. Speakers had been discreetly positioned around the room. Einstein would have marveled at his calculator. Teenagers would have lusted over his state-of-the-art cell phone. I bet he drove the latest model car, too. He continued, "I understand the ranch has had its share of problems lately."

"Yes," I said, "That would be me."

He looked at me quizzically and so I elaborated by telling him about the drug farm and then being stalked and finally being shot at.

"I just feel like this is all coming to a head soon and I know this guy is going to put me to a test. He knows my talent lies in tracking." This drew a surprised look. Okay, I admit I don't look like your everyday tracker, but I can't help it. "And so this little game of his could take me far a-field. I just need to be findable. The last run-in I had with these people was three miles from a remote campground. I just want a little insurance."

"I see."

"If it's a service I need, then there are three men I would like you to give my coordinates to. If it's a device, I need two receivers and a bug of some kind for me to wear. The receivers need to be portable and easily used in the field."

"I see you have thought this out a little bit."

"Just tell me what the options are, or even if there are any available. Am I asking or expecting too much? I just thought it was smart to ask."

"Certainly," he said again. He took me into a showroom filled with gadgets and spyware technology, and then handed me a device similar to the one Paul had issued to me.

"This is a personal tracking device. You can leave the base unit at the ranch and carry this small transmitter on your person. The transmitter can be turned on with this little switch. The only disadvantage being that nobody knows you are in trouble. They only know your location.

Our other option is a service where you wear the transmitter and your location shows up on a screen here at CPI. Your family can then call our offices twenty-four hours a day to get updates on your whereabouts. The disadvantage to this option is that it requires communication. However a definite advantage is that you can press a button that automatically calls

911."

"I'm not sure I want to rely on cell phones out in the hills. I spend a lot of time away from the house so I know it's not always reliable. If someone from the ranch is looking for me, will they be able to get through?"

"We haven't had any problems yet. I wouldn't expect any connection problems except in the deep canyons."

"What about the coordinates. How do searchers out in the field use them to find a person?"

"In that case, they would find the latitude and longitude coordinates on a map to pin-point your location."

"And if they carried the portable receiver?"

"Then they would have the same coordinates, but also be able to see where the base unit is in relation to the transmitter."

"If I was out in the oaks, five miles from the ranch or town or any kind of help, how close would searchers be able to get using just the GPS device?" I asked.

"Ah, here's where we see the wonders of modern technology. With *our service* we know your position to within three feet. The handheld devices claim to be reliable to within ten. Realistically, I'd say searchers would definitely be able to find you but I'd put the distance at more like seventy feet. I've tested it myself. Occasionally places like roads and readings didn't match up, but *most of the time* it is right on the money."

"And how much money would that be?" I asked.

"There will be a two hundred dollar deposit on the equipment, which is refunded upon return of the devices. Then there is a ninety-five dollar rental fee per week. We find that the people who come to us frequently have temporary uses for our services. If you require a more permanent solution there is a package available for purchase, as well as a long term contract for a monitoring service. The tracking service is a bit more expensive because it requires more manpower. We staff the surveillance room twenty-four hours a day seven days a week, year round."

Golly, rich people are serious about their security, I thought!

"Okay," I replied. Then I thought that this system was less than buying a GPS device from Ron's that I couldn't use. The service was more accurate, but the hand held receiver was more useful to the guys. Seventy feet was close enough for me. "I'll go with the portable system."

"Certainly. You said you wanted to have two base units?"

"Yes. I don't want to alarm my family and there are two people I trust to make wise decisions without worrying them."

I left the offices carrying two boxes as well as a transmitter in my pocket.

I was feeling a little less vulnerable, just a bit poorer, yet satisfied I'd done everything I could. Hopefully the rental was a waste of my money and had only padded the Carr's pockets. It was a little difficult to put a price tag on my peace of mind.

I drove back to Ron's Sporting Goods and bought two topo maps of the area. It couldn't hurt to have more information. On my way back to the ranch I drove through Carl's Jr. and ate a Western Bacon Cheeseburger on the road.

Once safely back at the ranch, I went straight to the barn. Steve was discussing something with Old Frank so I waited until they were finished. Steve raised an eyebrow when he saw me waiting.

"What's up?" he asked.

"I went to town," I replied, "and picked something up. I don't want it used unless something comes up. You and Rusty are the only ones I trust to use these right. I don't want Mom to worry, so only you and Rusty will know I did this, okay?"

"Why are you being so secretive?"

"Because I have a feeling things are going to get worse. I think Peccati is getting tired of the easy stabs at me. It's boring him and he has real business to attend to. Here, keep this device in the office somewhere. Check on it a couple of times a day when I am out and about. If I show up on the screen, you'll know my location. It won't be turned on unless I need to be found. It's portable, so you can take it out in the hills."

"You're worried."

"Yeah, I'm worried."

"Why can't you just stay home? This guy's not going to break into the house and kidnap you, and you aren't going to go looking for him."

"Steve," I hesitated, "I can't promise that. Every time he pulls one of his stunts, I want to hunt him down. If he left a clear trail, I'd track him down right now."

"Okay, I feel better having a little information on hand anyway. I'll keep tabs on it. Just don't do anything stupid."

"Yeah, right. When have I done anything stupid?"

"I'm not gonna answer that."

I took the other unit to my room and hid it until I could talk to Rusty about it. He should be coming soon since Mom expected him in the afternoon.

I was getting antsy again. Nothing to do, no place to go. I walked the ranch and then I walked it again. I was going to my room to change into exercise clothes when my mom stopped me.

"Can you talk to Jesse? She can't seem to find Patrick. She said he was tracking rabbits and the next thing she knew he'd wandered off."

Mom didn't seem too alarmed, but I headed right over to Jesse's house.

My sister was outside in the yard holding Wyatt and calling Patrick's name in all directions. He couldn't have gone far, I thought. He probably just chased a rabbit out of the yard.

"Hey, Jess, mom says you're looking for Patrick?"

"Oh, Cassidy, I'm so glad you're here. I sent James looking for him but he's been gone for hours and I haven't heard anything. Pat said he was stalking a rabbit. He was so cute trying to sneak up on this cottontail in the yard. He'd sneak a few steps and it would hop a few steps. He'd never catch that thing. I went inside to fix lunch and when I called him to come eat, he didn't answer. And when I looked around the yard I couldn't see him. I called James, and he's been looking, too, but…" she paused, clearly worried.

"No problem, just show me where you last saw him."

I took a quick look in the tree house. If Patrick didn't want to eat lunch, he could have easily hid there. When that didn't pan out, I went back and Jesse led me to the spot where she'd last seen him. Yep, there were his little cowboy boot footprints, clearly stalking an enormous cottontail rabbit. Just like Jesse had said, it was sneak, sneak, hop, hop. I was thankful for the rain last night because it had left the tracks clearly visible. The rabbit had led him into the trees and then it had been startled and froze. Patrick had been pleased with that and rushed the poor critter, only to have it flee. He had stomped the ground a time or two and then turned to return home, but something had stopped him. His footprints mulled around in one spot and then headed in a different direction. He was following another lead now. His boot prints were then joined by a second set of prints and they had walked off toward the road. I memorized all the clues available from the new footprints, knowing it might prove vital: small men's casual shoes, not boots; worn across the ball of the foot; slow, careful steps. They weren't bothering to hide their trail. I followed them to the road and then the steps clearly showed that the man had picked up Patrick and put him in a car, then gotten in the other side and driven away. Alarm bells went off. I examined the car track, memorizing the tread pattern. The car seemed to be dragging something. Not a trailer, something like a chain. Maybe a branch? Why would they do that? Jesse was following along but I didn't want to alarm her.

"I'll find him," I said and sprinted off to the ranch house.

I ran up to my room and changed into camouflage gear. I strapped on my gun, then frantically dug out the tracking system and put it on Rusty's bed. I scrawled "ask Steve" on the business card, ran back to my room to dig out the transmitter from my jeans pocket, and then took off for the truck.

As I passed Jesse's house on my way to the main road James ran out, flagging me down.

"What did you find?" he demanded.

"Someone's taken Pat. I can show you where it happened and I know I can find him. This guy wants to be found. He's marking his trail."

I drove down to the pavement to search for the dirt road to Macaluso's house. James pointed it out. I drove to the spot where I'd last seen sign of Patrick and we jumped out of the truck.

I pointed out the signs, reading them aloud to James so he could get the picture. "They came up from your yard to this point on the road. You can see Patrick's boot prints. He isn't scared or fighting. He trusts this guy. They stop at the road here. The man picks Pat up and puts him in a vehicle. The tread marks go up the road. This must be the guy who has been messing with me all this time and he's using Patrick as bait to lure me in."

"Then don't go. Call the police."

"And send them where? I need to find him first."

I followed the tread marks. Every once in a while I'd stop to examine them again. Being short had some disadvantages when it came to driving big ranch trucks. I had to look way over the hood, and the trail was impossible to read. I couldn't take a horse, though, not knowing if I was going one, five or twenty miles; there was just no telling. It was stop and go, stop and go, always making sure I was still following the right tread.

After a while, I *knew* they wanted to be found. That was the only reason to mark their way so clearly. Surely, they realized something was dragging under their car. Dragging things makes a racket and any reasonable person would stop and fix it. No, these people were dragging something on purpose to mark the way. They wanted to be found, and I was almost ready to find them. I just wish it didn't involve Patrick. But if not Patrick, then who? Patrick had simply been an easy victim. Peccati knew I wouldn't turn my back on him. I was being baited. I was driving into a trap and I knew it. I took the transmitter and, turning my back to James, stuck it in my bra under my left breast. If I was searched, I had every right to slug someone if they touched me there. I could protect the device without it being obvious.

I came to Macaluso's driveway. That meant we'd traveled three miles. I'd better keep track of how far I'd driven to know the distance back if I was afoot again. I took note of the mileage on the old truck. Over 150,000 miles and it was still going strong. I stopped at Macaluso's drive to ensure the trail continued past.

Two and a half miles further down the road, we came to the corrugated metal garage that I'd visited the day before. I stopped and looked at the trail. It clearly made a wide left turn and then entered the garage. The door was down and locked. I checked the truck. There was plenty of room for other traffic to pass around it, so we left it there, in plain sight and easy to reach if needed. I circled the garage on foot and found the backdoor. Looking through the small window in the door, I saw the silver SUV. Shit. I glanced around at the footprints near the door of the garage. Men's casual shoes and little boy boot prints went up the hill. We followed.

"Cassidy, I can't let you walk into this. What are we going to do when we get there? There's just two of us."

"And Peccati wants it to only be one of us. I'm more concerned about you than I am about me. Peccati thinks this is a game, but he isn't going to be too happy that I brought you along. At least we know Patrick's okay for now, look." I pointed to the tracks so James could see.

Patrick didn't seem to be fighting his captor. He was just walking along. I expected to top the hill and to find a house or a compound similar to the one in the Angeles Forest, but their trail continued into the hills. I followed along, keeping my eyes on the landscape ahead, aware that Peccati would be watching for me. I strained my ears. Kids are usually noisy and I expected to hear Patrick's voice bouncing off the hills as he asked a hundred questions or yelled at his captors in anger, but the hills were silent. I was more disturbed by the silence than I would have been from any noise; even the click of a gun would have been more comforting than the silence I was walking into. All I could do was read the trail and follow deeper into the hills. The quick, scuffy cowboy boot prints kept stride with the casual stroll of an adult male. How much of a head start did they have on me? An hour? Maybe. Jesse had made lunch and gone to call Patrick to come in to eat. Then she'd looked around and called James. James had been gone for a few hours, she'd said. Shoot, that meant they could have a 3-hour head start, but it also meant that Patrick was getting hungry.

Peccati hadn't been in a hurry. If so, he'd have picked Patrick up or pulled him along, but he hadn't done either.

As the trail progressed, Patrick started acting more worried. His footprints would turn as if he was looking back down the trail. He was a long way from home, and he wasn't with his mom, an unusual feeling for a preschooler. Nice man or not, something didn't feel right. I didn't point this out to James however, since he didn't need to worry about Patrick being scared.

I was reading sign while James followed a few steps behind. Suddenly a bullet zinged by and James fell to the ground behind me. I rushed to his side.

"I'm okay," he said, trying to get up, but he wasn't okay. He'd been hit.

"Only the girl gets in!" we heard shouted from the treetops. Looking up, I saw several deer platforms in the trees. Men were stationed, guarding the way.

"They aren't going to let you in," I told him. "Peccati only wants me."

"Then we'll have to go back."

"No, I can't do that either. We're past the point of no return. These guys were sent here to specifically make sure only I get in."

I pressed the truck keys into his hand. I was glad to see he was armed like the other ranch hands. The men dropped from their perches, surrounding me.

"Hand over your gun," one of the men demanded.

I didn't have any choice. I unbuckled the belt and held it out to them. The leader of the group snatched it from me grinning. They pointed up the hill and marched me down the trail I was following. I prayed James wouldn't take a shot at their retreating backs. If he did, they would finish him off easily.

They brought me to a large fenced in area. They pushed me through the gate and vanished into the nearby trees. I knew the way was guarded. There was only one way to go and that was towards Peccati.

The fence was tall, nearly eight feet by the looks of it, built of vertical metal bars. It surrounded many acres of open land. In the middle of the land was a large, glamorous house overlooking a small lake. Peccati was sitting on a hill watching Patrick, who was out in the field. Milling around against the enclosure were about fifty large elk. He'd conned Patrick here by telling him he could stalk deer, and he'd kept his promise. Patrick didn't know how dangerous this was. If anything spooked the herd, they could trample him in a heartbeat.

So far, Pat seemed to be doing pretty good. Sure, the elk saw him and ran away from him, but he snuck up anyway with firm determination. I didn't expect much more out of a little kid. Grace and finesse would come later.

Peccati sat, just watching until he turned and pulled out a radio or cell phone. He spoke to someone, then turned to see me standing at his gate. I walked forward, firm determination in every step.

"Ah, good. You came," he said calmly.

"I should just kill you now," I said, "Why should I play this sick game of yours?"

"You could try. That might be fun. I'd prefer to take you on myself, but if you insist on bringing this to a close here and now, that can be arranged. Before you take that option, however, you should consider the boy."

"What about the boy?" I didn't want to use Patrick's name in case Peccati didn't know it. He couldn't use it against us if he didn't know it.

"You have a choice. You can leave the boy or you can take him. If you insist on finishing this here, then the boy stays here. If you take him with you when I hunt you down, the boy has a chance. Either way, one of my bullets is meant for you. Just remember, you can't go home and I'll take out anyone who stands in my way."

His words hit home. There was no way I'd let him near the ranch.

"The hunt starts very soon. When I go to the house, I will get my rifle and be on my way. I trust you will do the same."

"By now the ranch has called the police. Why don't we just wait here until the police arrive, and we can skip this whole hunt business?"

"Because that would force me to act quickly. The police would be much too late to save you or the boy. They would meet the same resistance that your friend did. My men are on call. They will come with a word from me, and enjoy being in on the action. Some of them are a little disappointed that I saved you for myself. They enjoy a hunt occasionally too. My recommendation is that you take the boy. It will be interesting to see how you try to get the two of you out of this. I've been looking forward to this hunt, and I think you better your odds by letting me have some fun with you. Just be warned, I find fun in some cruel ways. I want to see the fear in your eyes when I take you down."

I had no choice. It was Patrick and me against Peccati, armed and dangerous. All I could do was take him and run. Peccati stepped toward the house indicating the conversation was at an end. The hunt was on. I ran to pick up Patrick. Peccati smiled.

"Pat," I said running up to him, "We've got to get out of here. That man wants to kill me."

"He won't. He's nice. He let me see his deer."

"Pat, kiddo, he only did that so I'd come find you, and now he is after me. I need you to come with me. Your mom is worried sick and we have to go."

He still didn't want to leave.

"I'm not kidding," I said, anger rising. "You must obey me. The longer you don't listen to me the worse the danger is. You wanted to be in a Cassidy adventure, well here you are and it isn't going to be fun. It's going to be scary, but you have to listen to me."

That got his attention. An Aunt Cassidy adventure! Hoo, boy.

"The first thing we need is speed and distance. Can you ride piggy back?"

I knelt down and he reluctantly climbed on. I jogged off to the gate, talking to him all the way.

"I need you to hang on tight. If you need to adjust your grip, tap me on the shoulder. I'm going to be running, so hang on tight. Second, I need you to be quiet. Don't say a word unless I tell you it's okay. Bad guys can hear really good, and we don't want him to find us, so quiet is the way to go. Any questions?"

"I'm hungry."

"I'm sorry, sport. I don't have any food. Sometimes staying alive is more important than eating. When the bear had me stuck in the tree, I didn't have any food. We'll get you something to eat just as soon as we can. Now, stay quiet and hold on."

I approached the gate. It wasn't locked. Peccati had left it that way on purpose. He was giving me time and must have been confident he'd catch up to me.

I had to check on James, but I didn't want Patrick to see his dad, so I ran down the trail within sight of where I'd left him but James was gone. I prayed he'd made it to the truck and worried that the men had returned and finished him off.

I broke the route I had planned to take into stages. Goal one: Tony Macaluso's house, two and a half miles by road. I could shave a little off the trip back to the road by cutting due east. I took off at a jog, with Patrick clinging for life to my back. I was glad I had put in my laps on the track wearing the backpack. My knee ached horribly but I pushed the pain away. There was nothing I could about it, so no use worrying. At this point, I was more concerned about distance than stealth. Peccati would not be running through the woods. He was on a hunt, and he was confident he would find me. Slow and steady would be his mode. Methodical.

I was aiming for the Macaluso place because I needed water. I knew there'd be water there, and perhaps some help. I also needed to get Patrick to a place of safety. I thought about having him hide with the transmitter, but then I wouldn't have it for an emergency. So far this wasn't an emergency. This was just the urgency part.

I jogged along with Patrick bouncing on my back. I smoothed my gait to make the ride easier on Patrick, but it made my knee hurt more. I dodged in and out of trees and followed animal trails. Finally we came to a big heavy bush and crawled underneath it for a minutes rest.

"If the bad guy is going to shoot you, why don't you shoot him first?" Patrick whispered.

I whispered back, "Because killing people is wrong. I won't shoot him unless I have to. Besides, his men took my gun away. I don't have anything to shoot him with. Now shush. We don't want him to hear us."

"I want to walk."

"You can't keep up if you walk. I'll give you a job to do. We'll turn you around and you can be the eyes in the back of my head. You can watch for the bad guy behind us, and if you see him you can give me a signal."

"What signal?"

"If you need to adjust your position, tap me on the shoulder, and if you see the bad guy, punch me on the shoulder. Okay? Show me a tap." *Tap.* "Now show me a punch." *Punch.* "Good boy, that'll work. Now, I want you to try and go to the bathroom. We are safe here for a few minutes. I won't watch."

He looked at me as if I was nuts.

"Patrick, you need to try to go now so you won't have to later when it might not be safe. Just pretend the potty's there and go on the ground. Animals do it all the time. Hasn't your dad ever taken you camping?"

He crawled around the back of the bush, pulled down his britches and peed. He came back, struggling with the snap and zipper. I fastened him up and we took off again. I pulled him up and he wrapped his arms around my neck, sat on my folded arms and peeked over my shoulder, being my lookout for the bad guy.

Soon we came to a long steep embankment with a road at the bottom. Sitting down I placed Patrick on my lap then scooted feet-first down the hill. Halfway down we began moving too fast and we both started rolling. I pulled up into a crawling position, stiffening my arms and legs to protect Patrick from the weight of my body. We rolled and tumbled to the bottom of the hill. We'd left a hell of a trail, but if people were looking for us maybe they'd see it. I checked the road and realized there were more car tracks than there had been earlier. I wondered if James had made it to the truck, or if the truck had been found by someone from the ranch.

"Are you okay?" I asked.

"Yeah, but that was scary."

"I know," I said, "but it's just part of having an adventure."

We jogged down the road, praying for a ranch truck to come along. Then I thought about how open we were and crossed to the trees on the other side. We left a clear trail into the trees, and then started hiding our trail. Peccati would follow us across the road and assume we had headed for shelter. With any luck, we could lead him into the trees and then make for the road again.

Punch. My heart lurched. I quickly found a large tree to hide behind.

Chapter 17

"Where?" I barely whispered, holding my finger to my lips in the universal hush sign.

Patrick pointed to the top of the hill that we'd just slid down. Shit. Peccati looked out over the land before him, taking in the wide picture, looking for movement. I wasn't going to give him anything to find.

We were in stealth mode now. While Peccati was searching for a way down, I picked my way toward the next two trees. He finally decided straight down was the way to go, and proceeded to scoot down in the same manner as I had, only slower. I made it past a couple more trees, hiding my tracks. He followed my trail down the road fairly quickly but then he slowed down. As with most people, he could follow a fresh trail when it was made by a person walking but he couldn't discern the subtleties of the job. I knew I could lose him if he studied my trail and I was covering my tracks. I chose my next destination spot, waited until Peccati was absorbed in my trail and then stepped lightly, using rocky places and roots to hide my passage. One thing about oak trees is that they left plenty of exposed roots. Sometimes I could just follow a root from one tree to another. If I stuck to the trees and kept the road to my right, I would eventually run into the Macaluso place. The trick was to do it one hiding place at a time.

I came across an area of dense brush which would hide us from view, so I ran behind it in a crouched position to the end. Putting the brush between Peccati and I helped a lot. I continued hopping from rock to root to hard pack.

Under the circumstances, Patrick was doing great. He would punch my shoulder whenever he saw Peccati behind us and he managed to keep his cool. Occasionally, we had to stop to get repositioned, but it only took a second and then we'd be on our way again. Eventually the seriousness of our situation settled in and Patrick became scared, but he hunkered down and did his job, fear and all. I guess Peccati looked a little more sinister when he packed a rifle. I wouldn't have expected it from most adults, so I was really proud of Patrick for showing such self-control under pressure.

It was hard to gauge how far I'd come when I was measuring the distance from one tree to the next. How long had we been out here? How many hiding places had I found? How many steps had I carefully hidden from Peccati's eye? How far to go? My knee was throbbing and I was dying of thirst. I knew Patrick had to be both hungry and thirsty. He hadn't had lunch and it was getting on towards dinnertime.

If I could have used the road, a half hour jog would have gotten me to the Macaluso place, but I didn't have that luxury. As it was, I almost passed the place in the fading light. I was looking over my shoulder for Peccati and choosing the next target spot when I found myself in the back of Macaluso's property. What had tipped me off was a total absence of trees. The land had been cleared to make room for his vineyards. Now what? No cover. To go around the back would add an extra hour and a couple of miles. We couldn't afford to waste that time and we both needed water. I looked down my back trail. No sign of pursuit. I wondered if Peccati had anticipated our need for water and had gone ahead to the Macaluso house. I had to risk it. I didn't think I'd make it another three miles, without water, carrying Patrick. My arms ached and my knee throbbed. I needed a rest.

I sprinted across the open ground, landing winded and worn at the back of Tony Macaluso's house. I found a dark, hidden corner behind a newly planted palm tree and pushed Patrick into it.

"Don't move from this spot," I admonished him. "Even if you hear gun shots, stay frozen here. I'm going to find water. If I can get into the house, maybe I'll be able to call for help."

Hugging the dark recesses, I made my way to a door. I tried the handle. Locked. I looked in windows, and there were no signs of life. Unfortunately there was no sign of a telephone either. The inside of the house still needed a lot of work. I made my way around to the front and tried the front door. No luck. I saw a hose lying on the ground and followed it to the faucet. I located a bucket and put the hose all the way to the bottom of the bucket so the sound of running water would be muffled and there would be no splashing. After filling the bucket partway, I turned off the water and took the bucket with me. On the way back to Patrick's hiding place, I spotted a small ice chest next to the garage. Somebody's lunch box left from the day's work. I opened it and pulled out some empty wrappers and a small plastic container of fruit cocktail. It was better than nothing, so I took it along, too.

I went back to the dark corner where Patrick had stayed hidden. I gave him the fruit cocktail, which he didn't particularly like, but I whispered that it was food and when you are on an adventure, you had to eat whatever food you could find. He didn't want to drink out of the dirty bucket either until after I did. He then reasoned that if it was good enough for me, it would be good enough for him.

"Besides," I pointed out, "we are dirty from head to toe. What's a little dirt on the inside going to hurt?"

"Mommy's going to be mad."

"No, she won't. She'll be so glad to get you back she'll hug you and kiss you, dirt and all."

"Ewe!"

I thought about what must be going on back home. Jesse was probably frantic. I worried about James again. Had he made it to the truck? If James hadn't turned up, they would have sent Steve down the road. He would have found the truck and figured out the garage had something to do with it. They had probably searched the area around the garage. Had they met the snipers? Had they found Peccati's house? The trail had been plain to me, but it wasn't a worn trail, simply a line of footprints through the hills. Would they be able to follow it? Maybe it was time to activate the tracking device.

Patrick tensed. I followed his stare to see Peccati walking out from the trees. He was bound to check the grounds. Keeping the house between Peccati and the two of us, we ran to the next building, a garage and office. I tried the door and it swung open. Quickly we stepped inside and locked the door behind us. I checked all the bay doors to make sure they were also locked. Then I checked the office to make sure there were no other doors.

I could relax a little now. Turning my back on Patrick, I slipped the transmitter from its hiding place. I pushed the button and allowed it to transmit for several minutes, which was just enough time for Steve to get a fix. And Rusty? Would Rusty be at the ranch? He should have arrived hours ago.

"Patrick," I said, "You have to listen to me. The man who is chasing us only wants to catch me. He will leave you alone if he can follow me. This device is used to call for help. I just pushed the button and Steve will know where you are. A dot will show up on a map, and that will tell him how to find you. I want you to wait right here until someone you know comes to the door. If it's your daddy, one of the ranch hands or Rusty, then open the door. Do you remember Rusty's voice?"

"I think so."

"Okay. If someone from the ranch comes, open the door and you will be safe. I am going to lead the bad guy away from here. I don't want the bad guy to shoot anybody from home. If the bad guy comes to the door, just stay quiet. He can't get in."

I looked down into his large scared eyes.

"Are you okay? Can you do this for me? You have to be a big boy and hide so I can get away. Somebody will be here soon."

I slipped out the door. Once I heard the dead bolt slide into place, I took off into the fading light. I did a circuit of the garage so that if Peccati followed our tracks he would think I hadn't been able to get in. Then I left a clear trail off the premises. I switched off the tracking device so searchers would go to the last known reading. I briefly made myself visible, just a shadow in the fading light, to allow Peccati a chance to refocus and then ducked into the trees.

Now the game was just between Peccati and me. I headed deeper into the hills. For a quarter mile or so I left a clear trail, just sprinting ahead, leading my stalker into country where I could maneuver better. The more cover the better. I knew a wooded place where the trees were thick and the ground cover would hide me. As a girl I tracked foxes there. Foxes were always fun to track. They led interesting lives and made instant decisions that would keep me guessing what they were going to do next. This trip into these woods, I would be the fox and Peccati would be the tracker.

I glanced behind me and saw headlights bouncing along the road. I hoped it was Steve going after Patrick.

It was dark by the time I reached the woods. They wrapped around me like a protective embrace. I made my way to a dense thicket, hiding my tracks. I crawled under the bushes. At night, in my camouflaged clothes, I was nearly invisible. All I had to do was stay alert and watchful. I lay in the soft leaves and stilled my breathing. Bugs crawled on me but I didn't move. Field mice scurried by and I welcomed their passing as proof there was nobody else near. As the night progressed, the thicket became pitch black. I caught myself dozing once or twice but was instantly alert, my ears tuned to catch approaching footsteps.

After a while I heard the forest noises. An owl caught a mouse and it cried out as it was being carried away. The whisper of wings was a comfort because owls would avoid Peccati too. I played mental games, trying to stay awake. Surely dawn was just around the corner. If I'd been on guard duty, staying awake wouldn't be a problem. I could walk and think and stay active. Here, I was trapped. If I moved, I would be a target. My mind was my only tool available to help me stay awake and alive.

At last, a faint glimmer of light appeared on the horizon. Time to track down my stalker. I crawled out from under my hiding place, keeping an eye out for movement.

I couldn't just run from Peccati. He would continue to pursue me until he found his chance to shoot me. Now it was up to me to end this game but I required a plan. I needed a way to disarm him, and to even the playing field. To disarm him, I needed his location and decided it would be best if I found him first. I headed down my back trail, keeping to the side, hiding my tracks and watching ahead for movement, always keeping cover between myself and the route I expected Peccati would take. If Peccati followed me into the woods, he would be somewhere along my back trail.

I found him just inside the woods. He knew why I was there and he didn't want to be trapped on my turf at night. He had waited out the dark and then with dawn's light had slowly followed my trail again.

A trap, I needed a trap. Now that I knew where Peccati was and where he would be going, I felt freer to examine the woods more closely. I went back to my original hiding place before continuing on further into the woods. I nearly hit my head on a big, thick branch. My break! I could use that branch. One thing I noticed about Peccati was that he focused on my trail. If I could keep him focused on the tracks, I could lead him right into this spot. I went back, placing my footprints down the trail directly below the branch. I then climbed the tree and waited for him to pass under me.

When he finally appeared, the sun had almost risen. He walked head down, concentrating on the trail. He was tired, his feet moving sluggishly. I sat in the tree, silently praying that he'd keep his head down. He appeared to notice that something was now different with my trail, and this caused him to study it more closely. I tensed. Was I really going to be ready for this? Once I started it was going to be a fight to the finish. As he passed under the branch, I brought my foot down and swung it forward as hard as I could. I caught him with a kick that jerked his head back with a sickening snap. I was worried that I'd killed him right then and there. The rifle flew from his hands, landing in the brush behind him. He fell back, dazed. I waited a second, clearing my head, readying myself for the fight ahead. As he rose I launched myself at him from overhead, sending him careening back into the ground with a grunt.

"So," he gasped, "you think a little girl like you can take me on?" He rose, smiling. I brought a punch to his face but he blocked it. "I spar with my men. I will enjoy the slow method even more than the fast one I had planned. I can do it with my bare hands this way. I can feel the struggle."

"You said you wouldn't underestimate me again," I snapped back. The rifle was out of the picture so I hit the button on the transmitter. "But here you are, doing it again. It's easy to underestimate me, but you've ticked off the wrong person. I could take it when you just picked on me but when you endanger other people, that's where I draw the line. When you rigged the barn door you created an enemy and I'm not letting you go so easily this time. You're stuck with me until this is finished and it's going to be finished sooner than you think."

Okay, Cassidy, I thought, you've made your silly little speech, now here he is, the punching bag in real life. You need to cream him before he creams you. This is the war all over again. This is life and death. You did it then, you can do it now.

He wasn't expecting me to be a fighter. I was quick and shoved my fist right up into his face and felt his nose crunch. He smiled, reaching up and taking hold of his nose. He was enjoying this. We circled a bit. I shouldn't have let him up. I should have kept him pinned down but now it was too late. Watch for your break, Cass, don't jump in too soon. Just as I had stalked the deer, I stalked Peccati, except this was a different kind of stalking. I feigned punches so he would avoid them and I moved smoothly and quietly. My circling was guiding him ever closer to a tree directly behind him and when he tried a swing at me I launched myself at him again, bashing him into the tree with all my one hundred and fifteen pounds. I pummeled him just like the punching bag, one hit after another until he was just holding his hands over his head, trying to protect himself. I stomped on his foot and threw a fist into his stomach which doubled him over. The punching bag work was paying off. I could actually do this. I closed in, not stopping, not letting up, but then he rushed me and I found myself tumbling on the ground.

I rolled to my feet in one fluid motion, taking stock of the situation again. Peccati stood, winded but whole, blood flowing from his broken nose. He was tiring. That was good. I was wired. I'd been through this fight so many times in the barn that I was ready. This punching bag however was just a little more unpredictable than the other one. I ran through all the reasons this guy could not escape and that only fueled my determination. This guy needed to be locked up. I just had to hold him here until help arrived and I'd do it. He wasn't getting away this time. I rushed him again before he had a chance to rest. He brought a fist up and caught me in the jaw. A point for him. I swung back, determined not to let him back off. I pushed forward, connecting, but I closed in too soon and he grabbed me, spinning me around until he had an arm wrapped around my neck. This was the break he had been waiting for. He squeezed and I felt my air supply slow. I stomped his instep quickly and shoved an elbow into his stomach. He bent forward but didn't let me go. I twisted, anything to get free of that grip. I was seeing stars by the time I wrenched free, gasping for air. Okay, another point for Peccati. This was getting dirty so I had to fight dirty too. He was still hunched over waiting for his stomach to settle down, so I drove another fist into his jaw and brought my foot up and into his groin which sent him to the ground groaning. I rushed over to the brush, searching for the rifle. I dove into the undergrowth, searching around quickly. I had seen where it flew. I just had to locate it. I hit something with my foot that felt a little too solid and grabbed at it. I came out with the rifle in my hands. I aimed the rifle at Peccati.

"Don't move! Don't even think about moving," I said. "I don't have much patience right now and I'm likely to blow a big hole in you. You know what this gun can do. You used it on me, so you know. I suggest you just sit there."

The sun rose in the sky. The day started heating up and I stood there. The longer I stood there, the more tense I became. I was totally exhausted from being up all night. My arms ached from holding the rifle up and I could feel flight mode still boiling under the surface. I wanted to put Peccati behind me and run, but I knew the police needed to catch this guy. I wanted him in jail for a long, long time.

After a while, I heard horses. Several horses. I was standing there, Peccati still in my sights, when Rusty stepped in from the side. The group of riders formed a line facing our altercation.

"Cass, put the gun down," Rusty said, sensing the tension in the air.

I looked around. Two ranch hands and several men in uniform had guns trained on Peccati. I slowly lowered the rifle and took a weary step towards Rusty. As soon as my attention was diverted Peccati made a lunge for me. Rusty tackled me and an explosion of gunfire exploded around me. I hit the dirt. Peccati fell in a cloud of dust beside me, my pistol still in his hand, the barrel inches from my face. One flick of his finger and I would be finished. I grabbed for the gun, yanking it out of Peccati's loose hand and stared into his unseeing eyes. I turned away and lay there in the dirt, shaking.

Rusty gently removed the pistol then knelt in the dirt beside me. I released the rifle and Rusty handed it to another officer. I sat up slowly and looked at Peccati's blood-spattered body. I scrambled away from the scene, walking quickly in an attempt to distance myself from the sight of him. I circled the group of men, trying to find some sense of peace. The gunfire still echoed in my brain. The men then closed in to check Peccati while Rusty closed in to check on me.

"Cassidy, what did you do to this guy?" someone asked.

"He was going to kill me. What do you think I did to him? Where's James? Is James all right? And where's Patrick? I hid him at Macaluso's. Please tell me you found Patrick."

"Patrick is home. He's fine."

"And James?"

"James will survive." My heart sunk. That sounded serious.

"Patrick did so good. He obeyed everything I said. He didn't complain. I never met a little kid who would go without food and water for most of a day and not complain. He helped spot when Peccati was catching up to us. I didn't want to leave him in the garage but it was the safest place for him."

Someone said, "It would have been the safest place for you, too. You should have stayed there with him."

That statement made me angry. They had no right to judge my decisions. If they had been in my shoes they might have done the same thing. If I had stayed at the garage they might all be dead now. I turned my back on all of them and walked towards home. I didn't even know who had said it, but it sure set me off. Rusty tried to stop me, but I pulled away and ran. I ran until I couldn't run any longer, and then walked until all I could feel was exhaustion and pain. I found a rock and sat stewing.

Rusty appeared and sat beside me. It seemed that he was the only person who understood me now. He was the only person who could see why I did the crazy things I did.

"Water?" my voice cracked. "Did you bring any water?"

"We were more worried about just finding you. As soon as that dot appeared on the receiver, we just took off."

I looked around and saw that he had a horse with him. I stood and walked over to the horse. Buck. The horse was Buck. I mounted up and Rusty got on behind me.

"Let's go home Buck," I said, and gave him a gentle kick.

I didn't even use the reins. I didn't pay attention to his speed; I only followed the movements of the horse just as I had from the time I was old enough to sit on one. The movement continued and Rusty didn't push the horse to go faster. I was tired, so tired. I'd been awake all night.

It was over. It was finally over, and I should be able to relax again, but I couldn't. I was still wound up so tight from the fight that I needed to run. I wanted to hide in the woods and never come out. My mind was drifting in little frightening circles and then, somehow quite suddenly, the barn appeared in front of me. I was home.

My mom came rushing out of the house and ran down to the barn. Rusty stopped her and then spoke to her gently. I slid down and walked the horse into the barn. Water, where's some water? Finding a hose, I turned on the water and took a long drink. I was so thirsty. Three long, hot miles with no water. I stripped off Buck's saddle and blanket and then set them on a stall wall. The weight of the saddle almost pulled me over but somehow I did it. Then I went through the motions of wiping him down and brushing him out, not even realizing I was doing it. It came so natural. I was acting on instinct and this was routine when you finished riding. You take care of your horse before taking care of yourself. Rusty fell in beside me, but I was too worn out to react. I didn't mean to ignore him, but the images and the tension crowded in until that's all I felt.

I walked up to the house. Water, I needed more water. I went to the kitchen and filled a glass from the tap, barely noticing Martha's shocked gasp at the sight of me. I drank half of it on the way to my bedroom. I left the door open, flopped down on the bed, and just let the images flow until I couldn't stand it any longer. I lay there dazed and exhausted until sleep came and took me away.

When I woke up I was stuck to the bedspread. My arm had bled. When had I hurt my arm? Rusty stood up from a chair next to my bed, disappeared into the bathroom, and then returned with a wet washcloth. With a gentle touch, he separated the bedspread from my shirt and arm. He still hadn't spoken. He appeared worried that if he said something I'd run off again and he may have been right. I was in flight or fight mode, and it was difficult to let go of the impulse.

"I'm sorry, Rusty, I'm trying." I didn't know if it made sense to him but it was all I could think of to say.

I took out a sleeveless shirt from a bedroom drawer and then went into the bathroom to change. When I returned I sat on the bed again and looked at my arm. I couldn't see it very well until Rusty brought over a clean cloth and washed the area.

"I don't even know how I did that," I managed to say.

"I do," he said sadly. "It's a graze from a bullet."

Okay, now it made sense. I felt my knee. It was the size of a grapefruit. How had I run all that way with my knee like that?

Over the next few days there seemed to be a bubble around me, this protective layer of silence. If someone did happen to mention the incident, it brought back a flood of memories that I couldn't push back and I'd go off to my room. Loud noises made me jump, and I woke in the night from nightmares. One night I woke shaky and frightened. I couldn't shake it. I tiptoed to Rusty's room and slept on the floor beside his bed. The next morning I awoke to find him sitting beside me.

"Come back to me, Cass. Would you, please, just come back to me?"

I curled up into a little ball and just wept because I really wanted to. I wanted to come back, but I didn't know the way.

When I was all cried out, he helped me up.

"How will I know? How will I know when I'm back?"

"I don't know, babe. I just need to see you smile."

"How long have you been here?"

"Four days."

"And what about the case? When do you have to go back?"

"There's a lot that needs to be done, but most of it's up here now. I'm supposed to get a statement from you, but I haven't had the heart."

"Okay, I'll try." I paused, thinking. How much could I remember without falling off the ledge? "I was baited. I knew it when I went up there. I knew it was coming. That's why I went to town and picked up the GPS systems. I just didn't know it would happen the same day." I managed to get through the part about why I went, and then I had to stop.

Rusty seemed to understand that I could handle the logical part of it, but the emotional part would set me off.

"Why didn't you use the GPS after you got there? We could have helped before things got out of hand."

"Peccati's men shot James. He said they would shoot anybody who got in the way. That's why I left Patrick in the Macaluso's garage. So you could take care of him without getting in the line of fire. Then I led Peccati away to the wood. I went there because I knew there was lots of cover. If there was a place where I could beat Peccati, that was it."

It took Rusty a few more days to get the whole story out of me, and I think he is still the only person who knows everything. Patrick came to see me a few days after I got back. I think mom had talked to Jesse beforehand because Patrick was all good manners and matter-of-fact. He still wanted me to talk to Ricky Mallory so he wouldn't be called a fibber anymore.

I asked about James every day, but didn't go to visit him. I felt like it was my fault, and to see him in the hospital would just be too much. I was told that he had made it back to the truck and had been found heading towards the ranch. Paramedics had been called.

Seeing Patrick again reminded me of the tree house. I took Rusty down there and we both climbed up into it and talked for an hour. After watching me Patrick had also tried to climb the rope but without success. I knew that with some practice he'd eventually catch on.

Finally, it just seemed like it was time to go home again. Not to the ranch, but to my own home. I just wanted one more day to enjoy the area before I left.

"Rusty?" I asked the next morning when we were bored, "Can we take a drive up Highway One? I need to get out and have a fun day. I think a fun day would do wonders for me."

"Do you promise not to meet any drug dealers and try to steal their beach pails?"

I smiled.

"I promise."

Chapter 18

I went upstairs and changed into a carefree, fun outfit; something that would make me feel pretty. I put on make-up, curled my hair and then made a solemn promise that I'd go buy some sandals. Hiking boots, moccasins, and tennis shoes just weren't appropriate some times.

Rusty's Explorer wasn't the same as flying around the curves in the BMW, but it was higher and provided better glimpses of the ocean.

We had a wonderful time. We drove through Big Sur, stopping at overlooks for marvelous views of the ocean. The wind-swept soaring heights blew some life back into me. Cliff swallows flew in aerodynamic bliss around the buildings. It reminded me of Jack and the way he'd always tell me that I had to find my own way to fly.

We found a place where elephant seals came up onto the beach, and we stood together freezing in the ocean wind. We pointed out the antics of the few interesting seals and the odd expressions on the adults with their strange floppy noses and staring eyes. We visited Cannery Row and poked around in the tourist shops, then walked on the beach at Carmel-by-the-Sea. We even bought swimsuits and played in the water. It was too cold to swim, but we tried nevertheless. I realized that I was smiling a lot.

At last, sitting lazily on the beach, I broached the topic on my mind.

"How's the work going on the case?" I didn't want to bring up anything negative that day, but I wanted to talk about going home, and this led up to it.

"There's still a lot to do, but I don't have to be the one to do it. We got Peccati. I think that will put an end to all the trouble at the ranch."

"I meant your work. What do you still need to accomplish up here?"

He paused. "My mission? Is that what you are going for here?"

"If you want to put it that way."

"My mission is to bring you home, whole and happy."

"That's it?"

"That's it."

"So you've just been staying up here for me?"

"No, I've been staying up here for me. I choose my own missions."

"Okay. Well, I think I am ready for the home part. When can we go home?"

"As soon as you wrap things up with your family. You can't just pack up and leave. They've got to see that you are ready, too."

"Okay, I'll talk to them."

"You really like it up here, don't you?' he asked hesitantly. "The ranch is the life you were born to and you take to it. You enjoy the horses and the area and being with your family. Why go home?"

"Mom told me I could stay." I fidgeted, drawing little figures in the sand. "Jesse tried to talk me into staying. But I can't."

"Why not?"

I paused for one long breath. "Because the ranch is missing something that means more to me than the life up here."

There was a long pause while he contemplated what that might be.

When we got back to the ranch I talked to my mom about leaving. She repeated that I could stay as long as I wanted to, and then I explained why I needed to go home.

"Mom, I need to find my own way. If I stayed here I'd be stuck in my childhood forever. It wasn't a bad place growing up. It was wonderful, but it isn't where my future lies. I want to do something useful. I need to go home and discover what that might be."

She could understand that. She knew I needed to stretch my wings.

"Before I go, can we have Jesse, James and the kids up for dinner? And can Patrick bring his little friend along? I promised Patrick that I'd talk to his friend, Ricky. I just want to see everybody together and happy one more time before I go."

"Of course. I'll talk to Martha. You know, everybody misses you when you are gone."

"Yeah, I bet it's really boring around here. No daily emergencies. What do the guys bet on when I'm gone?"

"Very funny. Cass, they all love you. You're like family to them, too."

"That's why I want to see them all together one more time before I leave. And I'll be back. It's not like I won't visit."

The next evening was almost like my birthday party all over again, except that I missed Kelly's booming laugh. I also had to face James who was all bandaged up, but recovering. He seemed happy to just have Patrick back in one piece. This time I didn't get all dressed up, although I had thought of it; eventually I decided to dress the part for Patrick and Ricky and wore camouflage pants with an olive drab t-shirt, and my moccasins.

When I finally met Ricky, he looked me up and down and then asked, "*You're* Pat's Aunt Cassidy? I thought you would be big and tough!"

"A person doesn't have to be big to be strong on the inside," I told him. "If you do what you think is right, and stand firm in that, everyone will think you're big and tough no matter what size you are. They might not take you seriously at first, but if you stick to your guns, they can see what you're really made of. Did Patrick tell you that he got kidnapped? He did just what was right, and he is home safe again. If he had done the easy thing when he was in danger, he wouldn't be alive right now."

"But Patrick says you have done all these crazy things. I don't believe him. I don't think you could have done all those things."

"Well, Ricky, it isn't always a matter of choosing what I do. Sometimes, things happen that force me to do things that other people don't get to do. Yes, I really got charged by a bear. Was I brave? Was I a big hero? No. Hell, I ran like crazy and climbed up in a tree. But it was the right thing to do.

When I became a Marine, that forced certain things to happen to me. I learned how to fight. I jumped out of airplanes. Does that mean I am brave? No, it means I could follow orders.

When I went looking for Mr. Green, I didn't know I would run into trouble. I just had to deal with it when it happened. Getting through tough times changes a person. Hopefully, it makes them stronger and better able to cope with the next challenge they face. "

"Did you really catch a bank robber?" Ricky asked.

"I tracked a bank robber, and I found him, but I didn't catch him. Detective Michaels caught him. Sometimes these things take teamwork."

The dinner was great. Everybody came and spoke with me, wishing me well. The stories flowed again, more for Patrick's sake than my own. When the evening was over, we all knew it was time to say good-bye. Randy asked me to write, knowing he'd get all his news secondhand from my mom. Steve gave me a firm handshake, then a quick hug and a wink. Jesse said she'd see me off in the morning.

When it was all over Rusty and I sat by ourselves in the living room.

"You're sure about tomorrow?" he asked.

"I'm sure. I'm almost done packing. Will everything fit in the truck with Shadow's crate?"

"We can fold down the back seats."

In the morning I went down to the barn to say good-bye to Shasta. Then I took Shadow to the agility course my dad had built for me and put him through the obstacles, one by one.

"You know you could take all these with you if you want." My dad said.

"I don't have the space, but thank you, Dad. Maybe one of the boys will decide to train a dog. And it'll be here for me again if I leave it. I like building stuff. I'll build the pieces at home that will fit in my yard."

He gave me a rare Big Wayne hug while my mom gave me her teary good-bye hug. Jesse talked on and on about all the things we could do if she came down to visit.

At last Rusty and I took our places in his heavily loaded Explorer, then drove quietly down the long driveway and off to our own destiny.

We took the long way home down the 101. There was more to see and share, and less time to dwell on the future. We stopped in Solvang, walked Shadow through the little Danish town, and bought a pastry in the bakery there. We walked Shadow on the beach in Santa Barbara. We bought oranges outside Fillmore.

At last we pulled up to my house. The grass was overgrown and the weeds needed pulling. I'd have a lot of work on my hands in the days to come. I opened the back of the Explorer and Shadow dashed out, running in circles in his familiar front yard. I let him through to the back, where he sniffed and marked all the corners. The wild birds were gone. They had given up on me ever feeding them again. The house didn't feel familiar to me anymore. I felt like I was trespassing. The house hadn't changed, but I had.

When I had asked to come home, I'd forgotten that I would need to say good-bye to Rusty, too. We stood facing each other in my living room, a seemingly large chasm between us.

"We need to talk," I said.

We'd talked for days, but he knew this was a different kind of talk.

"Give yourself a few days. I want you to think first."

"Okay, I'll clean up around here and you need to get back to work. When you have a day off and if you want to do something together, let me know. There's still something I want to show you."

I spent the next few days mowing and pulling weeds. I had to clear out all the agility equipment in order to mow the grass in the backyard and then put it all back again. I went grocery shopping, without incident this time, and restocked the house.

Shadow was happy to be in his own yard and back into his familiar routine. I wasn't as happy, though I had enough to do and didn't get bored. When all the work got caught up, what then? What would I do when all the work was finished?

Kelly had a big party at his house and I got to meet his wife, Rhonda. He called it his "coming out" party because his casts had been taken off. He still used crutches, but planned to gradually give them up too. I made a date with Kelly to let him drive the BMW, as promised.

Rusty called every day, but we had slipped back into the same old routine of him checking up on me. This just had to stop.

I cleaned my house and took down the pictures of Jack, carefully placing them in a photograph album. I rearranged all the decorative things around the house, knowing Rusty would notice the changes. Then, one evening I drove to his condo and parked a few doors down. Sitting on a rock beside his doorway, I waited for him to arrive. He wasn't expecting me and was distracted, so I slipped in behind him just as he unlocked the door and placed my hand on his shoulder.

"Where did you come from?" he asked, amused that I'd surprised him. My actions seemed to confirm something in his mind, but I didn't intentionally sneak up on him.

"Like Crocodile Dundee," I said.

He opened the door and motioned for me to come in.

"Long day at work?"

"A little. Tying up loose ends. Catching up on new cases that came up while I was gone. Meetings."

"Sounds like you're going to be busy for a while," I said.

"Why, are you ready for that talk?"

"When you're ready to take me there."

"Take you? Where are we having this talk?" Rusty asked.

"I can't tell you. I have to show you."

"How about Friday? I need a few days to arrange my schedule."

"Friday's good. Morning?" I asked.

"Pick a time."

"Anytime in the morning is good. The earlier we leave, the more time we will have. Will you have the whole weekend? Do you have a daypack? Sleeping bag? I have an extra if you don't have one," I offered.

"Got it."

"And a change of clothes. I can have everything else we'll need."

His eyes were smiling.

"What?" I asked.

"It's just good to see you," he responded.

Over the next few days I went to the sporting goods store and bought backpacking food. Only one day's meals would keep while hiking, so like it or not, backpacker meals were the fare most of the time. At the grocery store I bought a nice thick steak, soy sauce, brown sugar and ginger. I chose grapes and apples; fruit that was easy to eat and didn't require any clean up. Usually I never bothered with fruit because it was heavy, but I felt the need to add a little variety since Rusty was coming. I bought oatmeal and hot chocolate mix for mornings, then picked up powdered eggs with bacon in them just in case Rusty liked oatmeal as much as I did. I made trail mix out of M&Ms, dried fruit and mixed nuts. I was being extravagant for Rusty's sake, but he'd still be amazed at how light we traveled. At the last minute I remembered I only had one cup and one fork, so I returned to the sporting goods store for another set of each.

On Friday I got up early, showered, then dressed in khaki shorts and a brown tank top. I wanted to show I was comfortable in the woods. I wore my moccasins so I could feel the ground under my feet. I curled my hair for a carefree look, but skipped the make-up since it would only look bad in the morning.

I mixed soy sauce, sugar and ginger together and then slightly thawed the steak. I crammed the steak into a mayonnaise jar and filled it to the brim with the sauce. I put it in the fridge until Rusty arrived at seven.

When he arrived, I unpacked his gear and then repacked our two packs with everything I'd just bought. You can't go backpacking with a guy and take the bigger pack. That's just a law of backpacking, so I strapped his sleeping bag to his pack and packed the insides of the two packs about equally. He looked at the packs with skepticism. It didn't look like much. I took the jar out of the fridge, stuck it in a gallon-sized Ziploc bag, and added it to Rusty's pack. I added a small bag of dog food to my pack.

"Ready?" I asked.

"If you are," he replied doubtfully.

We tossed the two packs in my Jeep. Shadow rode in the back, pacing nervously. His seat had been usurped. I drove quickly to Creekside Campground, passing up the crowded sardine camp and heading to the trailhead. Friday was the worse day to try and get a camping spot. I was glad we weren't competing for a spot there. I hung my Adventure Pass on the Jeep mirror and pulled out the packs.

"No tent?"

"We won't need one."

"No sleeping bag?"

"Don't worry about it. Have you ever seen me go into the woods unprepared?"

"You always *look* like you're going unprepared, but somehow you always manage to survive."

"I'm bringing a lot more than I usually do for this hike. Don't worry."

I clipped Shadow's leash to a belt loop so I'd have my hands free. There would be a lot of city folk on the trail. City folk had city dogs, so I didn't trust them.

The weather was already hot and the sun was bearing down as we hit the trail. I made sure we each had a water bottle. We had two easy miles and two rough miles to go. Rusty let me lead, since I knew where we were going. I also think he expected to walk too fast for me, but he didn't have to worry about that. After all that track running at the ranch I was ready for anything.

"Are you going to tell me anything about this?" he asked.

"What do you want to know?" I replied as we hiked along.

"Where are we going?"

"Camping."

"Okay, how far is it?

"Four miles."

"Why?"

"Why is it four miles? Because the camp happens to be about four miles from the trailhead."

"I meant why are we doing this?"

"I'm doing it because I need to share this with you, and you are doing this because you want to see it."

"It better be worth it."

"If it's not, then that will tell us both something."

When the trail crossed the creek we filled our water bottles and stopped to soak our feet. I took out the trail mix and we each picked out our favorite ingredients. I dropped my pack beside the creek and walked downstream a little bit. Creek-side stops were always cool and refreshing. I was looking for raccoon tracks, but I didn't find any.

"Our turn-off is just a half mile further. Are you ready for some off roading?"

I found my pack and shoes again.

"Are you sure you know where you're going?" Rusty asked.

"I wouldn't bring you along if I wasn't sure."

"That's not very encouraging. That means you hike off trail by yourself."

"So?" I answered.

We occasionally met other hikers until we turned off the trail, and then they magically disappeared. I unclipped Shadow's leash and he took off up into the canyon.

"He's gone," Rusty observed.

"He's never far away. He knows where we're going."

"I wish I did."

"It's not far." I said, finding my way between a boulder and dirt bank.

We found the joining creek again and followed it up and into the canyon. We climbed over rocks and weaved in and out of the dense trees as we climbed ever higher.

We came to a rock wall where the creek cascaded down into a small pool.

"You rock climb, right?"

"Yeah, with Kelly."

"Then this should be easy."

I looked at the rock, found a foothold, felt the rock for a handhold, and hoisted myself up. I continued up the rock, feeling for the small cracks and bumps that offer support while Rusty watched from below. I pulled myself over the top of the rock, then he started up. One thing about rock climbing is that one person's handholds don't necessarily match what is right for another person. Each has to find his own way.

"You come down this way, too?" he asked as he pulled himself up over the top.

"There are a lot of ways to get there. We just happen to be following the creek and that rock was in the way. All we are really doing is following the canyon. You can't get lost. You turn where the creeks come together and you follow the canyon up to that huge pine tree. Can you see it? That's where we're going."

"Yeah, I see it," he said, taking off his denim shirt jacket. How he managed to stand it for that long, I'll never know.

"Let's stop for a second," I said, sitting down on the lip of the rock. "I want to check something before we go on and you should be rested when we go there."

We sat and caught our breath and looked out over the forest with the desert floor stretching far and away into the distance.

"Leave your pack here," I said, "No one will touch it."

I crossed the creek at the top of the waterfall and continued weaving between trees until I came to a small clearing. Parting the brush we saw a single buck grazing on the bushes beside the clearing.

"Later in the afternoon there will be more of them. I just wanted to make sure they still came this way."

A half hour later we made our way to the lonely pine tree. There were many other trees around, but this ancient tree towered over the others, making a clear landmark.

"Remember this tree and this flat rock overlooking the creek. When you get here, you've arrived."

"Okay, where are we?"

"Camping. Just remember this spot. Okay?"

"Okay," he replied.

"Here, let me put the meat in the fridge," I said, burrowing around in the pack. I took the mayonnaise jar and set it in the icy waters of the creek. I unstrapped Rusty's sleeping bag and carried it towards the hideout.

"Follow me," I said, looking around for the flap that was the door to my hideaway. I found it buried under weeks of fallen pine needles, sticks and leaves. I lifted it up and crawled inside. I turned around and poked my head out.

"Are you coming?"

I backed inside, found the lantern, and lit it so Rusty could find his way. Rusty crawled in, filling the small opening. I rolled out his sleeping bag and then produced my own from another corner. He looked around.

"You've got to be kidding," he said. "You built this place up here?"

"I wouldn't exactly use the word *built*. *Scrounged* would be better. Here, lie down with me. I didn't realize how small the place was until you got here."

He looked around.

"I've got a stove and food. I keep a sleeping bag up here and books. There's water just outside and a wonderful view. About two years ago I built this place as a way to escape. I would come here when I needed to get away; when I needed to feel the earth beneath my feet. I spent 10 days here once and lived off the land for three of those days."

"Cass," he said astonished, "Why did you bring me here?"

"I wanted you to see me for who I really am. I don't feel like the same person who was trapped in a house with a carjacker. I don't like the part of me that was able to shoot a person. The real me can be found in the woods, following a track, piecing together hints and clues and allowing myself to be at one with my surroundings." I started to fidget. I was getting in deeper than I'd planned. "I don't get along with the city well. It is a place to live, but so is this."

"You can't live up here like this all the time. You know that. You aren't the hermit type either. Come back to Joshua Hills with me and we'll figure this out together."

"This is where I came after you took Silva in. It was the one time this place didn't feel like home."

"Why?"

"I don't really know. I did all the things I usually do when I come up here, but you weren't here. When I saw deer in the clearing, I wanted to point them out to you. And when I couldn't identify a birdcall, I wanted you to hear it. It wasn't home because you weren't here."

"But you didn't even know me."

"You don't need to know someone to miss them."

"I know. I missed you, too."

We crawled out into the sunshine again. I dug around in the bushes and finally pulled out an old, dirty barbecue grate. I washed it in the creek and we cooked our mayonnaise jar steak over the fire, then ate it with backpacker rice and fruit.

"This steak is great."

"Thanks. I think it has something to do with the surroundings. It must soak up the atmosphere while it marinates."

The next day we climbed up into the canyon, found some animal tracks and then followed them. I taught him how to walk silently in the woods by reaching out and feeling the ground before transferring his weight. He tried sneaking up on me once and I couldn't hear him, but I knew where he was because he was predictable. Then I taught him to do the same kind of walk in a crouch and in a crawl, using his hands the same way he used his feet, to feel first, then transfer.

I took him back down to the clearing and the buck was back, along with several other deer. I could see five does and knew there were many more out of sight. We went into our stalk and immediately had better luck in the small clearing than we had in the deer flats at the ranch. We entered on silent feet, inching forward with each dip of the deer's heads until we were on the outskirts of the herd. These deer were used to me. I stalked them every time I came up here, and that helped Rusty's first real try, too. I knelt down in the grass and pointed out a doe with my eyes, telling Rusty to go for it. I laid in the grass, peeking up just high enough to watch his progress. He was doing well for a beginner, but his size made it hard for him to hide. He looked back at me and I gave him a signal that meant *lower*. He lowered into a crawl, the doe about twenty feet away. Since that was as close as I thought he'd get, I rose to a crawl and came around the other side of the doe so she was slightly boxed in. Rusty laid flat and I continued inching in. Several of the other deer skittered to the side, but I wasn't concerned about them. I came around the backside of the doe, silently; using only my gentle movements, I urged and coaxed her to step towards Rusty lying silently in the grass.

I lay down, allowing the doe to become accustomed to grazing with people around her. I soaked up the sun and smelled the earth beneath me. After a while, I inched to a crawl and started in, closing the gap. It was her own decisions that brought her ever closer to Rusty's side until she was nearly standing over him.

All of a sudden the doe became alert, her ears swiveled and she bounded away. Rusty and I stood up. Shadow walked over carrying a pinecone in his mouth. I took the pinecone from him and threw it. He raced after it.

"Which do you like better, stalking or tracking?" I asked.

"Stalking. I like to see what I'm after."

"I thought a detective would like figuring out the clues."

"First you have to be able to see the clues."

"I can show them to you. We could track an animal until we see it and then you could stalk it. Have you ever seen a fox in the wild? Or a bear? Don't stalk bears. I only tried it once and I kept a distance. They are too unpredictable. Have you ever seen a wolf?"

Again he asked me, "Why did you bring me up here?"

I thought the answer would be the same, but I found a different one coming to mind. He had asked me following the Silva capture if I didn't tell him where I was going because I didn't *want* to be found. At the time, I simply didn't know how to tell him, but I was still keeping this place a secret. I wondered if he would remember. I paused.

"I brought you up here because now I *want* to be found. I never want to be lost from you again."

That night, side by side in the hideout, a wave of contentment enveloped me. I unzipped my bag and scooted over, close to Rusty. He put his arms around me and drew me closer.

"Rusty?"

"Mhm?" he answered sleepily.

"Your mission's accomplished."

"All of it?"

"Mhm, all of it."

He got up on one elbow and looked into my eyes and I smiled back. He leaned forward and gave me a gentle kiss. A shiver went through me and I responded eagerly. I was whole and happy, I was finally home.

www.ingramcontent.com/pod-product-compliance
Lightning Source LLC
Chambersburg PA
CBHW020322260626
47156CB00004B/1329